LOVE HER OR LOSE HER

LOVE HER OR LOSE HER

A NOVEL

TESSA BAILEY

AVON

An Imprint of HarperCollinsPublishers

HarperCollins books may be purchased for educational, business, or sales promotional use. For information, please email the Special Markets Department at SPsales@harpercollins.com.

FIRST EDITION

Designed by Diahann Sturge

Library of Congress Cataloging-in-Publication Data has been applied for.

ISBN 978-0-06-287285-2 (paperback)
ISBN 978-0-06-300435-1 (hardcover library edition)

20 21 22 23 24   LSC   10 9 8 7 6 5 4 3 2 1

For Esther

ACKNOWLEDGMENTS

When writing a romantic comedy, definitely pick a failed marriage as your subject matter. It's *such* a funny topic. Kidding! I'm not sure what I was thinking when I set out to make this story happen, but I'm so glad I buckled up and went for the ride. Having been married for twelve years myself, I felt like I was working out my own insecurities on the page, alongside Rosie and Dominic, and that made this whole process very cathartic. This story and these characters will always hold a place in my heart.

This book was inspired by three things. One, the podcast *Where Should We Begin?* with Esther Perel. Two, the song "Apple Juice" by Jessie Reyez. I wouldn't have been inspired to write Rosie and Dominic's journey without the voices of these strong women and the different ways they explore the vulnerabilities and pitfalls of relationships. Not to mention how beautiful relationships can be when treasured accordingly. My third source of inspiration was the book *The Five Love Languages* by Gary Chapman. It's amazing how differently you can see the person you know the best when you consider them a little more closely.

Thank you to my family; my readers; my editor, Nicole Fischer; my agent, Laura Bradford; and the publicity team at Avon for helping get this book out into the world.

LOVE HER OR LOSE HER

CHAPTER ONE

Rosie Vega: a department store shopper's worst nightmare.

Really, that's what her name tag should have read, instead of COSMETICS CONSULTANT. In order to fulfill that title, someone would be required to *consult* her first, right? Problem was, no one ever asked to be spritzed with perfume. And really, that's all it was. Just a little spritz. Why wouldn't customers let her make them smell good? Was it so much to ask?

Rosie hobbled over to the Clinique counter in her high heels, watching out for her supervisor, Martha, before performing a casual lean against the glass, groaning as the pressure on her toes and ankles lessened. One might surmise that Rosie was in the military, instead of a perfume girl at the mall. If Rosie was caught taking an unscheduled break, she wouldn't be docked pay or anything so serious. She would just get the shittier-smelling perfume to demonstrate tomorrow. Martha worked her evil in backhanded ways.

Rosie leaned over the counter and checked the clock on the register: 9:29. A little over half an hour to go and she was exhausted from standing on her feet since three o'clock. The only customers left in Haskel's were buying last-minute birthday presents or shopping for impromptu job-interview clothes. There were no pleasure cruisers at the mall this late, but she was required to stay until the very end. On the off chance someone wanted to smell like begonias and sandalwood right before bed.

A squeal rent the air and two children holding giant mall pretzels came tearing through her aisle, their mother sprinting after them with no fewer than three bags on each arm. Rosie managed to lunge out of their way, but one kid's legs got tangled in the other's and they went sprawling, both pretzels turning end over end like tumbleweeds into a Dior display, which tilted, wobbled, and crashed onto its side. Perfume bottles hit the floor with a cringe-inducing smash, the scents of several fragrances pooling and combining in what could only be referred to as too much of a good thing.

"Kill me now," the mother wailed at the ceiling, turning bloodshot eyes on Rosie. "Help us. Please."

Feedback screeched over the department store PA system. "Janitorial services to cosmetics."

Both kids burst into noisy tears, neither one of them making a move to get up off the floor.

The PA system sent a ripple of static into the atmosphere, forcing everyone to plug their ears, which Rosie could only accomplish with one finger since she was still holding a perfume bottle. "Bring a mop," the man on the speaker finished sleepily.

Rosie chewed her bottom lip for a moment, then set down

her fragrance, thus committing a cardinal sin in the eyes of her supervisor. *Don't dawdle, always have a bottle.* Those words were on a plaque in the employee break room in size 72 font. Desperate times called for desperate measures, however, and with her hands free, Rosie could stoop down to help the children to their feet, while their mother lamented the fact that she no longer smoked.

A teenager appeared on the scene dragging a mop behind him, music blaring in his earbuds, and Rosie ushered the kids over to their mother, waving off her gratitude, knowing she needed to find her bottle before—

"No perfume, I see," Martha drawled, rising from behind the glass counter like a vampire at sundown. "How are we to entice the customer?" She pretended to search the immediate area. "Perhaps our commission will appear out of thin air."

Smile in place, Rosie picked her bottle back up and gave it a shake. "Armed and prepared, Martha."

"Oh! There it is." Martha sauntered off to go terrorize someone else. But not before calling to Rosie over her shoulder, "You're sampling the Le Squirt Bon Bon tomorrow."

Rosie ground her molars together and threw a thumbs-up at her supervisor. "Can't wait!" No one had ever sold a bottle of Le Squirt. It smelled like someone woke up with a hangover, stumbled into their kitchen without brushing their teeth, and housed a cupcake—then breathed into a bottle and put it on shelves.

She was debating the wisdom of paying the janitor to hide every bottle of Le Squirt—an inside job!—when the sound of footfalls coming in Rosie's direction forced her spine straight, as if on command. She pushed off the glass and held her perfume bottle at the ready, a smile spreading her mouth and punishing her sore cheeks. A man turned the corner, and her smile eased somewhat, her hands lowering. Even if he were to buy the scent as a gift for his wife, the dude definitely wouldn't want to go home reeking of women's perfume.

Rosie assumed the man would pass on by, but he stopped at the counter across the aisle, peering into the glass case for a moment. Then he straightened and sent her a warm grin.

"Hi." He shoved his hands into his pockets, and Rosie performed her usual customer checklist. Nice watch. Tailored suit. Potential for an upsell if she could convince an obvious businessman that the three-scent gift box was a must-have for his lady. "Shouldn't they have sent you home by now?"

Was he talking to her? Weird. On the cosmetics department floor, most people passed by Rosie as if she were an inanimate object. A minor annoyance they had to successfully avoid for 3.7 seconds, unless they needed directions or help wrangling their kids. She had an urge to glance over her shoulder to confirm the man wasn't addressing someone behind her. Maybe Martha had doubled back to make sure she was spray-ready.

"Um." Rosie tried not to be obvious about shifting in her heels, transferring the ache between feet. "No rest for the weary, I guess. The mall closes at ten, so . . ."

Speaking to a man felt strange. Foreign. She hadn't even talked to her husband, Dominic, about anything of real importance for years. And, God help her, someone giving enough of a damn to ask why she was terrorizing people with a perfume bottle at nine-thirty did feel important. Someone asking about her, noticing her, felt important.

For a split second, Rosie let herself notice the man back. In a purely objective way. He was cute. Had some dad bod going on, but she wasn't judging. With both hands in his pockets, she couldn't look for a wedding ring. Some intuition told her he was divorced, though. Maybe even recently. There was something about how he'd approached as if intending to go straight for the exit that told Rosie he was only pretending to be interested in the jewelry case now. His tense shoulders and stilted small talk suggested he'd actually stopped to speak to her and wasn't overly comfortable doing it.

"Have you been working here long?"

This man was interested in her. In the space it took Rosie to have that realization, she noticed her own wedding ring was hidden behind the perfume bottle. Without being obvious, she curled the bottle into her chest and let the gold band wink at him from across the aisle. The light in his eyes dimmed almost immediately.

Rosie had been faithful to Dominic since middle school and that wouldn't be changing anytime soon, but she allowed herself the feminine satisfaction of knowing a man had found her attractive. Had she even allowed that simple pleasure for anyone but Dominic? No. No, she didn't think so. And in the years since Dominic had returned from active duty, she hadn't gotten that light, bubbly lift from him, either.

Everything between them was dark, lustful, confusing, and . . . so far off course, she wasn't sure their marriage would ever point in the right direction again.

Maybe it was silly, allowing this stranger's attempts at flirting to bring everything screaming into perspective, but that was exactly what happened. On a boring Tuesday night that should have been like any other. Suddenly, Rosie wasn't just standing in her usual spot beneath the fake crystal chandelier while boring piano music was piped in over the speakers. She was standing in purgatory. Whose life was this?

Not hers.

Once upon a time, she'd been a straight-A student. A member of the Port Jefferson High School volleyball team—B squad, but whatever. She'd been an aspiring chef.

Wait. Wrong. Rosie *was* an aspiring chef. She needed to stop thinking of that dream in the past tense. Something that faded with a long-ago wish upon a star.

Rosie set the perfume bottle down on the Clinique counter and sent the man a wobbly smile. "How long have I been working here?" She laughed under her breath. "Too long."

The man laughed, seeming grateful that she'd broken the wedding-ring tension. "Yeah, I can relate." He rubbed at the back of his neck. "Well, I guess I should get going . . ."

He trailed off but made no move to leave. It took Rosie a tick to realize he was gauging her interest level, even though she was married. With a quick intake of breath, she nodded. "Have a nice night."

Rosie stood there long after the man left, still trapped in

that out-of-body feeling. Whose life was this, indeed? In a few minutes, she would clock out from a job she hated and go home to a too-quiet house. A horribly, painfully quiet house where she would orbit around Dominic as if they might catch fire if they made eye contact. Where had everything gone wrong?

She didn't know. But twenty-seven was too young to settle for unhappiness. Discontent.

Any age was too young for that.

Yet that was exactly what she'd done. Professionally and personally.

"I think I'm done," she whispered, the words swallowed up by elevator music, the sounds of cash drawers being removed from registers and gates being pulled down at the entrances to Haskel's. Likewise, gates were coming down around a heart that was broken every time she passed through the living room and didn't receive so much as a *hello, how are you.*

I love you.

When was the last time she'd heard those words out of her husband's mouth?

She couldn't even remember.

She couldn't even remember.

Maybe Dominic was the reason she couldn't make the leap to step three of her aspirations. His lack of faith and encouragement—his utter lack of acknowledgment—was holding her back. She'd become content to waste away in this perfume purgatory. If she had more courage, she would tell Martha where to stick a bottle of Le Squirt Bon

Bon. That bravery was missing, though. It had been for way too long.

What happened to us? We used to love so hard. We used to be a team.

With a chest full of crushed glass, Rosie leaned over the counter and checked the clock again. Ten. She'd made it another day. Her marriage wouldn't.

CHAPTER TWO

Marriage to Dominic was complicated.

To say the absolute least.

Rosie pulled her car into the garage and shut off the engine, keeping her hands on the steering wheel as she breathed in and out. In and out. His truck was parked at the curb outside their house, so Rosie knew he was inside, probably nursing a beer in front of the evening news.

Tonight was not only the night she would tell her husband it was over.

It was their scheduled night to fuck like the world was ending.

She reached over and plucked her purse off the passenger seat, holding it in her lap as she considered the door just a few feet in front of the car's hood. It led into their kitchen. She would walk into the house like she did every single night, kick off her heels, and figure out dinner. Her own dinner. Dominic would have already eaten alone. Separate meals. Just another part of their marriage that should have signaled the end long before now.

With her heart pounding in her ears, Rosie left the car

and climbed the stairs to the kitchen door. She paused with her hand on the doorknob, anticipation heating her skin despite her common sense. Sense had no place in what happened between Rosie and Dominic once a week, when the sexual tension between them reached a fever pitch and they gave in. Gave in hard.

Their marriage might be cold, but the bedroom was not.

Ever since Dominic had taken her virginity on the night of her seventeenth birthday, sex between them had grown more and more explosive. That hadn't changed when he returned from overseas, but something important was missing. Something she needed for it to feel right and not just about slaking an urge. Affection. That had gone the way of her husband's warmth, caring, and support, leaving nothing but a brutally gorgeous man who knew her body's every single filthy secret.

Giving her lower lip a warning bite, Rosie opened the door and stepped over the threshold into the house, the familiar sounds of the news reaching her ears. There was already an empty beer bottle sitting by the toaster. An accusation. *You're late. I'm waiting.* Ironic that a man who showed so little awareness of her as a woman would keep such close tabs on her schedule. Enough to know she usually walked into the house at 10:15 and it was now 10:22.

Rosie toed off her high heels and loosed a silent groan of relief at the ceiling.

Before she could stop herself, she slipped her feet into her running sneakers, nylons and all, her heart starting to slam loudly in her ears. *This is it. I'm doing it. I can't take the lack of love anymore when it used to be so abundant.* There was so much slack in their rope now and nothing to pull it taut.

Even though her stomach was growling for something to eat, Rosie bypassed the refrigerator, stepping ever so slightly into the living room. Enough that she could make out her husband's profile in the flickering light of the television. Tonight was the night she got relief, and her libido knew it well. Sticky, sweet need meandered downward into her belly, turning her limbs fluid. Yes, Dominic was a gorgeous man. Even though he'd slowly, so slowly, broken her heart, leaving it limp and gasping in her chest, there was no denying how her body responded to the sight of him. Her husband sat shirtless on the couch, leaning forward with his hands clasped between his knees. Tattoos wove over his ripped shoulders, black ink on brown skin, including the single-starred flag of Puerto Rico she'd licked too many times to count.

His head was shaved, the cross around his neck gifted to Dominic at his high school graduation by his father. A Bronx man raised Catholic. Tradition, honor, respect. Those qualities were ingrained in him growing up, but only the skeleton of them remained. At least when applied to her. He provided. Worked himself raw day in and day out on the construction site, had never been late paying a bill or delayed the repair of something around the house. In her bones, she knew Dominic was faithful. Didn't have a single doubt. He might be the perfect husband.

If only he'd give her the time of day.

He was prepared to give her the time of night. That was

made obvious by his lack of shirt and socks—and when he leaned back, she knew the top button of his jeans would be undone.

A full bottle of beer rested on the coffee table in front of him.

Minutes had passed and he'd made no move to touch it. He knew she was there and hadn't gotten up to greet her. Hadn't even said hello. Just sitting there like a king, waiting for his queen to climb on and ride, so they could start the clock again. Another week of silence. Another night of rough sex. A cycle that would never end.

Unless she broke it.

When Rosie normally would have started stripping off her clothes on the way to the bedroom, she turned on the toe of her sneaker and reentered the kitchen. She opened the cupboard above the sink and took out her address book. She set it on the counter and stared at it before reaching back up and leafing through documents. Bills, financial records, things she wasn't sure why she needed, but certainly would. There was a folder with their marriage certificate and a deed to the house. All of it was coming with her. As much as Dominic treated her like a part of the scenery, he would never file for divorce.

It would have to be her.

"What are you doing?"

His voice climbed her spine like ivy. Endorphins rushed underneath the top layer of her skin and her body begged for the relief her husband doled out like a punishment. But as Rosie turned to face him, she reminded herself how lost and alone she'd felt in Haskel's that night. How she'd become a stranger in her own life—and she was done waiting for the old Dominic to come back and revive it. The man who used to share her dreams, make them his own? He was gone.

"A man was interested in me tonight."

Rosie had no idea where those words had come from. They were unplanned. As soon as they were out of her mouth, though, her determination to leave multiplied tenfold. *That's right, husband. I'm a badass. One you've taken for granted way too long.*

Dominic had gone very still at her statement. Within the boxed doorframe between the kitchen and living room, he seemed to expand, his muscular chest rising and falling as if he were winded. "Excuse me, Rosie?"

"You heard what I said. A man. Was interested. In me." She cocked a hip, feeling more like her old self than she had in years. "Tonight."

Charged silence stretched between them.

"If someone touched you," he said slowly, taking a step into the kitchen and filling it up like a hundred balloons, "that someone will regret it."

"There was no touching. Only interest," Rosie said. "And you know what? It felt so good. To have someone look at me and . . . see me. To make an effort."

A muscle popped in his jaw. "I've been sitting here waiting for you to get home."

"What we do doesn't require an effort. Not anymore." He raised an eyebrow at her, as if to say, *You sure about that?*

And her temper spiked. "It's good. We both know it's good. But . . ." Her voice threatened to crack, so she stopped to clear her throat. "It's just empty sex. There's nothing in it anymore."

His upper lip curled. "And you think it won't be empty with some fucking guy you just met? Some guy who showed interest?"

"I'm saying it'll be the same," she whispered, before she could stop the truth from emerging. It wouldn't stay packed in tight anymore. With every admission she made, honesty grew easier. Grew impossible to stay silent about everything that had been hurting her. For years. "The sex won't be as good. Maybe it never will be as good with anyone else and maybe that's why I—I thought there was hope? I don't know, Dominic. But being with a stranger will be the same in the ways that count. I'll feel like I mean nothing afterward."

He seemed to stop breathing, his skin turning chalky. "Rosie."

"What?"

Before she'd even finished the question, she'd whirled back around and started shoving her address book and paperwork into her purse. The back of her neck prickled and she knew Dominic was approaching. *Don't let him touch you or you'll lose steam.* Her sense of self-preservation kicked in and she turned, avoiding him on her way through the living room, down the hallway to the back bedroom. A total mistake, going anywhere near a bed when her body was involuntarily primed for contact. On Tuesday nights, they gave in. Like clockwork. Rosie steeled herself against the weakness of her flesh and ripped a suitcase out of the closet, throwing it open on the bed.

Holy shit. I'm doing this.

"What the hell are you doing?" Her husband stood outlined in the bedroom doorway, his heaving bare chest highlighted by the moonlight filtering in through the window. "You're not . . . Are you leaving?"

A strangled laugh found its way out of Rosie's mouth. "Are you really this surprised?"

"Yeah, I am!" he shouted. "Put the goddamn suitcase away."

"No."

That was the moment he recognized she meant business. This wasn't a fight. It was the *last* fight. Even fights had been few and far between, hadn't they? There wasn't enough passion for one. Not unless he was inside her.

Rosie started toward the dresser, prepared to clean out her underwear drawer in one sweep of her arm, but something caught her eye. A newspaper peeking out from beneath the mattress. For the past month, she'd been circling advertisements in the local paper for restaurant space. She knew through Georgie that Dominic had found her secret stash. He'd told his buddies on the construction site, but hadn't bothered to mention it to her.

"Dominic, do you know how hard it was to circle those advertisements?" She pinched the edge of the newspaper between her fingers and tugged it free of its mattress prison, dangling it in the air for him to see. "Do you know how hard it was to let myself believe, even for a second, that I could be capable of pursuing this dream I've had since we were kids? Really, really hard. Because I don't even believe in myself anymore. I forgot what it was like. To dream. To want something for myself. A-and you saw these. You knew they were there, that I'd started to hope again . . ." Her voice dropped to a whisper. "And you still didn't say anything?"

Dominic had the grace to look ashamed, color blooming high on his angular cheekbones.

Irked to the breaking point by his lack of response, she let the newspaper flutter to the floor. "I don't love you anymore."

Air rushed out of him, carried on an awful, wounded sound.

Sympathy tugged at her insides, but she staunchly ignored it. There was so much more she wanted to say. She wanted to comb through the last handful of years and hurl every nuance of her pain at him. Tell him how hurt she'd been when he'd shut her out, stopped communicating with her. How she'd felt like a failure when she couldn't reach him even though they shared a bed, a house, a life. But there must have been a part of Rosie that loved what they used to be, because she physically couldn't make him suffer any more. *Just get it over with.*

"I'm going to Bethany's."

He rounded the bed in her direction. "No."

Rosie moved away, her back coming up almost immediately against the wall of their small bedroom. "Don't try to stop me."

His body pressed hers hard into the wall and their moans

joined together, feminine layered on top of rough. God, his smell. It had changed over time. Matured. Gone from light and spicy to male and earthy. She hated the way her thighs turned pliant, her panties dampening, her womanhood preparing, squeezing, aching to be filled.

"Dominic," she whispered, her words muffled when he stooped down and pressed their mouths together.

He didn't kiss her, though. He never did anymore. Not unless he was inside her.

"Shhh, honey. I've got you. I know what you need." His fingers raked up the outsides of her thighs, disappearing beneath her work skirt and hooking in the waistband of her panties. He watched her under heavy eyelids as he started to peel them down. "My wife wants to fuck extra-hard tonight?" He caught the underside of her chin with his nipping teeth. "That's what you were getting anyway. You didn't have to put on a show."

Rosie's body was a traitor that had never stopped craving Dominic for a second. He knew every button to push, whether she wanted fast or slow, when to switch positions. How dirty talk made her extra-adventurous. When she needed a hard slap on the backside or a slow, drawn-out bump-and-grind session that left him sweaty and covered in claw marks. He could whisper to her sex drive, speak its language, make it babble like a brook. Make her scream, make her shake, make her beg.

His middle finger slid into the split of her sex, his lips peeling back on a growl when he found her soaked. "I've been hard all day waiting for this."

Waiting for this. Not waiting for you.

Still, when she should have admonished him, her voice emerged sounding like a plea. "Dominic."

His name ended in a whimper when he pushed that middle finger inside her, twisting the digit, grazing her clit with his thumb while in pursuit of her G-spot—and he found it, found it without delay and tickled it, bringing Rosie's back off the wall in a heaving arch.

"Uh-huh. There you go, honey girl. You're going to come right here, aren't you?" He looked down, leaned back to watch his finger drive in and out of her—but something made him still for a second. And then he was yanking up her leg with his free left hand, propping her knee on his hip. The warmth of his touch reached her ankle, lower. "Get these shoes off now."

"Make me."

Dominic lodged his hips between her spread thighs and hefted her up against the wall. The thick ridge of his erection pressed to her core—hard—making her cry out his name from behind clenched teeth. "Kick them off," he rasped, rolling, rolling, rolling his hips and looking her square in the eye. "You're staying."

"I'm leaving," she breathed, head falling back. "Accept it."

"Fuck that." His open mouth skated over her cleavage, his hot, quick exhales turning her nipples to tight points inside her silk blouse. "I need you."

Dominic reached between their bodies and lowered the zipper of his jeans. The *zing* of sound in the near-darkness had the effect of an ice-cold waterfall raining down on

Rosie's head. He didn't get to say he needed her. He didn't get the pleasure of her body when he gave nothing beyond their scheduled physical contact. She was more than someone's weekly gratification. With all the willpower she housed inside her, Rosie pressed both hands against Dominic's shoulders and shoved him away, her feet landing on the ground a split second later.

He stood a couple feet away—far too close—several inches of his arousal showing at the waistband of his loosened jeans. She had no choice but to acknowledge how breathtaking her husband was, one last time. He was a muscled warrior with a carved granite jawline—and for the couple beers he drank every night, none of the effects of that vice showed on his body. If she didn't know better, she'd think he kept in ruthless physical shape for her.

Yeah, right.

He didn't even say good morning.

"Don't touch me again." She quickly pulled her panties back into place, ignoring the fluttering in her belly when he tracked her movements with hot eyes. "How dare you call this a show?" She kicked the fallen newspaper out of her way and moved on watery legs back toward the suitcase. "I'll come get the rest of my things later."

He moved up beside her, panic beginning to creep into his usually stoic expression. For a brief moment in time, they locked eyes and she saw him. The Dominic who'd sworn to love her until the day she died. Sworn it until his voice went hoarse. She saw the man who'd indulged her with a smile when she insisted they match at prom. The man who'd asked her to marry him the day they graduated high school, kneeling on the football field with a modest ring pinched between his fingers, their bright future right there in his eyes.

And then he disappeared in the blink of an eye, a shutter slamming down into place, hiding his every emotion. She knew this man well. Too well.

"Go, then. No one's stopping you."

There must have been one tiny stitch holding her heart together, preventing it from breaking entirely. But it frayed and snapped at his words, leaving her reeling, hot moisture pressing behind her eyelids. Blindly, she packed a drawer's worth of clothes and unplugged her cell-phone charger, grabbing her jar of Curlsmith Curl Conditioning Oil-In-Cream and a nighttime head scarf. Everything went into the suitcase, and she zipped it up with sickening finality.

The cool fall air kissed Rosie's damp cheeks when she walked into the garage, and she realized she'd never closed the garage door. Made things easier, didn't it? She tossed her suitcase into the trunk and climbed into the driver's side, audible gasps escaping her mouth. *Oh my God, I'm leaving Dominic. Oh my God, I just ended my marriage.*

She'd almost backed out to the end of the driveway when Dominic appeared in the garage, still shirtless and more beautiful than any man had the right to be. Her headlights caused the cross around his neck to glint . . . and she noticed he was clutching the newspaper she'd kept hidden under the mattress. What? He wanted to talk now?

It's too late.

"Rosie."

Her heart seized as he shouted her name a second time, striding toward the car. No. No more. She couldn't take any more. Before she could change her mind, she whipped the car into a K-turn and floored it down the residential street, Dominic's voice booming through the dust she left behind.

CHAPTER THREE

Dominic caught his reflection in the door of his truck as he slammed it. His face was unshaven, eyes and cheeks sunken in. Lines that hadn't existed around his mouth before were prominent this morning, even partially hidden by bristling facial hair. All in all, he looked pretty decent, considering his fucking life was over.

He closed his eyes and leaned forward, pressing his forehead against the cool metal of his truck, breathing in and out through his nose, trying to quell the incessant nausea. He'd started drinking on Tuesday night after Rosie left and now it was Friday. He'd remembered to send Stephen Castle, his friend and boss, a text before going on the kind of bender that would make a rock star proud.

I'm sick.

That's all Dominic had had the presence of mind to type to Stephen—and it wasn't a lie. He was sick. Just not with anything that could be cured.

Dominic heard the crunch of gravel behind him and

braced for noise that would surely split his brain down the middle. "Jesus H. Christ," Stephen said, his voice obnoxiously chipper for eight o'clock in the morning. Or any time of day, for that matter. His work ethic made him a great construction foreman, but Stephen's smiling face was the last thing Dominic wanted to see right now. Unfortunately, he had a solid work ethic of his own and the guilt of missing two days on the job had him feeling like shit on top of everything else. "You still sick, buddy?" Stephen patted him on the shoulder. "Go home. I don't need the whole crew catching the plague."

Stephen turned Dominic by the shoulder, jerking back when he saw his face.

"What the hell did you catch? Malaria?"

"I don't have time for this," Dominic said, pressing a row of fingers to the center of his splitting forehead. "Don't act like you don't know Rosie is staying with Bethany."

"I . . . Oh. Shit." Stephen's hand dropped away. "No, I didn't know, man."

Why did that piss Dominic off even more? Leaving her husband wasn't a big enough event that this tiny-ass town with a rabid gossip mill didn't know about it? Swallowing the acid in his mouth, Dominic moved to the back of the truck and hefted out his toolbox, just in time for Travis Ford to approach with a shit-eating grin a mile wide. He had the swagger of a man who didn't need to work, just wanted a hobby in between commentating gigs at Bombers Stadium and getting heavy with his fiancée, also known as Stephen's *other* sister, Georgie.

The pair had accidentally hooked up over the summer after pretending to date in an effort to clean up Travis's "bad boy of baseball" image. It had worked in a way they'd never expected and the guy couldn't be flying any higher. Or be more obviously devoted to his girl.

I used to be like that with Rosie.

Right up until the day he'd joined the marines and left for his first tour, anytime he and Rosie were in the same room together . . . he saw nothing else. There was simply nothing and no one but the girl who'd held his heart since middle school.

It was still that way. Nothing had changed in that regard. Never would.

He hadn't been in the same room as her since Tuesday, and thank God. Thank God she hadn't seen him drunk and raging and calling her turned-off cell phone in between swigs of Jack Daniel's. He wouldn't have been able to stomach her seeing him weak.

The ex–baseball player propped an elbow on the raised back gate of Dominic's truck and took a long pull from his paper coffee cup. Then he lowered it, hesitating. "Heard your wife left you."

If he'd had an ounce of energy left in his body, he would have decked the cocky motherfucker. As it was, Dominic was too numb to move. Couldn't even feel the toolbox in his hand. "You have something to say about it?"

"Wait, wait. Hold up." Stephen stepped in between them with a look of outrage. "How come Travis knows and I don't?"

Travis grinned into another sip of coffee. "You don't really want a reminder this early in the morning that I'm moving in with your sister, do you, Stephen?"

"No." He held up a staying hand. "Please, God, keep it to yourself."

"Bought an autumn centerpiece for the dining room table last weekend," Travis continued undeterred, obviously enjoying himself. "Has little pumpkins and pinecones sticking out of it. Cute as hell."

"Are you done?" Stephen complained. "This man's marriage is over."

The cavern in Dominic's chest widened, but he hardened his jaw, refusing to let the turmoil inside show on his face. "Look, if you two assholes wouldn't mind? I'd like to go knock some walls down."

Travis tipped his coffee cup in Dominic's direction. "What you should have done is knocked your own walls down and let her in—"

"Oh, for fuck's sake." Stephen's voice was rife with disgust. "You've been in a relationship for one minute and think you're an expert?"

"Yes."

Dominic turned on the heel of his boot and headed toward the house, leaving his two friends to argue behind him. Today was demo day on their new flip, and he found sinking a sledgehammer into old Sheetrock cathartic most times. This morning, he physically needed the outlet. Already frustration was curling his fingers into fists.

His wife was supposed to be by his side.

He was working, but the money he earned would no longer provide for her. Knowing that was a constant punch in the gut.

I provide. That's the one thing I've never fucked up.

Dominic's father had been a quiet man, but he'd been driven. After his single mother had passed, he'd left Puerto Rico at age twenty to find a fresh start in New York, where he'd met Dominic's mother after only a month. With a young family to care for, he'd worked impossibly hard to make ends meet in the beginning. Sick days didn't exist for the man, and he'd managed to pass on the importance of dependability to his son. Wake up, work, create security for his loved ones. As long as he was doing those things, they would be content. Providing was a no-fail way to communicate love, wasn't it? So where exactly had Dominic gone wrong?

A few crew members were scattered on the porch when Dominic climbed the stairs and they called greetings to him, but he just kept walking, letting the roar in his ears build and block everything else out. He took a cursory glance at the markings made in thick black Sharpie on the walls, indicating where beams or pipes lay on the other side. And then he picked up the closest sledgehammer and buried it in the old Sheetrock.

Nothing. None of the pressure in his chest abated. If anything, it grew worse.

The sound of his breathing rasped in his ears as he picked up the heavy tool again, raised it over his head, and destroyed another section of the wall. In his mind, he could see Rosie packing her suitcase on their marriage bed. Her words that had split him wide open, sure as he was splitting open the wall.

I don't love you anymore.

His next assault on the wall absorbed the humiliating sound that left his mouth. Men didn't lose their heads like this. Or break down in front of other people. They were supposed to be rocks. Constants in the lives of those around them, never wavering. But he couldn't stop lifting the sledgehammer and driving it full force into the wall.

Finally, he had to quit thanks to his screaming muscles and the two sets of hands that ripped the tool away. Dominic tried to get it back, but the whiskey he'd ingested the night before chose that moment to rise up and set his throat on fire. He barely made it outside before throwing up his breakfast in the grass behind the house.

Dominic's legs wanted to give out. He needed to sit down. But he'd already shown too much of his hand with everyone watching. No, he'd stand, thank you very much. He'd given in to the pain enough for today. Hell, enough for a year.

As the rush of sound in his ears started to fade, Dominic heard himself laboring to breathe. Heard the passing traffic in the distance, the shift of the yellowing lawn around him. He wasn't alone.

"You're welcome," Dominic said, keeping his back turned to Stephen and Travis. "Saved you some work."

"Well, hold off next time, man. We like breaking shit, too," Travis returned. A few moments ticked by. "Look, I was, uh . . . trying to make light of the situation earlier.

Knowing you, I thought you'd appreciate me forgoing the one-armed, back-slapping man hug and an off-key rendition of 'Kumbaya.'"

Dominic cleared his throat. "Yeah, I'd rather die."

"But it has recently come to our attention . . ." Stephen said drily, "that you might actually need to talk."

"Nope."

"You sure?" Dominic glanced over at Travis, who toggled his eyebrows. "I'm willing to break my fiancé-fiancée confidentiality just this once." A shadow crossed his face. "When Georgie broke up with me, I would have sawed off my fucking leg to find out what she ate for dinner. Or what she wore to bed—"

"We get it," Stephen said, exasperated.

Travis held up both hands. "All I'm saying is . . . I have the goods."

Dominic ground his jaw together to keep from asking for information. Was Rosie upset? Did she give a shit at all? Was she still wearing those goddamn high heels that gave her blisters and made her hobble around the house at night? How many times had he hidden them in the back of her closet, hoping she'd put on the flat slipper-looking shoes instead?

Was she eating dinner at a normal hour?

Her boss at the department store used to let Rosie work straight through her legally required break, until Dominic had sent an email to the owner of the department store, not so subtly suggesting they review their employees' right to meal breaks.

The urge to pump Travis for the smallest, most trivial thing was so intense, Dominic had to bite down on his tongue. He was used to laying concrete over his impulses, but this was a test he couldn't pass. The woman he was supposed to care for forever was gone, she didn't love him anymore, and she'd felt something when another man showed interest. It might have been sheer feminine enjoyment, but he hated it with every fiber of his being. What if next time, the man asked her out on a date? Would she say yes even though they were still married?

No.

No, Rosie would never do that.

The fact that she might want to say yes, however, was enough to strangle him.

"Is she, um . . ." Dominic crossed his arms in a jerky movement. "She never warms her car up in the wintertime. She just gets in and drives. Someone has to wake up early and do it or it'll ruin the transmission and she . . ." He shrugged. "She loves that stupid car, so . . ."

Stephen stroked a hand down his beard, even though he didn't have a beard. "My wife makes me do this, too. Get the heater running."

"Rosie doesn't know I do it," Dominic muttered.

"What?" Stephen snorted. "Why miss out on those brownie points?"

Dominic didn't answer, but he noticed Travis scrutinizing him. "That's really all you want to know? Who's going to warm up her fucking Honda?" A beat passed. "I knew you were a piece of work, but you're just swinging for the fences now." He smoothed the cuff of his long-sleeve T-shirt. "And that's my job."

Stephen made sure everyone witnessed his eye roll.

"Here's what I want to say." Travis spread his stance and settled into it, like a team manager getting ready to level with his pitcher. "I might have implied before that I'm an expert on relationships now, but that was mainly to drive Stephen crazy."

"It's working," Stephen snapped at his childhood best friend. "Dick."

Travis grinned, but it dropped away just as fast. "Dominic, man. I just saw you tear down a wall single-handedly, so I'm taking a big risk saying this," he said, raising his eyebrows. "Get your shit together. Your wife just left. I don't know anything about your marriage, which is weird, because you're so damn chatty." He paused to smirk. "But I'm willing to bet you want her back."

Stephen stepped into Dominic's line of vision. "Give us a nod or something. Blink once for yes, twice for no."

"Of course I want her back," Dominic said in a rusted voice, shocking himself by saying the words out loud, instead of letting them ricochet around inside his skull. "She's my wife. She's supposed to stay. We said vows." Travis and Stephen made wishy-washy sounds, as if they disagreed. "What?"

"Yeah, marriages have ups and downs," Stephen said, obviously treading carefully. "But if a woman isn't happy for a long period of time . . ."

He trailed off, widening his eyes at Travis.

"Don't look at me. Me and Georgie aren't getting married for months."

"Well, well, well," Stephen drawled. "He's only an expert when it's convenient."

Dominic pinched the bridge of his nose and inhaled. Now that adrenaline had worn off from his wall-smashing activities, the pounding in his brain was back. "Do you two have anything useful to say, or what?" He dropped his hand. "If not, I'm going back to work."

"Yeah," Travis said with a nod. "I have something useful. Go get her back. There's a Just Us League meeting tomorrow night at Bethany's." He sent them both a pointed look. "Told you I had the goods. You're welcome."

The words *She doesn't love me anymore* were stuck in Dominic's throat. He couldn't say them out loud. Hearing them was terrible enough. And goddammit, on top of the horror of losing Rosie, he was embarrassed. What kind of a man lands an incredible woman like Rosie and doesn't do enough to hold on to her?

His jaw hardened. No. She was supposed to stay regardless. His parents weren't necessarily close, but they respected each other. His mother depended on Dominic's father, had always been confident in his ability to give her a comfortable life. They were a united front at the weddings, funerals, and barbeques Rosie and Dominic attended for his mother's side of the family. Bottom line, they'd *stayed* together, through hard times and good. Even now, they were back to living in the old neighborhood, so they could be closer to his mother's family in the Bronx. They'd sworn to stay together until the end and they damn well would. They didn't even sleep in the same bedroom, but they admired each other.

He and Rosie, they had a lot more than mutual admiration. Didn't they?

Some of his frustration slipped, giving way to doubt. Those nights he spent working himself into a sweat between her thighs were the greatest of his life. He would bury his face in her neck, lick her whipping pulse, and absorb the energy of her. Those cries she let out in his ear, the nail marks she left on his back . . . he'd taken those as proof that she was satisfied. Satisfied and provided for. How had he been so fucking wrong?

At that very moment, there didn't seem to be a way back into her life. She'd been unhappy too long—and he'd been blind to it. Dominic wasn't even sure he could keep his shit together around Rosie. Looking her in the eye and knowing she didn't love him anymore? He might as well go back to living in the desert, without a drop of water this time around.

But as Dominic split a look between Travis and Stephen, he recalled the times they'd come close to losing their women. They'd gotten them back, hadn't they? If there was anything in this world worth fighting for, it was his wife.

Fuck. Most of all, he just needed to look at her. Be around her. His world was off-kilter, his mental equilibrium shot to hell. So that's what he would do. He'd go remind her that marriage was forever and he'd ask her to come home. If there was even the slightest chance it might work, he had to take it.

Dominic swallowed hard. "What time is the meeting?"

CHAPTER FOUR

Rosie took a pizza cutter out of Bethany's cutlery drawer and laid it beside the bowl of chilled dough, squaring her shoulders and preparing to create. Some might find her process crazy, but unless she really took a moment to focus on the food, she could taste her worries within the fabric of flavors. And that was a waste of good ingredients—an egregious sin.

When she arrived at Bethany's house last night, her friend had answered the door with a sleep mask pushed up on her forehead, blond hair sticking out in eighty directions. She'd taken one look at Rosie's face and wordlessly led her to the upstairs guest room. No words had been exchanged, just a long hug—and that was enough to let Rosie know her friends had seen the implosion of her marriage coming a mile away.

She didn't know whether to be grateful or offended.

Good thing she didn't really have the mental energy for either.

Making good food? She always had energy for that.

When she'd woken up this morning, Bethany had already

left for work, but thankfully she'd left a house key sitting on the kitchen counter. Since Rosie had worked the early shift at Haskel's, she'd gotten home first, and being alone in the big, airy house had given her too much room to think about Dominic shouting her name from the garage. To combat the sound of his voice, which continued to echo in her head, she'd gone to the market and then worked out some angst making dough for her mother's medialunas.

Focus on the food.

Using the pizza wheel, she cut the dough in half and made two long rectangles. She stacked one rectangle of dough on top of the other and lined up the edges, cutting the dough into triangles, humming as she made strategic slits and molded them into crescent shapes, placing them one by one on a parchment-paper-lined baking sheet. Then she set them on the windowsill to rise in the sunshine, the same way her mother used to do.

There, her mom would say. *Now we sit, have a coffee, and savor our hard work.*

God, she missed that woman. She'd had a tried-and-true method for everything. *On Sundays, we wash and set our hair. Mondays are for cleaning and going through the mail. On Thursday evenings, we make asado—enough to get us through the weekend and share with the neighbors if they drop by.* And all the while, Rosie's father would smile indulgently, his fingers flipping through a car magazine or twisting a tool into a car part. It didn't seem fair that people who'd been so rooted to this earth with their routines could just be gone. A stroke for her mother, and weeks later, her grieving father simply didn't wake up one morning. So fast and jarring, but Rosie took comfort now in the knowledge they were together again.

The front door of the house opened and Bethany walked in, a camel-colored leather briefcase tucked smartly beneath one arm. "Why, honey. You cooked."

"I'm making breakfast, actually," Rosie said, gently poking one of her medialunas in the side to check the texture. "These will taste great in the morning with your coffee."

"I'm looking forward to it," Bethany murmured, hopping up on one of the stools surrounding the marble island. "How was your day?"

Rosie rolled a shoulder and went to preheat the oven, setting it at 395—an important component of her mother's crescent rolls. *Don't pressure the dough to grow up too fast, Rosie.* "It was good. I even managed to sell a bottle of Le Squirt Bon Bon. As a joke, obviously, but it still counts in the eyes of the commission gods. What about yours?"

"Fine." Brow furrowed, Bethany plucked at the arm of her blouse. "Making things pretty as usual. You know the drill."

"Still wanting to ditch your swatch samples and swing that sledgehammer?"

"Like a motherfucker." Bethany gave her a tight smile. "I'd rather talk about you, though. How are you doing?"

Again, she thought of Dominic and how panicked he'd looked when she started to pack. "I don't feel great. I probably won't for a long time, but . . . leaving was the right thing to do, Bethany. We're married and we don't even speak to each other."

Bethany shook her head slowly. "You used to, though,

right? In high school, the two of you always had your heads together, whispering about something."

"We used to talk constantly, yeah. Where we would travel when we made some money. We'd talk about our dream home on the water. All the parties we would host in our big backyard." Swallowing hard, Rosie took a bowl out of the cabinet and cracked an egg inside, beating it with a dollop of milk, preparing to make the egg wash to brush over the medialunas. "When he came back from overseas, I don't think I noticed right away how quiet he'd become. I had my mother. We were always in the kitchen together and . . . he'd been gone so long, his silence didn't register—I was just so happy to have him home safe. And then she was gone and it was *so* quiet. All the time."

"I'm so sorry." Bethany slipped off her stool and went to the wine fridge beneath the counter, selecting a bottle of white and twisting off the cap. "God, it's been almost four years since your parents passed, Ro. That's a long time to be drowning in silence."

"Well, I'm definitely not drowning now," Rosie said in a rush, hoping to ease the pressure in her chest. And that was the truth. Ever since she, Bethany, and Georgie had formed the Just Us League, not only was she surrounded with supportive women and a shitload of town gossip, but her dreams of opening a restaurant had been rekindled. Transformed from the pipe dream she'd set aside to reality. They'd signed her up for one of those crowdsourcing websites and people had *donated*. Invested in *her* dream. Or at least given her a push to get started.

Rosie wasn't sure how her mother would feel about benefiting from the kindness of strangers. Or if she would even see it that way, as opposed to charity. Growing up biracial in the predominantly white town of Port Jefferson, Rosie never had any friends who looked like her. Her father, Maurice, was African American, and her mother, Cecilia, was from Argentina, so they didn't resemble her friends' parents, either. Even unspoken, there always seemed to be a dividing line between them and everyone else. People were friendly, but not so friendly that they might accidentally invite real friendship. She'd witnessed the disappointment that treatment bred in her parents, whether or not they ever said it out loud.

Rosie had been aware of the Castles and many of the Just Us League members for a long time, but only enough to say hello on Main Street or if they happened to pass through her section at the mall. That dividing line between her and everyone else had remained for a while after her parents had passed, and it had taken some courage to step over it. Accepting the kindness of her friends only sat right with her now because she knew—and had experienced—how the Castles and the women of the club went out of their way for *everyone*. Rosie *herself* went out of her way, right alongside them, and it dulled any possibilities of taking a handout. She would do the same for them. Especially if someone needed a place to stay.

"Thanks again for letting me crash here until I figure out my next move."

"Stay as long as you want," Bethany said, pouring two

glasses of wine and handing one to Rosie. "I'm having my lawyer draw up a nondisclosure agreement about my snoring, however. You don't mind signing, do you?"

Rosie laughed. "I can keep your secret if you don't tell anyone I groan about my tired feet like a ninety-year-old."

"Deal." Bethany's smiling mouth met the rim of her wineglass for a sip. "Speaking of next moves, where are we at on opening your restaurant? Which I'm going to eat at five nights a week. Maybe six. Any more thoughts on that?"

Any more *thoughts* about it? She'd thought about opening her own place nonstop for almost a decade. Along with their plans to own a big, beautiful house and eventually have children, she and Dominic had talked about her dream of cooking for the public. Something her mother had always wanted to do—a desire she'd never had the chance to fulfill, thanks to money being tight while Rosie was growing up.

God, she and Dominic had entertained big dreams.

A forever home to grow old in, a family, lucrative careers.

Her biggest dream had always been Dominic, though. Sure, they'd settled on a smaller house that needed a lot of repairs and didn't have enough room to expand their family. Sure, the money for her restaurant was taking a lot longer to save. So long that they'd stopped talking about it altogether, the way they'd stopped discussing everything else under the sun. But if she'd had their love, she couldn't help but think it would have been enough.

Something sharp moved in Rosie's chest and she took a sip of wine. "I'm almost there." She took a deep breath. "Just waiting for the dust to settle and then . . . leap."

Bethany laid a hand on her shoulder. "You're not leaping alone." She pressed her lips together, like she was holding in a secret. "You know . . . Georgie called me today. She's had not one, not two, but *three* of her birthday party clients ask if you're open to catering their parties. Word is getting around, woman." She drank deeply of her wine and sighed. "I'm basically housing a future celebrity chef."

Rosie let out a long breath and allowed herself to feel the stirring of satisfaction. If she combined the Just Us League donations and the money her parents had left her, her dream of owning a restaurant was beginning to come into focus. Unfortunately, that dream was still difficult to fathom without her husband in the frame.

Give it time.

Not too much time, though. She'd waited long enough.

She clinked her glass with Bethany's and steeled her spine. "I'm going to start working on menu ideas."

CHAPTER FIVE

Dominic watched through the driver's-side window of his truck as women piled into Bethany Castle's house. They came in all ages, carrying bottles of prosecco and wine. One of them even had a bottle of tequila tucked under her arm. Just what the hell went on at these Just Us League meetings? Ever since Rosie and the Castle sisters had formed this unholy union, the men in town had been wary as hell—and Dominic was no exception. It couldn't be a coincidence that mere months after the club was formed, his wife decided to leave him. Today's club agenda: throw darts at a poster of his face.

He scrubbed a hand over his shaved head and cursed.

What the hell was he doing here? He wasn't even sure speaking with Rosie alone would earn him another chance. For damn sure, he was taking a risk approaching her in a roomful of women who might have encouraged her to ditch their marriage.

He supposed he could wait. Come back tonight, after the meeting ended.

Dominic brushed his fingers against the keys where they

still dangled in the ignition. Before he could bring the truck to life, though, he threw one more glance at the house. And there she was.

Rosie. In the kitchen window, smiling at whoever stood beside her just out of view.

It was impossible to swallow the lump that formed in his throat.

Fuck. His hand grabbed the keys and squeezed until his palm burned. She was so beautiful. Enough to make his pulse clamor in his ears. This was why he was here, sitting outside a meeting where—rumor had it—a man could get his balls chopped off for intruding. He'd come because it was Saturday and he hadn't laid eyes on his wife since Tuesday night. He hadn't gone that long without being near her since returning from overseas.

A memory of her waiting for him at the airport caught Dominic off guard. A war had been waging inside him that afternoon, between anticipation, love, yearning to hold Rosie again. He'd been battling against the mental weight he'd brought home, as surely as his standard-issue camo duffel bag. So many men had lost their lives, men he'd befriended. Their plans for the future were still circulating in his head when he'd spotted Rosie waiting at the bottom of the escalator.

Dominic had grown up with one vision for his future. Marry Rosie. Work hard. Give her everything she'd ever dreamed of.

When he'd seen her waiting for him, so insanely gorgeous in a loose summer dress, her dark curly hair in twin braids gathered in a crown on top of her head, he'd thought, *Oh God, she deserves more than I could ever give her. How could I ever make this woman happy? I'm just a soldier. The only trade I know is construction. How do I do this?*

At the bottom of the escalator, he'd reached Rosie, taken her hand, covering the meager engagement ring she wore with his palm—and kissed her like it would be the last time, like a dying man, because he had no idea how to speak the words in his head out loud.

So much time away from Port Jefferson had given him perspective. He'd sat back and listened to the rich futures his fellow soldiers had carved out for themselves. And they'd not only called attention to his own lack of grandeur, but that of his father. That man had worked his fingers to the bone and he'd earned respect, given his family security. Had it been enough for him? Maybe being depended on would have to be enough for Dominic. To work, provide, and give Rosie security, since he couldn't give her everything in the world. Everything she *deserved*.

What he'd given *wasn't* enough. At least now he had his answer.

Dominic shook off the dark trail of thoughts and leaned back, retrieving Rosie's red fall jacket from the backseat. Holding it beneath his arm, he walked toward the house, the sounds of laughter growing louder as he got closer to the front door. He debated knocking, but set aside that plan almost immediately. No one would hear him unless he pounded the goddamn door down and pissed-off husband wasn't the image he needed to portray. Even though he felt every inch the angry, resentful man, this close to carrying Rosie from the meeting over his shoulder.

For better or worse, wife. You said the words.

That thought gave Dominic the impetus to push open the front door and enter the house. He half expected to be spotted right away and possibly sprayed with holy water, but he stepped into an empty entryway unnoticed. He used the opportunity to hang the red coat on the hook to the right of the door, hiding it slightly behind a couple black coats. Up ahead, there was a crowd of women gathered in the living room around a makeshift bar and trays of appetizers. He immediately recognized the food as Rosie's cooking and the restlessness inside him expanded. Where was she?

An oven door snicked shut in the kitchen and there she was. All alone, but looking happier than he'd seen her in a long time. She used the back of her wrist to push a stray curl out of her face and went back to arranging empanadas on a tray, adding a little bowl of pickled onions as garnish and sprinkling parsley over the top of everything. The recipe had been passed down from her mother's Argentinian side and she'd perfected them in high school. Dominic had figured out quickly that the act of making the delicious, crusty meat pockets was a sign of Rosie's happiness.

It had been a long time since she'd made them for Dominic.

He knew the moment she sensed him because her movements slowed, hands pausing in midair. He forced his features to remain schooled as she looked up from her task, clocking him in the doorway. The corners of her mouth turned down and wobbled a little bit, delivering a swift kick to his stomach. God, she really didn't love him anymore. Couldn't possibly. Not when her first reaction upon seeing him was sadness.

He took a few steps toward the kitchen, acutely aware that the conversation in the living room had flatlined. "Can I talk to you outside?"

Rosie shifted behind the kitchen island, the smooth bronze color of her cheeks turning a deep rose. Lips rolling together, she cast a look toward the living room.

Bethany approached, stopping between them, clearly unsure how to proceed. "Uh, hey, Dominic." She tucked some blond hair behind her ear and widened her eyes at Rosie. "What brings you to our humble Just Us League meeting?"

Dominic held on to his patience. Wasn't it obvious why he was there? She was standing in the kitchen looking so fucking gorgeous, his hands flexed with the need to stroke her skin, head to toe. "I want to talk to my wife."

Bethany hummed. "Okay . . ."

"It's fine." Rosie nodded briskly and took off her apron, leaving it on the marble island top. "There are a fresh batch of spicy pork empanadas here, if everyone wants to dig in." With a reassuring smile in the direction of the living room, she breezed past Dominic and out the door.

He raised an eyebrow at the sea of disapproving faces and followed her out the door, closing it behind them. The first thing he noticed was her lack of coat. It was right inside, hanging on a hook, but he couldn't tell her that. She'd know he'd brought it.

When she rubbed her hands together to ward off the brisk

air, Dominic ground his back teeth together and started to shoulder off his leather bomber. "Put this on."

His wife shook her head. "Why did you come here?"

Dominic frowned at the goose bumps on her arms. "A bunch of strangers aren't going to stand between me and my wife."

She laughed. "Oh, I get it. You purposely showed up during the meeting to make a statement."

Until she said it out loud, Dominic hadn't even been aware of his own intentions. He couldn't deny it, could he? He'd wanted to make it known what was written in stone, as far as he was concerned: a marriage was forever and there was nothing more important than their commitment. "You were making empanadas."

Rosie opened her mouth and closed it before saying, "Yes."

He slid both hands into his pockets. "You haven't done that in a while."

"Actually, I have," she said, tilting her head. "I've been making them for months at these meetings. A few people are even asking about me catering birthday parties." She licked her lips, her gaze cutting sideways. "Maybe I'll say yes eventually."

It wasn't lost on Dominic that they hadn't spoken like this in far too long. His wife had been asked to cater birthday parties? Had he really known none of this? A montage of their silent evenings spent in separate parts of the house ran through his head and panic snuck in beneath his skin. Jesus, he didn't know what was happening in Rosie's life. At all. "Why haven't you said yes?"

"I don't . . ." She gave a jerky shrug. "It doesn't matter."

"It does."

"Seriously, Dominic?" Eyes squeezed shut, she shook her head. "You don't get to come here and act like you suddenly care."

Frustration welled up inside him, biting the heels of his already-frayed nerves. "You don't think your husband cares more than these women? You've only been hanging out with most of them for a matter of weeks."

"I don't know." She lifted her hands and let them drop. "I do know the club members like my cooking so much, they've . . . they . . ."

"What?"

A few beats of silence passed while she scrutinized him. "They've donated money on this online crowdsourcing site. To help me open the restaurant," she said quietly. "The GoFundMe was Georgie's idea and it . . . well, it's been pretty amazing. The response."

That knowledge made Dominic's esophagus burn. He was supposed to provide for his wife. That's what he'd been doing since the day they married, and he'd been attempting to go beyond the basics by setting aside a portion of his salary for the last five years. Would telling her about it now make any difference? "You're opening the restaurant with other people's money?"

"I haven't decided, actually. I might. If I don't, I'm going to give the money back, obviously," she said. "It's not the full amount I would need to buy the building I like outright, but maybe there's a chance the owner will let me make payments. It's worth finding out."

"Come home," Dominic pushed through his teeth. "You don't need to take donations. We'll find the money to open your place on our own."

"We've had years to try and find it. We didn't." She rubbed her hands up and down her arms. "Now I'm going to do it the way I choose, Dominic. I'm sorry if you don't like it."

He paced away from her on the porch and came back. What the hell was he supposed to say? She was . . . right. They'd stopped talking about the possibility of her restaurant years ago. He'd almost started thinking she didn't *want* to try anymore, so he'd set out to give her another dream. One they'd spoken about hundreds of times. By the time he'd found her classified ads for commercial space under the mattress, the money he could have given her to open the doors . . . it had been spent.

Christ, he was failing here. His wife was gone and she already had plans to pursue the future alone. He'd lost his chance to help. "Come back to me." Dominic took several steps in her direction, gratified when that familiar awareness smoked in her eyes. "Things haven't been great for you at home. I get that, all right?"

Bewilderment transformed her features. "Have they honestly been great for you?"

Dominic was too embarrassed to say yes. The privilege of caring for this woman was his reason for getting out of bed in the morning. If he'd sensed occasionally that she wanted more, he'd worked harder. Looked for other things that were making her unhappy and fixed them, because it was his job. The alternative was to acknowledge her unhappiness and his own shortcomings as a husband. That he was human. Inadequate. To admit he wasn't doing enough—that maybe someone *else* could have done better by Rosie. He didn't *want* to know if their marriage was leaving her unsatisfied; he just wanted to throw another dart and pray like hell it hit the target. "What do I have to do?"

She started at the vehemence in his voice. "I don't know if there's anything. Not now."

The hollow husk of his stomach filled with acid. "Think about it," he said firmly, stepping close enough that Rosie was forced to tip her head back. Fuck, he would have killed to kiss her in that moment, with the sun setting on the golden highlights in her eyes, her lips parted and plump from having him close. "While you're figuring out whether to give me a second chance, Rosie, I need to know you're not enjoying the interest of other men." He wet his upper lip and watched her eyelids flutter. "It won't be long before this whole damn town knows you're not sleeping in my bed, and trust me, a lot of men would like to take my place."

"Fine," she whispered, her attention flicking to his mouth. "Same goes for you. Until we figure out if this marriage is really—"

"Don't say it. Don't say 'over,'" he growled, lifting a hand to cup her face. When she flinched, he curled the fingers into his palm and let the hand drop away. "I've never had another woman and I'll never want another woman. Bet the fucking bank on it."

Her chest shuddered up and down. "You should go."

"Why, honey?" Ever so slowly, he allowed his fingertips to brush the curve of Rosie's hip and his cock reacted to the shape, the feel of her. "You starting to wish we'd gotten in one more Tuesday night?"

"No," she breathed, swaying a little on her feet.

Dominic hummed deep in his throat, pretty sure they had an audience watching from the front window, and not caring. "You have a good hard think about letting me try this again. Us again. In the meantime, if you come knocking in the middle of the night—any night—I'll scratch that itch, Rosie. It can be our little secret."

Fire kindled in her eyes. "Don't count on it."

"We'll see. I'll leave the porch light on."

Dominic had to physically restrain himself from carrying his wife to the truck. Taking her home and making her moan so loud, they heard it at the ridiculous club meeting. Instead, he catalogued her features one final time and left, his restlessness increasing with every step he took away from Rosie.

CHAPTER SIX

Rosie passed a rinsed dish to Bethany, watching in a daze as her friend tucked it neatly into her stainless steel dishwasher. The meeting had ended twenty minutes ago and Georgie had stayed behind to help clean, leaving the three Just Us League founders to tidy up the mess. Now if Rosie could only tidy up her scattered thoughts, that would be awesome. She'd been in a trance since Dominic left.

Scratch that. She'd been in a trance since he arrived.

She'd married a stubborn son of a bitch, and she'd never imagined him showing up unannounced to ask for another chance. It just wasn't like him. Was it?

Once upon a time, Rosie would have one hundred percent expected Dominic to fight for their relationship. When they were younger, he'd claimed the role of her protector, lover . . . all of the roles, really. They'd been consumed with each other. It wasn't like that now, though. There was still a sexual attraction between them—a wild, pulse-pounding, feverish attraction—but that couldn't sustain their marriage on its own. The fact that their sex life was mind-blowing had probably kept their relationship intact far past the point it had stopped being emotionally fulfilling. And that wasn't okay with her anymore.

Come back to me.

Rosie could still hear the raw quality of Dominic's voice as he said those words. Could still see the plea in his deep green eyes. God, she couldn't remember the last time he'd looked at her like that. Like the fate of his universe hung on what she said next.

"Does that sound good to you, Rosie?" Georgie asked, breaking into Rosie's thoughts.

"Oh. Um, yes. Sounds perfect."

"Really?" The birthday party clown turned entertainment company mogul wiggled her eyebrows at Rosie. "Because I just asked if you'd have a three-way with me and Travis."

Rosie almost dropped the plate in her hands. "What?"

Georgie burst out laughing.

"All right, you lunatic." Bethany hip-bumped her younger sister while battling a smile. "Stop teasing Rosie or she won't spill the goods about what happened on the porch."

"Ah, I was only kidding. Travis is all mine." Georgie chef-kissed her fingers. "Not that I wouldn't be honored to tap that, Rosie—"

"Jesus." Bethany laughed. "You're sexually liberated now, Georgie. We get it."

"I prefer the term 'bonkified.'"

Rosie snorted into the back of her wrist, grateful she'd come to stay with Bethany rather than check into the local motel. The banter between the sisters was a nice distraction from the sudden upheaval of her life. And when Georgie went home to her fiancé, the companionable silence she shared with Bethany was nice, too. Rosie didn't want that silence tonight, however. She wanted to be distracted.

"Have you ever . . ." Rosie pursed her lips at Bethany. "Had a three-way?"

"Rosie Vega, as I live and breathe. The nerve it takes to ask me such a thing." Bethany swiped some cookie crumbs into her hand and brushed them into the garbage can. "Of course I have. You have to kiss a few frogs to find Prince Charming. Might as well test them dicks out two at a time."

"Oh my God. My ears." Georgie snatched her car keys off the kitchen island. "That's my cue to head home."

Bethany leaned a hip against the sink, waving a paper towel at her sister's retreating back. "Look at that. And here Georgie thought she was bonkified."

"No one likes a one-upper!" Georgie called on her way out the door.

When only the two of them remained in the kitchen, Bethany and Rosie cleaned in silence for a few minutes, washing the larger serving trays and setting them out to dry, sweeping up chip particles and napkins. Rosie could feel Bethany's gaze stray to her several times and knew her friend would probably let her escape without giving the details of what went down with Dominic. But Rosie had been bottling up the problems with her marriage for so long, she couldn't do it any longer. And hell, now things with her husband were up in the air—and she didn't have a clue what to do about it.

Rosie set aside the broom. "He wants another chance."

Bethany dove across the kitchen island and propped her chin in her hands. "Oh my God. Tell me everything."

"I'm glad you're enjoying this."

"It's not enjoyment, so much as I'm utterly fascinated by relationships and how they work. You know, since I can't keep one going to save my life."

"You will." Rosie gave her friend a look until that sunk in. "He asked me to come home. I said no. I think." She winced. "I think I said no?"

"I understand. His sex-death-ray eyes wiped your memory clean."

Rosie's laughter was pained. "You saw that, right?"

Bethany straightened and crossed herself. "Woman, we all saw it." She slumped back onto the island. "The chemistry is clearly still alive and kicking—that's for damn sure."

"Yes. But like I told you, everything else is . . ." Rosie made the sound of a cartoon piano falling and crashing on the sidewalk. "It's supposed to be over. I've even dropped a few lines with people at work about available apartments in town. And now . . ."

"And now?"

"Now Dominic is asking for another chance. I'm supposed to have a good hard think about what he needs to do to earn one."

Bethany rolled her lips inward. "Do you want to give him another chance?"

A line formed between Rosie's brows as she thought back over the past five years since he'd been home for good. Moving around her own house like a ghost, trying to lure

Dominic into conversation and failing. Wanting more professionally—personally, too—and not knowing him well enough anymore to broach the subject. She definitely could have tried harder. The more time that passed, the easier it had been to let sleeping dogs lie. Focus on the daily grind and let her aspirations slip further and further until they were unreachable. Now the situation had reversed and the success of her marriage was the thing that felt unreachable.

"No," Rosie said, guilt settling on her shoulders. "I don't think I can try again."

Her friend gave her a sad look. "I'm sorry."

"That being said . . ."

Bethany perked up. "Yes?"

"I'm kind of surprised, but . . . I don't think Dominic is going to give up that easily. He wants his chance."

For long moments, the only sound in the kitchen was the clock ticking on the wall. Until Bethany inflated one cheek and let out a "Hmmmm."

"What?" Rosie narrowed her gaze at Bethany. "What was that?"

Bethany picked up a rag and started to clean off the counters. "Nothing. It was nothing."

"You're not saying something." Rosie searched the kitchen with a sweeping look and picked up one of Bethany's favorite fresh-cotton-laundry candles. "Spill or the candle gets it."

"You wouldn't," Bethany said, and gasped. "I had that shipped from Bali. They captured the essence of a sarong drying in the tropical breeze."

"You know that's bull, right?"

A noncommittal sound from her friend.

"Okay." Bethany pulled out a stool and settled into it, indicating Rosie should do the same. "I dated this divorced guy once. Way back in the day—like two threesomes ago." She winked to let Rosie know she was kidding. "He told me after several margaritas that when he was on the outs with his wife, they went to . . ." She lowered her voice to a whisper. "Extreme couples counseling. Like, I'm talking *extreme*. I think he even called it last-ditch."

Rosie waited for Bethany to say she was joking. She didn't. "Are you serious? Dominic talking to a stranger about his feelings? He gets uncomfortable when people cry on television."

"Okay." Bethany shrugged. "Say he says no. At least you tried. You gave him an option."

Unbelievably, the idea went from cockamamie to brilliant in the space of a breath. "But what if he says yes—" Rosie cut herself off with a wave of her hand. "Never mind. There is a zero percent chance Dominic Vega goes to counseling."

Funny, those words didn't comfort her whatsoever. When she asked Dominic to try counseling and he said no . . . that would truly be it. Their marriage would be over. There *must* have been a tiny part of her that was still holding out for an improbable reconciliation, because she was almost scared to set herself up for that one final disappointment.

Rosie tried to swallow but her mouth was dry as dust. "I'll think about it."

That night, Rosie barely slept, which was saying something, since—like everything else in Bethany's house—the

bed was decadent. High-thread-count sheets, cushy pillows, a mattress that swallowed her like a cloud. The kind
of luxury one would expect from Port Jefferson's premier
house stager. None of it lulled Rosie to sleep, however, and
by the time the sun came up, she was gritty-eyed, restless,
and ready to jump out of her skin.

She threw on some yoga pants and tiptoed down the
stairs, intending to go work out some frustration at the gym.
Her muscles were strung tight as a bow and no amount of
stretching seemed to help. No use in pretending she wasn't
horny. Her soon-to-be ex-husband had shown up with his
leader-of-the-pack swagger and eyes that could strip her
without removing a single stitch of clothing—and now her
body hated her for declining the pleasure he could provide.

On her way out the door, a flash of red brought Rosie to
a screeching halt. She tugged Bethany's white coat to the
side, only to find her red one hanging by the door. How had
it gotten there? Just yesterday, she'd been mentally kicking
herself for not taking it along the night she'd walked out on
Dominic. They were heading into October, and in a town
surrounded by water, the temperatures were starting to
chill fast. She'd considered buying a cheap one, rather than
return to the house and risk a run-in with her husband . . .
but apparently that wouldn't be necessary. Maybe Bethany
had gone and picked it up?

That seemed unlikely. Did Dominic . . . ?

No way.

Rosie shook her head as she donned the coat over her
workout clothes, locked the door, and strode across the

porch, her footfalls extra loud in the morning silence. She breathed in the crisp morning air deeply on her way to the car, spinning the keys around her finger. When Rosie unlocked the driver's-side door and slid in, she frowned, shifting her butt around.

It was forty-something degrees outside. No way the seat should have been so warm. As if someone had been sitting in it before her. Between her red coat appearing on the hook and this, she was starting to feel like the protagonist in a psychological thriller.

Physics had never been her strong suit in high school, especially because Dominic had sat behind her all semester, whispering in her ear when the teacher's back was turned, but maybe the beginnings of sunlight coming through the windshield had heated the seat? Seemed unlikely, but the alternative was that someone had been inside her car.

With a frisson of panic slipping into her bloodstream, Rosie leaned back to make sure there wasn't a seat-warming murderer camped out in the backseat. Finding it empty, she faced forward again with an eye roll and started the car. Rosie reached down and pinched the skin of her forearm, relieved to feel a jolt of pain. The lack of sleep was obviously taking a toll.

There were very few cars on the road as Rosie drove to the gym and parked in the rear lot. Itching to blow off some steam, she flashed her membership card at the sleepy teenager manning the front desk and headed straight for the cardio section. Normally, she would store everything in a locker, but since the gym was empty, she left her coat in a neat pile in front of the treadmill, popped in her headphones, and started running.

She had to make a decision today. Was she going to give Dominic a second chance or not? And if the answer was yes, did she have the strength or will to make an effort?

As if thinking about her husband had conjured him, a movement in her peripheral vision turned her head—and there he was, just on the other side of a floor-to-ceiling partition that separated cardio from weights. She almost tripped over her own feet, her hand slapping down on the treadmill's emergency stop button, before stepping off the treadmill on shaky legs.

Dominic hadn't seen her yet, but the sweat staining the back of his T-shirt told Rosie he'd been there for a while. He finished a set of biceps curls, then fell onto a bench press without taking a breather, his hips straining off the black leather every time he heaved the bar up. There was so much weight on either end, the bar appeared to curve ever so slightly. And when she heard the low rumble of his grunt, right before he released the bar back onto the rack, it sounded so familiar, her nipples tightened into points inside her sports bra. Yes, sir, she knew that grunt exceptionally well. She usually heard it in the dark, amid the creaking of bedsprings and her own screams.

Those were the thoughts in Rosie's head when Dominic sat up and they locked eyes across the gym. His surprise melted into outright hunger almost immediately. It was so potent and visceral, it almost knocked her back a step.

Damp warmth spread along the seam of her yoga pants and she could hear her own breath rasping against her eardrums. So, no—running a mile hadn't done anything to alleviate the sexual frustration. And now her body's tormentor was mere yards away, looking much like he did after one of their Tuesday-night marathons. Sweating, muscles prominent, intensely focused on her.

Why couldn't there be one single other person in the gym? A buff buffer, perhaps? Damn that new CrossFit that had opened in the neighboring town and left this place empty in the mornings when it used to be reasonably busy. Being near her husband when she was this needy wasn't at the top of any good-decision lists.

When one corner of Dominic's mouth lifted in a smirk, Rosie realized she was returning his intense focus and then some. As she watched, he caught the hem of his drenched T-shirt in one hand and stripped it off over his head, revealing a glistening wall of packed, ink-draped muscle. Never taking his gaze off her, Dominic scrubbed a palm over the mountain range of his abdomen, letting his hand drift down, just beneath the waistband of his sweatpants, dragging them down a single inch—and a hoarse sound left Rosie's mouth.

Based on Dominic's reaction, it might as well have been a gunshot. He was off the bench while the noise still hung in the air, closing the distance between them. Whatever thread of self-preservation was still alive in Rosie's body woke up, but in her weak-kneed state, she could only manage to back up a pace. At her retreat, Dominic halted in his tracks, but the scent of his musk and shaving cream continued to travel forward, teasing her senses.

"See something you like, honey girl?" He touched his tongue to the corner of his mouth. "Tell me to fuck off and I'll go. For now." Green eyes raked her body. "I can see that I'm catching you in a weak moment."

Rosie's mouth went dry. *Say something.*

Seconds ticked by. She gave him a pleading look, no idea what she was pleading for. Him to leave her in peace or . . . something else entirely. Something she *needed.*

"Okay, then," he breathed, reaching her in one step. His huge hands found her hips and squeezed hard before spinning Rosie toward the wall. Before she could guess her husband's intention, he'd tucked his lap right up against her backside, letting her feel his erection through the thin material of their workout clothes. His mouth pressed to her ear, breathing, breathing—and when she couldn't help but circle her butt on his hardness, he groaned, loud and long. "There's no one in the bathroom, Rosie. Let me get you straightened out."

"I don't need straightening out," she lied, trying not to be obvious about easing her thighs apart, giving him more room to mold their lower bodies together.

"Lies." His mouth opened beneath her earlobe, his tongue snaking out to taste her skin. And, oh God yes, he took the space she offered, thrusting Rosie up onto her toes, working a desperate sound from her throat. They stayed that way for several seconds, Dominic grinding up into Rosie, Rosie pushing down with her hips, the friction electric, both of them laboring to breathe. Dominic's hand slipped under the elastic of her sports bra and massaged her naked breast with a skilled hand. "Those nipples perked right up for your husband, didn't they? Always begging to get sucked."

A shudder passed through her. She struggled to find enough brainpower for a response, but the lust storm made it difficult to form words. "It's . . . it's, um, cold . . ." Until she opened her eyes, Rosie didn't realize they were closed, but the first thing she spotted was her red coat, still folded in front of the treadmill. "Cold, but I—I had my coat . . ." *Make sense, brain.* "Did you bring my coat to Bethany's?"

Dominic's hand stilled on her breast, but his breath remained shallow in her ear. "What?"

That was all it took for Rosie to have her answer. She'd known this man seemingly since time began and he never lied. He only evaded. "You did bring the coat."

She turned in his arms, sucking in a breath at the stark need on his face. His gaze was transfixed on her mouth for long seconds, before dropping to her right breast, which was still exposed thanks to his marauding hand and her lifted shirt. Dominic's nostrils flared as he pulled her bra back into place, making no move to give her space. "So what?"

"So what?"

Dominic dragged his fingertips down Rosie's sides and flexed his hips, catching her gasp with his mouth, but not kissing her. Never kissing her unless they were in that frenzied state. "I need to get inside you. I need to fuck my wife."

Her neck almost lost power. "Stop changing the subject."

"Your thighs are climbing my hips, honey girl." He thrust into the notch of her legs, slapping a hand on the wall above her head. "This is the goddamn subject."

Well, look at that. Her thighs were, indeed, treating his body like a gym-class rope. With an effort, Rosie forced her feet to flatten on the floor and braced her palms on Dominic's bare chest. It took her another gathering of willpower to push him away, to lose that rigid ride of hard flesh that would guarantee an orgasm if she gave in. God, she wanted to give in. But she knew from experience she would feel empty afterward. Sad. Because while they were so in tune with each other during the act, they disconnected when it was over. Such a steep drop that it never failed to make her uncertain. About everything, especially herself. "Why wouldn't you just say, 'Hey, Rosie, I brought your coat'?"

Dominic sighed and stepped back, crossing his arms over his powerful chest, making the tattoos dance over his muscles. "Did you give some thought to what we spoke about?" His jaw flexed. "A way for me to get you home."

"Yes, I thought about it."

His Adam's apple slid up and down. "And?"

Now it was Rosie's turn to cross her arms. "Answer the question first. Why would you sneak my coat into Bethany's house?"

Dominic's exasperation with the question was obvious. "Because I don't need brownie points for taking care of my wife. It's my job."

Rosie raised an eyebrow. "No offense, dude, but you could use the brownie points." She shifted. "Look, we don't talk anymore and . . . it's not okay. I need to know what you're thinking. Unless you can give that to me, a second chance is pointless."

For long moments, he scrutinized her, thoughts winging behind his green eyes. His head dropped forward and lifted to reveal her husband looking more uncomfortable than she'd ever seen him. "I don't want the credit. I don't know . . . it never feels earned enough. If you said thank you to me for bringing your coat, I'd just be irritated. Because that coat is three fucking years old and why haven't I given you nine to choose from?"

Getting a glimpse into Dominic's mind was like having an oxygen mask slapped over her face. She sucked every insight down greedily, letting the cool, sweet rush of them fill her lungs. Expand them. Was it possible she'd been wrong about some things? This man in front of her didn't seem indifferent at all. Not in the least.

She wanted to hear more. Was that enough to try again when she'd spent so long feeling useless and unhappy?

"Last-ditch therapy," she murmured, before she could stop herself.

Dominic inclined his head. "Come again?"

Rosie cleared the cobwebs from her throat. "Last-ditch therapy. It's for marriages that are in danger of being—"

"Don't say 'over,'" he gritted out.

She took a few seconds to breathe. "Well?"

"Therapy, Rosie? Christ." He dragged a hand down his face. "I knew this club would put ideas in your head. First you leave me—"

Without letting a beat pass, she sidestepped him, scooped up her jacket, and sailed out of the cardio area. Dominic caught up with her in the hallway leading to the lobby.

His hand closed around her elbow and tugged her to a stop. "Wait."

"I left you. That was all me."

A muscle jumped in his cheek. "Yeah. Fine."

This was familiar territory. This stubborn, let's-fight-until-we-fuck dynamic—and it made her angry to be back there after she'd gotten a glimpse of how his mind worked. After witnessing their potential to communicate. "You might as well say no to therapy, because I'm going to find the touchy-feely-est Zen master of them all. I'm talking incense in the waiting room and chakras and the whole nine."

The corners of Dominic's mouth turned down. "Fine. Let's do it."

"Crystal healing and—" She cut herself off. "What?"

"You heard me. Schedule the damn therapist." He leaned down, bringing their faces an inch apart. Whatever he saw there caused him to rear back a little. "You really thought I wouldn't take any chance—*any chance*—to get you back, didn't you?" His voice roughened. "Fuck, Rosie. You can't be serious."

He ran his gaze over her face one final time before turning and leaving her standing in the empty hallway. But not before she saw his determination.

This was real. It was happening.

The Vega marriage, round two.

CHAPTER SEVEN

Dominic leaned up against the side of his truck, pulling from a Newport cigarette and scanning the parking lot for Rosie's Honda. When he didn't see the familiar vehicle, he reluctantly faced the building again, which happened to be painted a bright robin's-egg blue, with a handcrafted sign atop the roof. It read ARMIE TAGART, RELATIONSHIP HEALING GURU.

"Fuck me," he muttered under his breath. "She followed through."

Was he annoyed as hell about having to parade his shortcomings in front of some hippie asshole? Of course. Was he also pretty turned on by his wife putting her money where her mouth was? Yeah. Enough to seriously dampen his irritation.

Dominic drummed his fingers on the roof of his truck, Rosie's show of defiance taking him back to their middle-school years. God, she'd been fierce. Brave. He could remember the first time he'd asked her out in seventh grade. It was lunchtime at school and boys were at one table, girls at the other. For a long time, Dominic had found that separation ridiculous, considering the guys wouldn't shut up about the girls and vice versa. For most of that year, Dominic sat at the end of the guys' table and bided his time, watching Rosie from afar. Every once in a while, she'd catch him staring, flip her hair, and grace him with an expression that said, *What are* you *looking at?*

Back then, she'd always been surrounded by friends. Girls he knew from his classes, but didn't know personally, since he'd moved to Port Jefferson from the Bronx the summer after sixth grade. For years, his mother had been complaining about the New York City congestion, the crime, the sounds of traffic. One day, Dominic's father had come home with the keys to a new home. She'd asked and he'd provided. That's what a man did. That's what kept a family intact. Maybe his father hadn't been an emotional man. Hell, Dominic could count on one hand the father-son talks they'd shared. His father hadn't been able to give them everything, so he'd given them the most *important* things. Security. A home.

Dominic's mind drifted to a very different kind of home than his childhood one. A house overlooking the water, with a sloping backyard and a dock extending into the water. With discomfort riding along the ridges of his shoulders, Dominic shook off the image and went back to thinking about the day he'd tossed the crusts of his ham sandwich into the cafeteria trash can and bridged the divide between the boys and girls of Port Jefferson Middle School. His ears recalled the hush that had fallen over the students, the whispered speculation behind hands.

Rosie had seen him coming a mile away and he'd liked

that. Liked knowing she'd been aware the whole time that he liked her, even though no words had been exchanged. She'd turned around on the bench to watch him approach and taken a deliberate bite out of her apple, chewing in that ladylike way of hers, giving him a once-over. All her friends had leaned in, chins glued to hands, eyes wide. He'd thanked God in that moment for the hours he'd spent listening to his older cousins talk about girls at family gatherings growing up, because while he'd been nervous, he also knew rejection happened to every guy and it wouldn't be the end of the world.

"That dance next Friday," he'd said, trying to keep his demeanor casual even though she was even prettier up close. "You coming with me?"

Gasps and giggles from every corner.

She'd tried to look bored, but Dominic could see the burnished rose on her cheeks and was already counting the days until he could kiss the spots where that color bloomed.

"Are all city kids this brave?" Rosie had asked, studying her apple.

"This one is."

"You've been looking at me a lot."

"Yeah."

When he didn't elaborate, she laughed. "I'll think about it."

Dominic had shrugged. "Better than a yes from someone else."

He'd started to turn and walk away.

She'd shot to her feet. "Yes."

They'd gone to the dance together the following Friday.

He'd worn jeans and a black button-down. She'd rocked a yellow strapless dress and white sandals—and when she'd come down the stairs of her parents' house, fingertips trailing on the railing, his palms had started to sweat, his pulse jackhammering, and he'd known there would never be anyone else. Never.

The sound of a car pulling into the lot broke into Dominic's thoughts. He experienced that same rollicking anticipation, just like all those years ago before the dance. His pulse still went crazy, his heart echoing in his ears, although the anticipation had a much more mature element now. The kind that made his dick grow heavy in his jeans just watching her climb out of the car, her tits shaking around in the neckline of her shirt. Fuck, there really was no one hotter than his wife.

Sunday morning in the gym, he'd thought, *This is it, she's giving in.* There hadn't been a doubt in his mind that he was going to fuck her up against the bathroom tile, one hand over her mouth to muffle her screams. They'd been at what he considered the point of no return, also known as that ass had been backed up in his lap, rubbing all over the wood he was sporting.

Yet she'd been able to put on the brakes. Last time, too.

Whenever he'd been worried about their marriage, their sex life had reassured him that Rosie still felt something for him. Without that reassurance . . . he was scared. Scared enough to talk about his emotions in front of some quack—and that was really saying something, because he barely acknowledged them himself. Keeping a stiff upper lip was a trait he'd always admired in his father. Whether he'd had a bad day at work or money was tight, Dominic's father kept his head down and grinded. No complaining, no showing signs of worry or stress. He simply got the job done and his family never wanted for anything. If there were cracks in his façade, he certainly never showed them. Wouldn't it have made everyone around him less confident in his abilities as a provider?

"Hi," Rosie said, drawing even with him. "You saw the sign and you're still here, huh?"

"That's right."

She shrugged her purse higher on her shoulder and started toward the building, leaving Dominic to follow behind her. "How was work today?"

"Fine. You?"

"Fine."

How many times had they asked the same question and given the same answers? Thousands? In a setting outside of their kitchen or living room, it really hit home how hollow the words sounded. An exercise in going through the motions. They rarely elaborated and the closer they got to the entrance of the shrink's office, the more Dominic's skin started to prickle. He didn't want to find out this therapist really was a last resort. And not just Rosie's way of making him suffer to get her back.

He stepped around Rosie and opened the door for her, trying to be subtle about taking in a lungful of her perfume. Coconut. The gold bottle with a crystal pineapple on top was still sitting on her dresser in their bedroom, so she must have sprayed some on at work. As she moved past him into the building, Dominic looked for the pulse in her neck and was pleased to see it pumping quickly. *Beat-beat-beat.* The proof of her awareness gave him enough hope to follow behind her into . . . the sixties.

Dominic came to a dead stop just inside the door and cursed under his breath. No. This couldn't be real. Each wall boasted a different mural, and if he wasn't mistaken, they were trying to celebrate the four elements. Earth, wind, water, and fire. A mélange of blues flowed into a nature scene, then erupted into flames, only to be blown apart by a cloud. With a face. A chandelier of purple feathers hung from the ceiling, so long it almost reached the floor. A bubble machine sent sprays of floating orbs throughout the room, and soft music played, some kind of combination of xylophones and harps.

"I had no idea you hated me this much, Rosie."

Was it his imagination or did she almost smile? Warmth in the center of his chest caught him off guard and he found himself needing to see that smile again.

"I didn't know it was going to be quite so . . . colorful," she murmured. "The reviews online were overwhelmingly positive."

Dominic turned in a circle, finding his rear end mere inches from a giant snap dragon plant and stepping away before it took a bite out of his ass. "There's a good chance his patients were high when they wrote those reviews," he muttered. "And one of them must be his decorator."

A laugh bubbled out of her, but she silenced it immediately, seeming almost surprised he could still get that reaction from her. How long had it been since he'd made her laugh? When no amount of mental searching landed him on an answer, his throat grew tighter.

"I don't know," she said quietly after a few seconds. "Maybe there's a method to the madness. In a place like this . . . how could anything we say be embarrassing?"

With a frown, he opened his mouth to ask what she could possibly be embarrassed about, but a door on the other side of the room burst open. Pungent marijuana smoke drifted out around a bald man in sandals and a Green Party T-shirt.

Dominic took Rosie's hand and pulled her toward the exit, but she dug in her heels. "You're free to leave," she said.

"Not without you," he gritted out, all too aware that the stoned hippie was strutting in their direction as if his hips were detached. "We can find someone else."

"I like it here."

"Jesus Christ, I forgot how stubborn you are."

"That's because I haven't been in a long time."

Dominic's mouth snapped shut. He wanted to take her face in his hands and dig into that statement before it drove him insane, but a hand settled on his shoulder. "Believe it or not, Team Vega, your reaction to my waiting room is not uncommon."

"Team Vega?" Rosie asked, waving away a waft of smoke.

"Yes. That's correct." The man clasped his hands together. "We have four sessions scheduled. During that time, we are all Team Vega. Rebuilding what is broken will be a collective effort. It will be daunting at times. But there's some good news."

"Enlighten us," Dominic said drily.

The man nodded. "At the end of our four sessions, we

should have an idea whether this marriage is worth saving." His eyes ticked back and forth between Rosie and Dominic. "I can already see we have conflicting opinions on that matter." Before Dominic could question the therapist's observation, the man stepped back and gave a slight bow. "I'm Armie Tagart. You can call me Daddy."

Dominic tried to pull Rosie out the door again.

"Only kidding," Armie called on his way into the back room. "Follow me into the epicenter of healing, if you would be so kind." He paused in the doorway. "That's not a joke. I really call it that."

There were times a woman admitted she was wrong. This wasn't one of those times. She was going to brazen this rash decision out if it killed her. Rosie had come home from the gym Sunday morning, her muscles locked with unfulfilled need, and she'd fired off an email to the most woo-woo-sounding marriage counselor on Long Island. Just to spite the man who'd turned her into an addict for his body while withholding everything else.

Rosie lifted her chin and sailed into the back room of the therapist's office, refusing to show an outward reaction to the lingering scent of pot. She didn't have to make eye contact with Dominic to know he was the poster boy for skepticism. She could see his body language in her periphery as she looked right and left, searching for a place to sit.

"On the pillows," Armie directed, indicating what appeared to be a blanket fort in the corner of the room. "Why not conduct our session in comfort?"

Having no choice but to soldier on, Rosie set down her purse on the corner of Armie's desk and crossed the room, dropping into a cross-legged position on a crocheted heart pillow. When Dominic made no move to join her, she arched an eyebrow at him and he sighed, toeing aside a stuffed crocodile and taking a place beside her.

Armie draped himself across the remaining pillows like Cleopatra preparing for a repast of grapes. "A little bit about me, before we start. Like I said, I'm Armie Tagart. I've been counseling troubled couples on Long Island for thirty years. I have no idea about my success rate, because I don't believe in weighing wins and losses. These are feelings we're dealing with. Hearts, minds, and expectations. They're messy and complicated."

He scratched the top of his bald head. "My methods are unorthodox. They might make you uncomfortable from time to time—and that's the point. To push past the limits of what you think yourself capable of as a partner and human being." A beat passed. "Nothing leaves the safe space of this room. Nothing you can say will shock me or make me think less of you. We're here for a common purpose. To save this marriage. And get high as hell." He pointed at Dominic, who was preparing to launch a protest. "I'm kidding. Lighten up, brother."

Rosie covered her mouth to trap a laugh. Dominic glanced over, appearing almost fascinated by her laugh, and his scowl cleared.

"Interesting," Armie murmured. "Face each other, please. We're going to begin by reintroducing your energies."

Rosie and Dominic remained unmoving.

Armie chuckled. "Sometimes we become so wrapped up in a routine, we forget to look each other in the eye. When was the last time you had even ten seconds of solid eye contact?"

"In bed or out?" Rosie said, heat staining her cheeks.

"Again I say, interesting." Armie made a wishy-washy sound. "Out of bed."

"Ten seconds of eye contact?" she whispered. "I can't remember."

Dominic sighed. "No one does that."

"We used to," she said, her memory zeroing in on one hazy evening in particular. They'd climbed to the roof of the school during summer vacation. She'd locked her thighs around his waist, her forearms propped on his wide shoulders. With the sun warming their skin and a breeze cooling it, they'd looked into each other's eyes so long they'd lost track of time.

Now his brow furrowed. And then he surprised her by saying, "You're right. We did."

"Excellent, Dominic. You heard her."

Rosie's husband's chest expanded on a measured breath; then he let it out and arranged his big body to face her. "Ten seconds?"

"Ten is an arbitrary starting point," Armie said. "There are no time limits or rules within this space. If something feels right, we'll continue with it."

Her heart hammered in her throat as she faced Dominic, their knees bumping, as they were both sitting cross-legged.

"Um . . ." My God, she was having a literal heart attack over looking her husband in the face. Honestly. She lifted her gaze to meet Dominic's. "L-like this?"

Armie hummed, but Rosie barely heard the sound. Her pulse was rioting too loudly in her temples. She had to focus on keeping her breathing even in the path of those green eyes. They were steady and lost at the same time—a combination she never expected—and it was hard not to turn away. So hard.

She only made it five seconds, her attention cutting down to her lap.

When she snuck a quick glance back up at Dominic, he was frowning, his chest rising and falling faster than it had before.

"What happened?" he asked gruffly.

"I don't know."

A few ticks of silence passed before Armie piped up. "Why don't we ease into this a little bit." He sat up straighter. "Rosie, are you comfortable with Dominic's touch?"

"Yes," Dominic answered for her, a hint of pleading dancing across his granite features, surprising her. "Please, just . . . give me that."

Feeling as if she were balanced on the edge of a diving board, Rosie nodded. "Yes."

"Okay. Rosie, close your eyes. Remember, you're in a safe place. Dominic, I want you to touch her face. It will be a little less intense than the eye contact, Rosie, but reestablishing the connection is what we're after here."

Dominic hadn't even touched her yet and goose bumps were already rising on every inch of her skin. She let her eyelids drop and held in a deep breath as Dominic reached out a hand and curved it to her cheek. The instant their skin touched, the breath rushed out of her on a whimper. Humiliating. Or it should have been, but she only felt a tenth of the embarrassment she'd consider normal. Maybe because her eyes were closed. Maybe because they were in a blanket fort with a high hippie. Whatever the reason, all of her focus raced to the hand on her face. Every nerve ending zinged in that direction, wanting attention.

"Learn her, Dominic."

"I know this face better than anything."

Rosie's heartbeat drowned out Armie's initial response, picking up somewhere in the middle. "Trace her eyebrows, her lips. Let her feel you looking at her and acknowledging her."

Her husband's thumb arched along her cheekbone, made a pit stop at her dimple, running the tip of his finger through it. Back and forth. He brushed his touch along the bow of her mouth, the crease of her chin. Moved higher and rubbed circles into the center of her forehead—and all the scattered parts of her calmed while it happened. For once, she was nowhere but right there, inside herself. So centered she could have fallen asleep. All because Dominic was looking at her and really trying to see? Was he? Or was this just an exercise?

"Thank you, Dominic," Armie said quietly.

His fingers lingered a few more seconds before their heat vanished. Rosie opened her eyes to find Dominic looking momentarily shell-shocked, before he hid it.

That made two of them.

When was the last time they'd touched . . . just to touch? Out of affection and without sex roaring in like an insatiable beast? She'd had no idea how much she'd been craving it.

"Dominic, how do you let Rosie know you appreciate her?"

It visibly took Dominic a few beats to focus and his voice was little more than a rasp when he finally answered. "I provide."

"That would have been my guess." Armie turned to Rosie. "When Dominic provides for you, does that make you feel appreciated?"

"I . . ." Her brow wrinkled. "I guess it does. In a way . . ."

"What would make you feel more appreciated? If he brought you a gift? Maybe your favorite incense?" She swapped incense for margarita mix or a standing mixer in her mind. Even though both of those items were super appealing, they didn't make her feel reassurance or warmth. "What if Dominic simply told you he appreciates you?"

"Yes," she breathed, her pulse thumping.

The therapist made a knowing sound. "You need words."

She thought of Dominic telling her he appreciated her. Out loud. And pressure on her chest she wasn't aware of eased a little bit. "Yes. I think I do."

Armie nodded vigorously. "I'm going to take a shot in the dark that neither of you is familiar with love languages." Silence. "As I suspected." He encompassed them both with a warm look. "Each one of us has a preferred way of expressing love. And having love expressed to us. Dominic expresses love through deeds. But you need to receive love through words."

"So . . . that's it?" Dominic asked. "Ten minutes and we already have a solution?"

"You would love that, wouldn't you?" Armie laughed, eyes twinkling. "No. You have an answer. The solution requires a lot more work. And practice." The older man was surprisingly spry as he jumped to his feet. Rosie and Dominic followed him toward his desk. "During one of these sessions, we're going to talk about what Dominic needs to feel loved and appreciated—"

"For chrissakes."

"For now, though, we're going to focus on Rosie, since she's the one who was troubled enough to leave the marriage." He paused. "I'm going to give you a homework assignment. A few of them, really. Since you've already separated, we're working on an accelerated healing track."

"He just made up that term," Dominic muttered in her ear.

"I heard that." Armie laughed heartily while leaning back against his desk, but he eventually grew thoughtful. "In my thirty years as a marriage counselor, I'm not sure I've ever witnessed such a raw sexual charge between husband and wife. I hope you don't mind me saying so." He whistled under his breath. "It's quite breathtaking."

Rosie was suddenly much more aware of Dominic's nearness. The scent of sawdust and male and menthol. How large he was in comparison to her and how one step backward would press their bodies together.

"Unfortunately, I think sex is getting in the way of really seeing each other." He stared down his nose at them. "Being partners out of the sack."

"We aren't . . ." Rosie licked her dry lips. "Doing that now."

Behind her, Dominic muttered something about putting their business on the street.

"Great," Armie said.

"Says who?" Dominic asked.

"Says me. One of your homework assignments is to keep not having sex." He split a speculative glance between them. "I will allow kissing."

Anticipation almost swallowed her whole. Kissing. God, she hadn't been kissed in so long, without sex happening at the same time. Oh, there was an occasional hard press of mouths or brief, cursory pecks, but one of her favorite pastimes with Dominic had been making out. Getting hot and bothered, just for the sake of *needing*. They were professionals at it. Had gotten that way by waiting until she turned seventeen to have sex. They'd dry humped through their first three years of high school and had so many orgasms with their clothes on, she'd truly lost count. And she'd never felt more connected to Dominic than when their mouths were communicating like that. Eye contact wasn't something that made her uncomfortable back then; it was expected. Craved, along with the words he used to whisper in her ear.

I love you.

I need you, honey girl.

We're in this forever.

"Kissing is often more intimate than sex and it breeds further intimacy, such as talking or looking into each other's eyes. Tapping into one another's energy," Armie was saying. "Now. For the next assignment. Dominic, you're going to write Rosie a letter."

"Come again?"

"Call me crazy, but I don't think words come that easily to you. Just like Rosie with the eye contact, we're going to ease into it. Let's try verbalizing on paper first."

Dominic shifted behind her. "What am I supposed to say?"

Armie smiled broadly. "That's up to you to decide."

CHAPTER EIGHT

Dominic had never written a letter in his life. Mainly because of technology. Text messaging had been around since he was old enough to spell, so there'd never been much of a need to put pen to paper, apart from the odd note. When he and Rosie were younger, they passed a couple of them between classes, but they were short and sweet. *You look cute in that skirt. I missed you this weekend. Come to the movies with me on Saturday.* Et cetera.

He couldn't help but remember that she'd looked kind of . . . excited about the prospect of receiving a letter from him, and, God, he'd missed that expression on her face. It brought back memories of the morning they'd run hand in hand through the rain into the courthouse, determined to tie the knot before he was deployed. Raindrops had still been lingering on her eyelashes when they'd presented their marriage license moments later, holding each other and rocking as they waited for their turn to say "I do."

Well, if she *was* excited about the letter, she was about to be sorely disappointed with the results.

Dominic tossed the pen onto the lowered gate of his

truck, scrubbing a palm over his shaved head. About fifteen minutes ago, Stephen had called a lunch break and everyone spread out on the job site, sitting in groups with their foil-wrapped sandwiches while Dominic retreated to his truck to get started on the letter. After therapy yesterday, he'd gone home and attempted to get his thoughts on paper, but nothing came—and he needed to get it done today. The urgency gnawing at his gut wouldn't allow for any further delay.

She couldn't even look him in the eye.

Every time he thought about that moment she'd ripped her gaze away like she was in pain, he felt sick. Hadn't even packed a lunch this morning because his appetite had dwindled to nothing. Sex was off the table. He couldn't make her feel better with his body. She needed this letter. She needed words. And he had no idea where or how to find them.

A rock bumped against Dominic's shoe, and he turned to find Stephen and Travis approaching with a third man, someone he was seeing for the first time. The guy was young—probably younger than all of them—but he made up for those missing years in height and walked with a shit ton of confidence that only someone in a cowboy hat could pull off.

"Dominic," Stephen said, "this is Wes Daniels. He's going to be working with us for a while. New in town."

Dominic reached over and shook his hand. "Where from?"

"San Antonio," Wes returned, giving him a firm shake and a flash of white teeth. "Good to meet you."

"Same." Dominic frowned at the empty piece of paper he'd weighted down with a rock. "Don't hear a lot of those accents on Long Island."

"Then I take pity on Long Island. This here is poetry coming out of my mouth."

Travis coughed into his fist. "Wes is a little cocky."

Dominic raised a brow. "Pot, meet kettle."

"He's got family in town, but he's not sure how long he'll be in Port Jefferson." Stephen gave him a nod and knowledge seemed to pass between them. "Let's make him feel welcome."

Wes jerked his chin at Dominic's non-letter. "You working on something?"

"Nope."

"Looks like you're working on something," Travis observed, stroking his chin. "Skipped lunch to do it. Must be kind of important."

Dominic stared unflinchingly at Travis. "If you already know something, pretty boy, I suggest you spit it out. I'm not in the mood."

Wes let out a low whistle.

"I know everything. All the business," Travis said, slapping a hand to the center of his chest. "It's amazing."

"You know what might be fun?" Stephen smirked at Travis. "Telling Georgie that you're not keeping this shit to yourself."

"You're just mad because your wife doesn't have the gossip."

"My wife has baked goods. I've made the correct choice."

"You two remind me of my aunts. Brenda and Julie," Wes said, adjusting his hat. "They would bicker on their way into hell over who gets to go first."

"You've just been compared to someone's aunties," Dominic drawled. "Can you two shut up now?" He picked up the discarded pen and tapped it on the rear gate. Maybe therapy wasn't total bullshit, because he had a minor urge to talk. To other people. About information he normally would keep guarded unless under threat of death. "Me and Rosie . . . we're in therapy," he muttered. "My homework is to write her a letter."

Wes crossed himself. "This is why you'll never get me down the aisle."

A crunch of gravel turned all of their heads. A silver Mercedes parked amid a lingering swirl of dust, and Bethany stepped out of the driver's side. Dominic was well used to seeing Stephen's sister on job sites. She usually showed up in the middle stages of a flip to get an idea of the layout, so she could begin deciding which furniture to use for the stage. He liked her. She was tough as hell and good at her job, but all he wanted to do now was ask about his wife. His throat actually burned with the repressed need. In an attempt to prevent the pressing questions, Dominic looked away from the approaching decorator—and found Wes with his jaw on the floor.

"Who is *she*?"

"Oh no. No." Stephen shook his head. "Everyone needs to keep their interest in my sisters to themselves, starting now. Especially if you're on my payroll. Leave me an ounce of pride."

Dominic didn't miss Travis sending Wes a warning slash across the neck. "You don't want to go there, man."

"I think I do," Wes disagreed, tucking a tongue into his cheek. "I definitely want to go there."

Stephen buried his face in his hands and groaned.

Bethany joined the group, and Wes smiled. "I'm Wes, ma'am. Nice to meet—"

"Roll your tongue back up into your mouth before one of us steps on it, pudding." Bethany threw an incredulous look around the circle. "Who is this guy?"

"I was telling you when you cut me off." Wes looked her up and down. "Pudding."

Dominic, Travis, and Stephen all took a collective step backward.

"Forget I said anything." Stephen waved a hand at Wes. "I want to see how this plays out."

Bethany and Wes were still attempting to stare each other down.

"I thought we only hired college kids in the summertime," Bethany said brightly, smoothing the sleeve of her black coat.

Wes crossed his arms, as if he had all the time in the world. "That must be hard, considering you probably create winter wherever you go."

She gasped. "Are you calling me an ice princess?"

"If the tiara fits."

"I'll take a tiara over your Clint Eastwood hand-me-downs."

Wes tilted his head to the side. "Remind me who that is? He might be better known among your generation."

"My—" Bethany cut herself off, closing her eyes and visibly composing herself. "I didn't come here to play verbal tennis. I'm here to work. Stephen, do you have a spare hard hat?"

Dominic reached for the one in his truck bed, handing it to her. "Avoid the back bedroom. There are some loose floorboards."

"Chivalry is not dead after all," she said, popping on the yellow hat and tapping the top to press it down. All while smiling sweetly at Wes. "I wasn't sure."

Wes smiled back, but it fell away as soon as Bethany turned toward Dominic.

"Whatcha got there? Some kind of letter?"

His lips gave a wry twist. "Sounds like you know something about this."

"I might," she said breezily, patting his arm. "Need some help?"

"Depends." Dominic swallowed, studying the blank page and willing words to appear. "Are you pulling for us?"

"I'm pulling for my friend's happiness."

He lifted his eyes to find Bethany wearing a serious expression.

"And I know you want to make her happy. I know it."

Dominic could only nod. "I'll take the help."

Travis propped a hip against his taillight. "Roses are red. Violets are blue—"

"Shut it," Dominic said, jabbing the pen into Travis's side.

"Boys. If you please." Bethany held up a hand and waited for silence. "You know what always gets me? When a man proves he's paying attention." She glanced back over her shoulder. "You taking notes back there, pudding? I'm assuming your knowledge of women is a zero. We can tick it up to one."

"I already know what a woman like you wants. A sturdy broom to ride around on."

"I hate him, Stephen," Bethany whispered tightly.

"That's enough, you two," Stephen huffed, waving at the blank page. "Continue. I'm interested to hear this."

"Right." Bethany patted Dominic on the forearm. "A man who pays attention. I'm not just talking about knowing her favorite movie or how she takes her coffee. I'm talking about details. Little things that would slip under the radar—unless you're the one who loves her. You would notice them." She smiled. "Yes, the devil is definitely in the details. Did that help?"

"Not even a little bit," Dominic answered.

"Well, I tried!" She whipped her coat back and swept toward the house. "Texas called, Wes. It wants its rodeo clown back."

"Oz called. They're missing a witch."

Travis laughed. "Told you not to go there."

"Are you crazy?" Wes said, taking off his hat and fanning himself with it. "I want to go there even more now."

The voices around Dominic faded out until he couldn't hear anyone's but Rosie's, traveling to him from the past.

In the darkness of the Montauk hotel where they stayed on their honeymoon. Over the phone when he called her from Afghanistan, his heart tearing in half while listening to her try not to cry, telling him to be safe. In the mist of a breathless meeting in their shower, her back squeaking up and down on the tile. Details. Details. He had those.

Swallowing hard, Dominic picked up the pen and started to write.

CHAPTER NINE

Rosie's heels clicked in the silence of the mall parking lot. The night breeze swirled around her calves and caressed her neck. She breathed it in deeply, grateful for fresh, clean air after eight hours of sucking in various perfumes. There was no respite from the cloying odor except for the break room, and that smelled like reheated chicken and stale donuts. This afternoon, she'd gotten stuck behind a stalled school bus and arrived three minutes late, so she'd been forced to demonstrate a scent called Green Monster.

Two bottles had been sold.

Both to female customers who wanted to play a joke on their boyfriend.

Rosie didn't even bother waiting until she'd reached her car to take off the heels. She gripped them by the stems and cooled her feet on the chilled asphalt, one step at a time. She'd have to remember to wash them off before getting into Bethany's dream bed.

Weirdly, she wasn't quite as excited to sink into the exquisite mattress tonight. It might be perfect and ergonomically designed, but . . . a lot was missing. Things she'd grown used to and possibly, maybe, taken for granted. Such as Dominic's breath in her hair, steady and deep and reliable. The way he'd brush their knuckles together when the night was too dark to see each other's face. And just that simple touch would lull her back to sleep. Even the dip of the mattress when he turned over, the one that used to wake her up and annoy her . . . She found herself waking up in Bethany's bed, troubled by the absence of it.

This was normal. Any kind of change was hard. It wasn't that she missed him. She needed to remember that. What would she miss? His brooding silence? Their total lack of a social life? Seriously, he hadn't taken her out in . . . years. They had friends, but those relationships never got nurtured because they always stayed home. Dominic didn't expressly ask her to stay home, but growing up they'd done everything together. Now they were adults and going out separately never seemed like an option. Almost like there was an unspoken rule between them and it was cemented by Dominic's possessiveness.

If she hadn't gone to Zumba class one night over the summer, she wouldn't have been there for the formation of the Just Us League. It might never have been formed at all.

Rosie stepped on a pebble and winced.

"You okay, Rosie?" called the security guard from the mall door. He'd been supervising Rosie's walk to her car since she'd gotten the job years ago. Such a sweetheart. His watching over her was slightly odd, considering he didn't do it for anyone else, but he was such a harmless grandfatherly type, she never questioned it.

Hopping on one foot, she waved back. "I'm fine, Joe!"

Lost in her thoughts—and the twinge of pain in her heel—it took Rosie a moment to see the envelope on her windshield, tucked beneath one of the wipers.

Her name was written across the front in a familiar hand. Dominic's.

Rosie's stomach winged up to her throat like a startled bird as she plucked the envelope out of its place. With it in hand, she looked around the empty parking lot, as if her husband might be leaning against a lamppost, but there was no one there, save the McDonald's wrappers and shopping bags blowing in the wind.

She took out her car keys and unlocked the door, waving one final time to Joe before climbing into the driver's seat and locking the Honda. After a moment of deliberation, she set the letter down on the passenger seat and started the car. She'd read it when she got home and changed into her pajamas. But she made it two feet before she slammed on the brakes and threw the car back into park. With a deep breath, she retrieved the letter and switched on the overhead light, sliding the folded piece of paper out of its home.

Rosie,

You have a freckle behind your ear, in a place that's impossible for you to see. I'm not sure if anyone has ever told you about it, but sometimes I pretend it's my secret. The first time I kissed it, we were at homecoming. Beginning of senior year. I pulled your back against my front and the lights went up. The dance was over and it felt like we'd just gotten there. We looked around and everyone was gone. When you turned your head, that's when I saw the freckle, right in the crease where your ear meets your head. I leaned in, kissed it, and you told me you loved me for the first time. Whispered it while they stacked the chairs around us. Do you remember that? I was convinced that freckle was magic. The secret way I made you fall in love with me. When you left, my first thought was, I should have kissed that freckle more. I bet you didn't know you married a ridiculous man. Will you please just consider the possibility that I love you more than you realize or than I'm capable of expressing with words?

If that's too much to ask, suffice it to say, I'm proud to have you as my wife.

I'm proud of the person you were that night at homecoming, the person you became when I was away, and most of all, the person you are now. You're incredible. I'm sorry I didn't tell you often enough.

Yours,
Dominic

The letter fluttered into Rosie's lap. Her fingers were tingling too much to hold the piece of paper for a second longer. *You're incredible.*

In that moment, that's exactly how she felt. Light and heavy all at once. Substantial.

Rosie was a strong woman and liked to think she didn't need a pat on the back. But Dom's letter was just truth. It was revealing and she couldn't deny the new energy flowing through her, knowing she made someone proud.

I should have kissed that freckle more.

She could almost feel Dominic's lips behind her ear, whispering those words that made her feel so desirable. Not as a sexual object, but as a singular woman. As Rosie. A hot mudslide seemed to break loose inside her, traveling all the way to her stomach. She suddenly felt so full. So aware of every inch of her skin and every breath entering and leaving her lungs. Her thighs felt uber-present on the seat, covered in goose bumps, and she moved them around, just to feel the soft, worn-in material of the driver's seat rasp against her panty hose. She tipped her head back and recalled that night at homecoming, her lips lifting into a smile. This was how she'd felt then. Like a woman. Like the object of someone's notice.

Important.

Real.

She could do anything when she felt like this.

Heart trapped in her throat, Rosie read the letter again. And again. She was preparing to read it a fourth time when a knock on the window shaved approximately nine years off her life.

Joe the security guard waved from the other side of the glass. Thankfully he kept his flashlight averted, because she didn't need the sweet older gentleman getting an eyeful of what Dominic's letter was doing to her body. Her nipples were in rigid points, her thighs squeezed together, those tiny muscles inside of her bearing down, searching for that invading thickness her husband usually provided.

"You all right in there, Rosie?" came his muffled voice through the window.

"Yes," she croaked, stuffing the letter back into the envelope. "I was just getting ready to leave—thanks for checking on me."

Joe nodded. "Wouldn't want to catch hell from Dominic," he said almost absently, throwing her a wink. "Or miss out on that extra fifty dollars a week he gives me to make sure you get to your car safely."

"He . . . what?"

"I've been putting it into a college fund for my granddaughter." He chuckled. "She wants to do something with computers. Hell if I understand any of it. You take care, Rosie!"

Shell-shocked, Rosie stared at Joe's retreating back. Until he turned around and waved her into action. Fingers still tingling, she started the car and pulled out of the lot, grateful the road back to Port Jefferson was mostly empty this time of night, because no way should she have been operating a motor vehicle. On her way through town, she found herself taking a detour down one of the side streets, just off Main, and stopping in front of the empty commercial space she'd been dreaming about since it appeared for sale in the classifieds.

Tonight was the first time she'd actually come to see it in person—and it was everything she'd hoped. It was out of her price range, even with the GoFundMe donations, but it had been sitting vacant for a while. At the very least, she could afford to make an offer, even if it was significantly lower than the asking price. The storefront might be a little closed off, but eventually, when she had the capital, that could be fixed, turned into a restaurant that beckoned customers closer. Open windows, music pouring out, the scent of Argentinian spices wafting onto the street. Lights. There would be so many lights, all colors, strung from the ceilings, hung from the rafters of the patio in back. Plants. Green, lush plants would be placed all over, giving diners the impression they'd gotten on a plane and traveled a long, long way from Port Jefferson.

If Rosie's mother were still alive, she would have wanted the waitstaff to be impeccably dressed. It was one of her mother's pet peeves—going out to eat and being served by a waiter with messy hair or an untucked shirt. She'd send Rosie and her father a sniff and an eye roll. God, she missed that eye roll. Missed having them both around so much. Maybe when . . . if Rosie opened the restaurant, she would give a nod to her mother by making an all-black uniform mandatory. She'd add a splash of red, though. That would be for her.

What was she doing here? Lingering at the curb at this time of night, weaving dreams through her car window? Rosie didn't know for sure, but there was a confidence sitting on her shoulders—a sense of self that hadn't been there at the start of the day. Or even when she'd finished her shift. It had come when she read the letter. Words. She really did need them. Her friends had been encouraging her verbally since they'd formed the Just Us League and that had gone a long way toward helping her realize she deserved more. More out of her life, her relationship, her career. But there was something about hearing Dominic's voice, even on paper, that made her feel more like her old self than anything else could. And the further she traveled toward her core, the more her self-esteem built.

Rosie took one last look at the storefront and pulled her car back onto the street, hesitating a moment before turning at the end of the block toward Bethany's house. She had to resist the temptation to drive the opposite way. To her home. To Dominic. He would be inside her before the click of the lock faded from the air. They would have sex instead of talking, which really, really didn't sound terrible at the moment. Afterward, though, what would happen? Would unspoken—necessary—words be forced into the open if they gave in to that other, extremely satisfying outlet?

Before she climbed out of the car, Rosie groaned up at the ceiling, all too aware that the seam of her panty hose was damp. It was only Thursday night and they didn't have therapy scheduled again until Monday. Would they get the all clear to be physical? Would she take it? God knew her body was ready, but her mind . . . she wasn't sure.

One thing Rosie knew for certain?

A few things couldn't wait until Monday for clarification.

When Rosie walked into Bethany's house, the blonde

was lying prone on the couch with a cold eye mask draped across the top half of her face. She lifted a hand and wiggled her fingers in greeting. "Hello, gorgeous."

"Hey, yourself." Rosie took off her red coat and dropped it on the hook, staring at it for several long seconds. "I'm going to head up early, okay?"

"Long day?"

"Something like that," Rosie murmured, heading for the stairs. "See you in the morning."

Bethany hummed, thankfully picking up on Rosie's need for a quick exit. As soon as she was in the guest room, she toed off her shoes and started to pace. Her purse sat on the bed, cell phone visible in the inside pocket. One button and she'd be connected to Dominic. The prospect of hearing his deep, cigar-ash drawl sent a rush of heat through her belly, and although she told herself to ignore those bubbles of yearning, she unzipped her skirt and let it drop to the floor, followed by the hose. Her silk blouse came next, the buttons feeling extra-smooth on her finger pads. It joined her skirt on the floor, and Rosie was left standing in panties and a strapless bra.

Biting down on her lower lip, she inwardly cursed the warm exhilaration creeping up the insides of her thighs. God, she was needy tonight. Every inch of her flesh was sensitive and restless. Hungry. Before she could stop herself, Rosie slid her feet back into the high heels, unable to suppress the naughty tickle of pleasure it gave her, being dressed so provocatively. Ignoring her blaring common sense, she snatched up the phone and called her husband.

"Rosie."

She covered the bottom half of the phone and let out a shaky exhale. Oh my God. One word out of his mouth caused the wetness to spread in her underwear, sent her nerve endings into chaos. "Hi, Dominic." In the background, she could hear the familiar slide of their living room curtain rod. "I'm not outside."

The frustration was evident in his lack of response.

What if he'd found her walking up the brick pathway? He'd already be unzipping his pants, stripping off his shirt to reveal all that honed and hardened muscle—

"So . . ." Rosie licked her lips, toes flexing in her high heels. "Let me get this straight," she breathed. "First, you sneak my coat into Bethany's house. Now I find out you've been paying the security guard to watch over me?"

Silence passed. "Joe was supposed to keep that between us."

"Dominic . . ." She shook her head. "Don't you think I would have liked knowing that?"

His low, noncommittal rumble reached her ear. "You should assume I'm doing everything I can to keep you safe."

Her laugh sounded dazed. "But it would have made me feel special. It would have told me that I'm special to you." Pressing the phone to her ear, she lay down on the bed and trailed light fingertips around her belly button. "A lot like your letter." Her body might be in full protest mode that she hadn't gone to see her husband tonight, but her brain could acknowledge how important it was for them to talk. Like this. So even though it was hard ripping off Band-Aids, she forced herself to do it. To be revealing. "Your letter made me feel like . . . the old me. I read it three times."

There was a change in the nearness of his breathing, as if he'd moved the phone away. He came back almost as fast. "I wasn't sure I did it right."

"What were you hoping to do? With the letter."

"Truthfully? I wanted it to make you come home."

The raw quality of his voice made her throat temporarily close up. "Don't you agree there are things we have to straighten out way before that happens?"

He cleared his throat and fell silent for a moment. "You couldn't even look me in the eye for ten goddamn seconds, Rosie. I know we've got a big problem now."

Their marriage might have gone radio silent, but she knew this man better than anyone. Enough to know he'd been holding on to this one thing, possibly even obsessing over it. Should she have been more sensitive to that? "I'm sorry. I'm still not sure what happened."

"I hate this." She heard him swallow. "I want my wife home. We can work out what's wrong right here. We don't need to separate."

"Do you want me back because I'm your wife and I'm supposed to be there? Or do you miss Rosie?" Her chest lifted and fell. "Can you imagine how hard it is to believe you want me home when . . . you barely seemed to register I was there before?"

His laugh held no humor. "Jesus Christ. If you only knew."

"Tell me. How am I supposed to know anything unless

you talk to me?" She closed her eyes and evened out her breathing. "We can start easy. Even you telling me about your day would mean so much to me. Actual details. Not just it was good."

A floorboard creaked on the other end of the line and she knew exactly which part of the house he was in. The hallway. Right in front of the pictures of them together. High school graduation, the day of his first deployment, on the steps of the courthouse on their wedding day, Dominic looking serious with an arm wrapped around her waist, pulling her into his side. She'd stood in that same spot thousands of times, listening to the echoes of the past, wishing they'd carried into the future.

"Stephen hired a new guy. Wes from Texas. He wears a cowboy hat."

"Get out of here."

"It's true. Bethany didn't mention him?"

"No, but she's wearing her heavy-duty eye mask. It only comes out of the freezer when she's mega-stressed."

"Trust me, he's the cause." She heard the scrape of a picture frame being adjusted. "Count on him being the topic of discussion at an upcoming Just Us League meeting."

That same sensation she'd experienced in the mall parking lot was back. That sense of fullness, being grounded. Talking to Dominic, hearing his words, reminded her who she'd been when talking to him hadn't been such a rare event, but a constant. It brought back that optimistic, anything-is-possible state of mind. Made her loose, light, and woke up every section of her body from the tips of her breasts down to the softening flesh between her thighs. Before she knew her own intentions, Rosie slipped her fingers into the waistband of her panties, running her middle finger through the slickness Dominic had created with his voice. His words.

"Um." She shuddered as her fingertip grazed her clit. "A-anything else?"

Dominic's breathing cut out. "What are you doing?"

"Nothing," she said too quickly.

"Where are you?"

"Bethany's house."

"Where are you in the house?"

"Lying on the bed," she rasped.

"Fuck, Rosie. I knew it."

Her breath caught at the sound of his fist hitting their hallway wall.

"I knew it. You think I'm not well aware when that pussy is wet?"

This had been a mistake. They weren't on solid-enough ground yet. For all she knew, the therapist would consider phone sex a violation of his rules and . . . and she didn't want to mess this up. Walking into Armie's office, she'd been prepared to plow through all four sessions just to say she'd tried. Now, though? Trying seemed like a real option. Dominic was in this. And it seemed like every day they were apart, she was discovering new things about him. Things that made her wonder if the old Dominic was there, right under the surface. So yeah. She didn't want to do something to jeopardize what little progress they'd made. "I'll go—"

"You hang up this phone, honey girl, and I'll kick Bethany's door down to get to you," Dominic growled, that dominant side she knew so well coming out to play. "When you're being a hot little tease like this, I find a way to make you come. Don't I?"

"Yes," she whimpered, adding a second fingertip and rubbing her clit in slow, unhurried circles. "You do."

"You want to talk, Rosie? Let's talk about Tuesday nights."

She heard his belt hit the floor, the buckle clacking off the wood, and moisture rushed between her thighs.

"With the exception of last week, you usually come home those nights and go straight to the bedroom. Strip down to your thong and pretend like you left the door cracked by accident. But you know. You know I'm watching you and getting hard. Christ."

He grunted a curse and Rosie knew he'd wrapped a fist around his erection, could picture his tattooed knuckles stroking up and down that thick column of flesh.

"I should have known something was wrong when you took off your high heels at the door. You usually leave them on Tuesday nights, don't you? They're the very last thing that come off when I fuck you, aren't they?"

Rosie cast a look down the writhing form of her own body, the breasts spilling out of her bra, the panties hiding her moving fingers, ending at the pointed black leather encasing her feet. "I'm wearing them right now."

"*Rosie.*" He made a choked sound and she could hear the pace of his strokes pick up. "If you were here, they'd have come off by now. Never can keep them on when I'm thrusting, can you? When I'm hitting you deep and your legs can't stay still, those size sevens hit the floor faster than your panties."

If there was one fact that was infinitely true about her husband, it was that he had no problem talking a blue streak when they were like this. Whatever filter he usually kept in place evaporated, and pure, raw sex rolled right off his tongue. She craved his filth. It was a constant between them. His obsession with her body was the one thing she could count on one hundred percent. Tonight, though? Tonight, after having read his letter, talked to him, Dominic's filth was even more effective. The insides of her thighs were coated with the evidence of that. She wished she could smell that faint tobacco scent he carried everywhere. The one he seemed to think she minded, but she actually craved. Her heartbeat echoed in her ears, and her hips arched, circled, arched, two fingers using the ample moisture to massage her swelling clit.

"Dominic," she gasped, feeling her walls start to quicken, that low, low thrum in her belly going from a ten to an eleven. "I want you to come."

"That right? I was starting to wonder." He groaned, and Rosie bit her lip, listening to the wet stroke of male fist on flesh, happening across town and in her ear at the same time. There was a twang of bedsprings, too, the sound achingly familiar. "I'm in our room, honey girl. Kneeling on your side of the bed. I'm picturing you in front of me with your thighs wide open."

Rosie rolled over onto her stomach and moaned into the mattress. With that erotic imagery in her head—Dominic pleasuring himself on their bed while she posed in front of him—Rosie bore down on her fingers, pumping her hips and rubbing up and back at the same time. "Dominic, Dominic, please . . ."

"Please, what?"

"Come all over me," she sobbed. "Paint me in it."

His growl almost hurt her eardrum. "Come home and I'll do it. I'll cover you in what I've got, all over that incredible body. And soon as I'm hard again, I'll flip you over and remind the neighbors how loud you can scream."

Even though his words warned her to put the brakes on, Rosie couldn't help herself. She sunk two fingers inside the weeping opening of her flesh and cried out, riding her own hand in earnest. "Please, I'm so close. I want you with me."

"No. No, I want you with me," he gritted out. "I want you home."

"Dominic!"

He made a low, hungry sound. "Would you suck my cock between those pretty lips if you were here, honey girl?"

A ripple moved through her sex and she rode harder, faster. "Yes. Oh my God, yes."

"Yeah, I know you would, Rosie." His breath was turning more shallow by the second. "You'd suck it like you know the pussy-licking is coming next. You always do."

"I'm coming," she wailed into the comforter. "I can't stop."

Sexual frustration dripped from his voice. "I'm not finishing until it's inside my wife."

Pleasure slammed into Rosie before those words could register, her flesh spasming around her fingers as the orgasm tore through her body, head to toe. Jesus. Jesus. She couldn't drag in oxygen fast enough, but at the same time, her lungs felt full to bursting. Dominic's harsh breathing on the other end kept her hips grinding down on her stiff fingers, milking the climax for everything it was worth.

"Say my name, wife," he instructed.

"Dominic," she managed, rolling her forehead side to side on the mattress. "Please. Please, don't hold out like this."

"Why not?"

Denial reared its head at thinking of him going to bed unsatisfied. Getting up in the morning and going to work without relief. "It's cruel to both of us."

"Good-bye, Rosie. I'll see you Monday." He took a sharp inhale, and she heard his jeans zip back up. "If you want to see me sooner, you know where we live. I won't lay a finger on you until you're ready. But I'm not going to let you settle into this. Living apart. Fucking over the phone. Understand how serious I am about bringing you back to me. Don't doubt me when I say I'll fight dirty to get you back through this door."

The phone line went dead.

Rosie stared at it with an open mouth for long moments before collapsing facedown on the bed with a closed-mouthed scream. Her husband had come out swinging. But she had to fight to make sure when—if—they reconnected, they would have the tools to succeed. Even though Rosie was annoyed as hell with Dominic as she slid under the covers . . . she found herself looking forward to their next therapy session. Looking forward to seeing him. A lot.

CHAPTER TEN

Dominic sat at the end of the dock and looked out over the water. Apart from the low hum of boat motors and the light breeze rustling the trees around him, it was quiet. So quiet. That lack of noise was what had appealed to him most the first time he'd come here. Where he lived with Rosie, there was noise from Port Jefferson's busiest avenue, which was a mere half a block away. He could often hear horns honking while he showered.

Not here, though. How many times had he pictured Rosie at the end of this dock? Sitting there with her bare toes brushing the water, a mug of coffee in her hand, smiling over her shoulder at him as he approached. When he closed his eyes at night, he thought of her outlined by the sunset's reflection off the water, fireflies dancing around her naked calves in the summertime.

Dominic turned and glanced at the house behind him where it sat on the slight incline. To someone who remodeled homes for a living, its stillness was almost accusatory. *When are you going to make me look nice?* it seemed to ask.

Summertime. Maybe he would tell Rosie about the house then.

He curled his hand around the set of keys so tightly, they abraded his palm. As always—lately—when he thought of showing Rosie the house he'd bought them over a year ago, that familiar panic crept in and burned his throat. Had he made the right decision? When he'd returned from overseas and started saving to buy this place, the kind of home they'd always talked about growing up, he was so confident that purchasing it would make Rosie happy.

His confidence in that was long gone. When Stephen handed him the keys a year ago, he'd come out of a fog and thought, *Jesus, I have no idea if she wants this anymore.*

I have no idea what *she wants anymore.*

He'd followed in his father's footsteps, making the move that would give Rosie security, happiness. The way it had done for *his* family. But when Dominic had finally saved enough money and purchased the house overlooking the water, doubts had begun burrowing their way under his skin. Rosie had always dreamed of owning a restaurant. He'd *known* that, but he'd believed the house was more important. It would be their foundation. A place to expand their family. A place to grow old together. On some level, Dominic wondered if he'd elevated the importance of the house to satisfy his own needs.

He could have given her what she *really* pined for a year ago, but he hadn't.

Now he couldn't.

Forcing his breathing under control, Dominic paced along the dock, looking toward the two-story house where it sat elevated on a small hill, hugged on either side by pine trees. Twilight was his favorite time of day to come here and formulate renovation plans. Come up with ideas and discard them as not good enough. Rosie would want a back patio with a pergola. A fire pit. Some Latin touches, for sure, to honor both their heritages. He might have been born and raised in the Bronx, but with two Puerto Rican parents—one first generation, one second—the island's influence had been sprinkled into most customs, meals, and holidays. When he was young, his mother would have her side of the family over for birthdays or simply because the weather was nice. The party started in the kitchen, expanding until, most nights, they ended up on the porch of their house. But he'd moved from the Bronx at a young age. His parents had entertained less with the distance between Long Island and the city, so he'd grown used to the relative quiet. The first time his parents came to the new house, though, he would love to see pride reflected in their eyes. An echo of the upbringing they'd given him, which included a place to gather. To be together.

His wife was sentimental about her mother, too. Come to think of it, she had a photo album stored in the closet with pictures of her mother's childhood home in Buenos Aires. Maybe he could get some ideas for the renovation from there . . .

His thoughts trailed off and he gave in to the impulse to light a cigarette, taking a long drag and leaving it clamped between his lips.

"You have to tell her," came Stephen's voice from behind him, and Dominic turned to find his boss and friend joining him on the dock. "'Hey, honey, I bought you a dream house.' Problem solved. Separation over."

Having heard the same song and dance from Stephen on numerous occasions, Dominic shook his head. "It wouldn't solve the problem." He sighed. "At this point, it might even make the problem worse. I waited too long."

His friend was the only living soul who knew about the new house, out of necessity. Five years ago, Dominic's initial plan had been to surprise Rosie with a house. To that end, he'd begun giving Stephen a small percentage of his paycheck each week to set aside, until he'd hit his goal. He didn't want Rosie to miss the money or worry about all the overtime he worked to make up for the missing funds. He'd just wanted to give her something she could *see*. Something that would serve as proof that he would never let her down. Or forget about their mutual goals.

In playing the silent hero, though, had he ruined Rosie's chance of reaching her own?

"Why are you waiting to tell her?" Stephen leaned against the post opposite Dominic. "I mean, I know you want it to be perfect when you bring her here. But you can't decide on anything. I've drawn up nine sets of plans."

An unsettled feeling weighed heavily in Dominic's stomach. One he'd learned to live with. It had moved in during his time overseas and never left. He'd met so many soldiers during his service who had bigger, more elaborate plans for the years ahead. The money to make them all a reality.

They'd put rocks—instead of small, simple diamonds—on their fiancées' fingers before being deployed. They'd gone on weekend getaways with their in-laws and already had plans for tech startups or to take over the family business. While Dominic had . . . nothing to give. Just himself.

His father's work ethic had once been more than enough, but the harder Dominic worked, the more the results seemed unworthy of his wife. The house included.

Especially now, when it was becoming obvious a restaurant could have made her happier.

Dominic took another drag of his cigarette and blew the smoke upward, making it look like it had come from the chimney. When this house had shown up on the market, priced to sell fast, Dominic had taken a leap and asked Stephen for the money he'd been setting aside. He could still remember writing the check and sliding it toward the realtor, thinking, *I won't let our engine stop roaring.*

But he had. He fucking had.

Acutely aware of Stephen's scrutiny, Dominic looked back out at the water—and he let disappointment wash over him. Those men he'd served with in the marines who didn't make it home . . . what would they have done with this time? These last five years? They probably wouldn't have bought a house and hidden it from their wife out of fear it wouldn't be the right one. The one that would make her happy.

That memory of Rosie at the bottom of the airport escalator snuck in and made him swallow hard. He could feel the weight of those extinguished futures on his shoulders the closer he got to her, could feel how unprepared he was to make them count. Nothing had changed since then, either, had it? Now it was extremely possible he'd waited too long to make every day of this life with Rosie count.

"You ready to pick a set of plans? Things are quieting down for the winter. We could get a lot of interior work done . . ."

It was on the tip of Dominic's tongue to say, *Yes, the fourth plan you drew up, with the Spanish tile floors and wide, arched doorways. That's my wife. My wife would love that.*

Instead, Dominic ground out the cigarette under the toe of his boot, gave one last look at the house, and strode toward his truck. "Not yet."

Rosie pressed a finger to the center of her crumbly biscuits and deemed them cooled enough. She peeled the plastic wrap off two bowls containing a homemade blackberry jam, another brimming with fresh dulce de leche. She'd added a touch of lemon zest to her alfajores, trying to put her own twist on her mother's recipe. If the sighs of pleasure coming from the living room were any indication, they were going over amazingly well. She couldn't get them out of the oven, cooled, and sandwiched with homemade topping fast enough.

"Let's begin, ladies!" Bethany said, clapping her hands in the center of the crowd of women. Their Just Us League meetings continued to expand every time they got together. Some of the newbies weren't even residents of Port Jefferson, having driven from neighboring towns to be there. Since Rosie happily did most of the cooking—and now baking—

for the meetings, Georgie had been thoughtful enough to start a weekly collection to fund her food supplies.

Rosie was loving every second of it. Being selective over the freshest meats for her empanadas, adding her own twist to classic chimichurri dipping sauce, testing out new recipes in Bethany's kitchen. It was a built-in weekly focus group for her skills, and tonight . . . yes, tonight she felt a little bit closer to setting foot inside the empty restaurant off Main Street. Originally, her idea had been small. An indoor empanada stand. A counter where people could order and take meat-filled pastries to go, but the more Argentinian dishes she tested and perfected, the more her dream expanded and took on new life.

"Who had something good happen to them this week?" Bethany asked her rapt, wine-sipping audience, a smile stretching across her pretty face. She held her dry-erase marker in front of the whiteboard she'd erected—or the Positivity Board, as they'd collectively begun referring to it. "Anyone?"

"I got a good deal on having the brakes replaced on my Chevy," said one of the women. "The mechanic tried to highball me. I turned him down and he started singing a different tune."

Bethany wrote "brakes" in loopy script on the Positivity Board.

"Er—um, a new position at my job," piped in another member who rarely spoke up. As soon as everyone turned to look at her, she tried to sink into Bethany's plush white couch. "I was promoted. You're looking at the new head loan officer at Town and Center Bank."

"Oh shit! That's amazing." Bethany did a little dance as everyone applauded. "Congratulations. Did you ask for the promotion or was it a surprise?"

"I asked for it." The loan officer sat up a little straighter, visibly bolstered by everyone patting her on the shoulders. "I don't mean to be sappy, but I don't think I would have if it wasn't for this club."

Rosie smiled to herself as she moved the alfajores onto a serving plate and carried them into the living room. She set them down on the coffee table, laughing as Georgie pulled her backward into an empty seat on the couch. Their resident clown was slightly tipsy tonight, but she was charming. Earlier, she'd greeted newcomers with a juggling act on the porch until Bethany dragged her in from the cold.

"You smell nice." Georgie sighed, laying her head on Rosie's shoulder. "I love you."

"You say that to all the girls."

"But I *mean* it with you, baby."

Rosie pressed her lips together to subdue her smile. "Are you celebrating something with your six margaritas?"

"Nope. Yes." Georgie hiccupped. "Eh. Just needed a little liquid courage."

"Care to share your conversation with the class, ladies?" Bethany called with a mock-stern expression, everyone laughing at her halfhearted reprimand.

"It's now or never, I guess. I have something." Georgie put

her hand up, then seemed to realize that hand was holding a sloshing margarita on the rocks and lowered it. "Me and Travis picked a wedding venue."

"What?" Bethany dropped her dry-erase marker and didn't bother to pick it up. "Excuse me, Georgette Castle, why was I not brought along as a consultant?"

"I didn't want to play referee. You would have disagreed with all of Travis's choices just to exasperate him."

Bethany waved that off. "Ah, come on. I've stopped needling him so much." She slumped. "Hard to hate the guy who proposed to you live on the air."

"With several adoring high school kids in tow," Rosie added, patting Georgie on the shoulder. "The man has flair."

"Damn right, Ro. And I'm sorry we ruined your fun, Bethany," Georgie said, taking a long sip of her drink. "But we decided on Oheka Castle—"

Gasps all around the room.

"—and we're going with kind of an unusual theme. It's called 'famous baseball player turned famous announcer marries local clown and everyone thinks he's crazy.' Or has that theme been overdone?"

Sensing a deeper layer to Georgie's flippancy, Rosie sent Bethany a look and noticed she was concerned, too. Actually, the silence in the room said everyone was concerned. They'd witnessed Georgie and Travis fall in love and watched his proposal during a Just Us League meeting. Everyone had skin in the game.

"I'm kind of freaking out," Georgie said, sweeping the room with wide eyes. "When we were looking at churches,

I just kept thinking about how everyone is going to be staring a-and comparing me to who he dated before. And how I never dated anyone before because I was like, this total scrub."

Rosie put an arm around Georgie's shoulders. "It's okay to be nervous. Everyone gets nervous when they're about to take a huge step," Rosie said, squeezing her. "Except Travis. Travis would have already married you six times, because the man is crazy in love with you."

Georgie started to respond, but the front door of Bethany's house blew open and the object of their conversation stood outlined in the frame, all six foot three inches of the rangy ex–baseball player.

Someone yelled, "Intruder!"

Travis ignored them. "Where's my girl?"

Everyone pointed at Georgie, who turned on the couch to face her fiancé. "Oh, hi, Travis. What are you doing here?"

Eyes narrowing, he took his cell phone out of his back pocket and held it up. "You're being weird in your text messages."

"No, I'm not," Georgie sputtered. "Weird how?"

"I asked what flavor of ice cream I should pick up at the store. Your answer was . . ." He looked down at his phone and read from the screen. "'What if we pick a flavor now and want something totally different down the road? It's too risky picking just one. Sometimes vanilla is great, but what if people expected to see you with rocky road? They'll wonder if you regretted it and it'll be too late to dress up vanilla. Toppings don't count.'" He lowered his phone and raised an eyebrow at Georgie. "And then you sent a GIF of a cat licking ice cream and getting brain freeze."

Georgie pursed her lips. "Still waiting for the weird part."

"All right, listen up." Travis advanced on the couch, and women scattered out of his way. Rosie scooted sideways, thinking Travis would want to sit beside her, but he knelt at Georgie's feet instead, taking her hands in his. "Today was the best day of my life. Seeing the place where I'm going to marry you. Talking about it made it real, you know?" He brought her hands to his mouth. "Do not freak out on me, baby girl. Please. I was scared enough you made a huge mistake picking me, but you made me believe I deserve you. Now I'm demanding you stand by that decision." An exhale rushed out of him. "I just really, really need you to keep believing I'm not a mistake."

"H-how could you think that's why I'm freaking out?" She shook her head slowly. "I'm just . . . the place we picked . . . it's so big. It's too big," she blurted. "You're famous and everyone knows you and the venue should reflect that, right? But it feels too grand and foofy compared to me, and I wondered if maybe that's what you want—"

"Jesus. Okay." He let go of her hands and dropped his head straight into her lap. "First of all, Georgie, I would marry you in a fucking shed. I can give you a big, foofy wedding, so I thought I should. If you don't want that, we'll get married in your parents' backyard or—"

"Really?"

"Yes." He lifted his head and searched her face. "Did I fix

this? Please tell me it was that easy. I just want to marry you any way possible."

"Oh God," Bethany groaned dramatically across the room. "You've gone from tolerable to lovable. Every belief I hold dear has to be reevaluated now."

"You fixed it," Georgie said on a watery laugh. "I'm sorry about brain-freeze cat. I've had like fifty margaritas. I love you so much."

He slid a hand around the back of her neck and pulled her in for a kiss. It started as an innocent peck. It did. But Rosie coughed into her fist and had to look away when Travis slipped Georgie the tongue and she curled her hands in his collar, pulling him closer. It made her think of Dominic and how he used to reassure her with touches and words when she got overwhelmed. Or vice versa. And it opened a pit of yearning right in the center of her stomach. It might have been the tequila warming her blood, but she couldn't help aching for the feel of her husband's mouth against hers, taking, giving.

"Take your time. I'll be outside in the car," Travis murmured to Georgie, loud enough for the dead-silent room to hear, nuzzling their noses together. "Ah, baby girl. You just wait until I get you home tonight."

No one said anything for a full minute after Travis left, but several women fanned themselves and at least half freshened their glasses of wine—filling them straight to the brim.

"Well," Rosie said, clearing the rust from her throat. "We definitely have to talk about sex now."

"Seconded." Bethany sighed, finally picking up her dropped marker and placing it on the silver tray of the Positivity Board. "We're all thinking about it."

"Not all of us are allowed to have it, though." The words were out of Rosie's mouth before they'd fully formed in her head. Heat climbed her neck and cheeks as every head swiveled in her direction—and she had zero choice but to elaborate. "Dominic and I are in couples therapy and we've been given homework. And rules. One of them is no sex."

"This is the best meeting yet," someone whispered at the edge of the room.

"So let me get this straight," one of the older members said, moseying forward. "You're so active in the bedroom that you need a rule against sex . . . and you still need therapy?"

Rosie tucked a curl behind her ear. "It's complicated."

"I'll say."

Georgie handed Rosie her margarita, and Rosie drank half before handing it back. "He wrote me a letter," she said, smiling as Bethany picked up the marker and wrote "love letter" on the board with a flourish. "He told me this old memory. About us. And I . . . I don't know, it made me remember myself somehow. I feel like me today, even if things aren't perfect."

"And what does Rosie want?" Bethany encompassed the room with a sweep of her arm. "That's what this club was founded on, right? Going after what we want?"

"I want to make an appointment with the realtor," she breathed. "To tour that restaurant space on Cove Street."

"The old diner?"

Rosie nodded.

A beat passed.

"Well, let's make the call," Georgie said, sitting forward, her face still flushed from Travis's kiss. "There's no better time to take the leap than when you're surrounded by all this support. Someone grab Rosie's phone. She keeps it charging by the coffeemaker." Georgie bounced, bumping Rosie with her hip. "Restaurant! Restaurant!"

Everyone joined in the chant, but they quieted down when Rosie dialed the number she'd been keeping stored in her phone for a month. Her heart was going a million miles an hour . . . and somewhere around the third ring, she got the sinking feeling that something was missing. No, not something. Someone. She was in a room full of people she adored, but there was only one person whom she needed to hold her hand. And so, while she wanted to be ecstatic as she made the viewing appointment and everyone cheered, a sense of wrongness continued to eat at her.

Someone approached and laid a hand on her arm, jarring Rosie from her thoughts. "These cookies are amazing, Rosie!"

"They're called alfajores—and thank you." Desperate for a distraction from whatever foreboding gnawed at her gut, Rosie shot to her feet and escaped the living room. "I'll just, um . . . whip up a fresh batch."

CHAPTER ELEVEN

When Dominic arrived for their second therapy appointment, Rosie was already inside the office, her skin cast in a purple lava lamp glow. Today had been a particularly messy day on the job, so he'd chanced a quick stop at home to shower and change, but unfortunately that decision had made him three minutes late. He searched her face upon walking into Armie's office, surprised when she seemed relieved that he'd shown up. Did she actually think he'd bail?

Every day that passed made him even more determined to fix what was broken, by whatever means necessary. The other night, when her name had popped up on his cell-phone screen, the world around him had come spinning back into motion. It did the same now. Being near his wife simultaneously settled the chaos in his blood and stirred it with lust. He knew damn well they were in therapy to talk, but tell that to his excess testosterone. He'd been on the verge of insanity since he made Rosie come over the phone, closing his eyes and trying to conjure her taste at the oddest times. Like during a foundation inspection that afternoon.

Focus.

"I was covered in grout," he muttered, sitting down beside her on the floor in the pillow fort, unable to keep himself from absorbing the sight of her. God, she always looked fucking fantastic, but after a few days away from her? The way she curved and dipped in all the tastiest places made him dizzy. His gaze ran hungrily over the juncture of her thighs, climbed up her belly, and clung to her tits. "I didn't want to show up dirty."

"Could have fooled me," she whispered, widening her eyes at him. "Dominic."

With a low sound in the back of his throat, he faced Armie, who was watching them with unabashed amusement. "I see you've been taking the rules seriously."

Jaw tight, Dominic crossed his arms and leaned back beside Rosie. He might have started to see the merit in these sessions, especially after hearing how much Rosie liked his letter, but that didn't mean he'd stopped wanting to simply be alone with her. She needed words. He got that now and he was going to work on it. What else could they possibly iron out?

Armie clapped his hands together. "Laughter. We all need it." He split a speculative look between Rosie and Dominic. "During our first session, Dominic, you seemed almost startled when Rosie laughed, which tells me it has been a while since you shared your humor with her." Armie raised an eyebrow at Rosie. "Would you call that accurate?"

Rosie dipped her head, but nodded, sending Dominic an almost apologetic look.

His gut clenched.

"Did you used to laugh together?"

"All the time," Rosie murmured. "He used to do this thing where he blew air into my neck and made kind of a . . ."

"Fart sound?" Armie supplied.

A laugh huffed out of Rosie. "Yes. Or he would tell me stories about his parents. Or over the phone, he'd talk about the men he was deployed with and their habits." Her eyes softened. "When we were in high school, he drew sketches of our least favorite teachers sinking in quicksand or being chased by a goat and he'd leave them in my locker. Yeah. We laughed all the time."

"What about you, Dominic? Did Rosie make you laugh?"

"Sure she did," he said, meeting her eyes for a not-long-enough moment. "She can do the Minion voice. You know, the little yellow guys from those *Despicable Me* movies?" His lips jumped. "That was probably my favorite. She'd do the voice when I was having a shitty day."

He caught a small, reminiscent smile from Rosie and his heart missed a beat. His hand itched to reach over, to trace the curve of her mouth with the pad of his thumb, but Armie distracted him by pulling a giant bag of marshmallows out from behind his back, dangling them in midair. "Who's up for a game of Chubby Bunny?"

Rosie whistled long and low. "That took a left turn."

"Hear me out." Armie ripped open the bag and popped one of the extra-large marshmallows into his mouth, talking around it. "We build resentments toward our loved ones. Sometimes we're not even aware of them. But they grow so strong, they prevent us from remembering what we loved about our partners in the first place. Maybe one or both no longer wants to give their significant other the satisfaction of showing their amusement, so the other person stops trying. And the laughter dies." Armie handed Rosie the bag, which was a good move considering Dominic would have handed it right back. "We can fix this by laughing at *ourselves*. If we stop taking ourselves so seriously for a moment, our partner can do the same. There is relaxation and acceptance in laughter. It's the anti-resentment drug."

Dominic wouldn't lie. He was still skeptical as hell about therapy—and this therapist in particular. Once upon a time, he might have stuffed his cheeks full of marshmallows to make Rosie laugh, but the idea of doing it now, in front of a near stranger, was so far outside his comfort zone, it wasn't even funny. The exercise also seemed . . . inadequate. He didn't want baby steps, he wanted her back. Wanted everything fixed now.

"Rosie, I can see your husband is somewhat hesitant, which frankly I find *shocking*. Why don't you begin?"

She blew out a slow breath. "So just . . . stuff them in my cheeks?"

"And talk like a Minion. Yes."

Marshmallows in hand, Rosie turned wide eyes on Dominic. "If you say *I told you so*, I'll stuff them somewhere else entirely."

Dominic crammed a fist against his mouth to stop a chuckle from escaping. Goddamn, he loved her feisty like this. That light in her eyes made his blood crackle. "I wouldn't dare."

Rosie gave a skeptical hum and studied the white, sugary confections. Her shoulders squared and she sat up straighter, stowing them away in her cheeks, one by one. Then she looked over at Dominic with a proud, lifted chin and said, "Banana."

The laugh burst out of him like helium leaving a popped balloon. His vision blurred with mirthful tears, his throat aching from the sheer force of his amusement. The most incredible thing happened while he was laughing, too—Rosie joined him, looking ridiculous and adorable with her full cheeks.

"Dominic," Armie said, humor lacing his tone. "Would you like to reciprocate?"

Dominic's laughter faded into a groan. He couldn't leave her hanging, though. Shaking his head at his wife, he took the bag and tucked six marshmallows in total into his cheeks. "Dr. Nefario," he said, doing his best Gru impression, though his bad German accent emerged so garbled, he might as well have been speaking into a pillow. "Prepare the torpedo."

P words were a bad choice.

Dominic barely covered his mouth in time to catch the spit, and Rosie's head fell back on a belly laugh. Armie might have joined her in his own silent laugh, but Dominic was too busy absorbing the sight of his wife's pleasure to confirm.

God, she was so beautiful when she was happy. And he'd made her that way by playing Chubby Bunny. Not by handing her his paycheck. Not by working overtime. Just by being himself. Or, rather, the self he'd been when they'd fallen in love. The guy who'd had nothing to offer.

He was still contemplating the meaning of that when Armie interrupted his thoughts.

"Let's talk about Dominic's homework." Armie nodded in his direction, fingers steepled. "Did you write her the letter, Dominic?"

"Yeah." He rolled his eyes when he realized the marshmallows were still in his mouth and they all had to sit there while he chewed and swallowed, Rosie doing the same with lingering humor in her gorgeous eyes. "She seemed to like the letter."

"I loved it."

Dominic kept his features schooled, but those three words made him feel winded, like he'd just finished a race.

Armie split a smile between them. "What did he write about?"

"Homecoming. Our senior year homecoming dance, but . . . it was more than that. There were all these details and I . . ." Rosie paused, her fingers twisting in the hem of her black-and-white wool skirt, one of his favorites, because it seemed to keep her warm. "I could see the proof in his words how he felt about me. Like I was . . . I don't know. Coveted, maybe? I remember I used to feel that way about myself, too."

"Used to?" Dominic turned to study her, those words winging around his head like fired bullets. "You don't think I covet you, Rosie?"

"Lately I do," she whispered. "All these nice things I keep finding out you do behind my back." She wet her lips. "Last time we were here, I found out you express your appreciation for me through deeds and now that I know about them . . . yeah, I'm starting to feel coveted again. But it was the words, more than anything. I really liked reading them."

"I'll write you more if you come home."

Rosie blew out a breath. "We keep ending up here," she said to Armie. "Can you please tell him I can't come home yet?"

"He's sitting right there," Armie said patiently. "You tell him."

"I have."

Armie studied them. "Let's come back to this. I want to explore what you said, Rosie, about the deeds Dominic does behind your back. What did you mean?"

"Well, he snuck my coat into the house where I'm staying. The night he left the letter on my car windshield, I found out he's been paying the security guard at my job on the sly to protect me."

"Interesting." Armie tapped his fingers against his lips. "Dominic, you're here to accept responsibility for your role in this relationship. That takes a lot of courage. Why not accept responsibility for the good as well as the bad?"

A pit started to open in Dominic's stomach. "I'm getting tired of being asked this question."

"You don't seem tired of it. I hope you don't mind me saying, you seem agitated."

"Because it's nothing. It's nothing to bring a coat or pay a guard," Dominic said, a lot louder than he'd intended. "I could always do better. Someone else would do better."

"Ah."

"'Ah'? What's that?"

Dominic realized Rosie was staring at him with a frown marring her forehead and closed his mouth, replaying what he'd said and searching for a way to play it off. But he couldn't find anything to say amid the crackle of static in his head. Like two live wires had struck by accident. "Can we move on?" he said, uncomfortable with the ripple his admission of insecurity had created in the room. Why the hell had he said anything? Rosie needed a strong man. Mentally and physically. Not one who worried. "I want to know what's been going on with my wife."

Armie crossed his legs. "In what way?"

"In every way. She used to sleep next to me. I could tell the kind of day she had by which pajamas she put on. Silk for good days, big T-shirts for bad. On her days off, she played the radio and danced to the salsa station while making breakfast. That's gone. When I walked into the bathroom in the morning, it used to smell like coconut, and now it's gone. I just want to know how she's been spending her days and nights. Is that not reasonable to anyone else? She's my wife."

A beat of silence passed wherein he could hear his pulse scraping in his ears.

"Rosie, do you think you can appreciate that this separation has been hard on Dominic?"

"Yes," she whispered, sounding awed. "I can."

Dominic couldn't look at her after sounding like such a train wreck. "Just tell me what you've been up to, Rosie."

He heard her swallow. "I mostly just work and go back to Bethany's. We had a Just Us League meeting on Saturday night, and I, um . . . I made an appointment to go look at a commercial space. The old diner on Cove."

That brought Dominic's head around. She was moving at the speed of light, and his feet were encased in drying concrete while he watched her shoot off into the atmosphere. His focus had been on keeping her happy and content for so long—but he'd done the opposite. Now she was reaching for her goals on her own. Was it selfish of him to want a hand in her getting there? Or would he only hold her back again? He wouldn't be able to bear the latter. "A commercial space for the restaurant?"

She shrugged a shoulder. "It's just an appointment."

Armie cleared his throat. "I take it you want to open your own restaurant, Rosie?" He waited for her nod to continue. "And why is it significant that you made the appointment this week to see the space?"

"I've been putting it off," she said haltingly.

"Why?"

"I don't know. I . . ." She glanced over at Dominic before lowering her gaze. "I just wasn't confident I could run my own place."

"Why did that change?"

"I thought it was the club. The women supporting me—and I think that has a lot to do with my boost in confidence—but it wasn't until I got the letter from Dominic that I felt prepared to take the chance."

"Earlier you said Dominic's letter made you feel more like Rosie. The Rosie you want to be, that you felt you used to be." He went quiet for a moment. "Your success is your own,

Rosie. You did something brave. But a marriage is about support. Would you like to acknowledge Dominic's letter—and support—might have helped push you toward your goal?"

The back of Dominic's neck tightened. "She doesn't need to do that."

"I want to." She looked down at his hand a moment before covering it with her own. "Your letter helped. Thank you."

Satisfaction wove around his lungs and it took him a long time to draw a decent breath. "Okay," he said hoarsely.

"And, Dominic," Armie continued. "Would you like to acknowledge that Rosie needs words and they are supremely important to her and thus vital when it comes to making this marriage work?"

"Yes," he rasped.

"Well done, Team Vega." Armie nodded and all three of them seemed to let out a long breath.

Crazily enough, Dominic felt a change in the air as if something had cleared.

"Time for your next homework assignment." The therapist winked at them both. "Still no sex. Sorry, folks. But I'm giving you the next best thing." He clapped once. "Mother Nature."

CHAPTER TWELVE

Twilight crept in as Rosie and Dominic hiked along the path toward the nature preserve. He thought therapy had hit peak weirdness during their game of Minion-themed Chubby Bunny, but he'd been dead wrong. Today they'd been assigned the task of setting up a campsite—together—as a means of learning to work as a team. And while he definitely didn't mind spending time with Rosie, he could admit to a growing impatience to have their problems solved. Every moment that passed meant missing her more, and this exercise felt like a damn waste of time when they could be moving her back into their home, where she belonged.

"Now seems like a good time to remind you that you picked the therapist."

Rosie lifted her chin and shot him a glare from beneath her eyelashes, knitting Dominic's stomach up tighter than a concrete slab. Back in the day, he used to refer to that look as the Death Laser. It meant she was not in the mood for his shit and he better tread more carefully than a man with size-fifteen feet crossing a field of land mines.

He hadn't given her a reason to grace him with the Death

Laser in a long time and he didn't like that realization one bit. There should be passion between them. They should get pissed at each other once in a while, shouldn't they? Every time they used to make up, he was only more grateful to have her. Their first argument in recent memory had happened the night she left.

That thought hardening his jaw, Dominic shouldered the bags of equipment he was carrying and picked up his pace, catching up with Rosie as they entered the nature preserve. Maybe now was a good time to remind her of the fire between them—and he didn't mean the sexual inferno that never waned. Was there anything at stake between two people who couldn't conjure up enough feeling between them to have a decent fight? Dominic didn't think so.

Their stakes had never lowered. They'd just been hidden. He'd have to jog her memory.

"Was this therapy technique listed in the Yelp reviews?"

She slapped at a mosquito on her arm. "Which technique is that?"

"The technique where we pay money to a therapist, and in return, he assigns us manual labor." He raised an eyebrow at her. "Maybe you didn't scroll down far enough."

"I scrolled." They entered a clearing and she turned on her sneakered heel. "Are you trying to pick a fight with me?"

Maybe. "Nope." He dropped the canvas bag filled with tent poles. "We've had some good ones, though, haven't we? Remember that romantic phase you went through when we were seventeen, reading those books about vampires and werewolves?"

"Of course I remember them." Rosie surveyed the area. "Actually, I've been considering a reread—"

"Christ. Please don't."

A laugh puffed out of her, genuine curiosity flitting across her gorgeous face. "Why?"

"You really don't remember, Rosie? The weeks you spent reading those books were the worst of my life. Nothing short of turning pale and granting you immortality would make you happy. You locked yourself in a closet and sent me one-word text messages until I was ready to lose my mind."

She winced. "Oh. Yeah."

"Oh yeah?" Dominic echoed, using his boot to kick aside some fallen leaves, creating a spot to pitch the tent. Then he started to remove the nylon shelter and poles from their bag, laying them out in order. "You remember how we worked that one out?"

"Yes," she murmured, brow furrowing. "You stopped texting me. You wouldn't even respond."

"And you showed up at my door breathing fire."

Color rose on her cheeks. "I think that's a minor exaggeration."

Dominic closed the distance between them, coming near enough to make her suck in a breath, but remaining far enough away that there was no chance of them touching. "I believe your exact words were 'Your thumbs better be broken, asshole.'"

Rosie gasped. "I never said that."

"I added the 'asshole' part. You said the rest." He chanced

another step closer, and the awareness between them grew to ten times the size of the forest. "I got angry, too. Remember?"

"Of course I remember." She stared off over his shoulder for a moment, then covered her face with her hands. "I think I said, 'If you loved me, you'd understand what I'm going through.'"

"And I said, 'I do love you, Rosie. That's why I want to go through it with you.'"

The intensity between them was building so much, Dominic was barely aware of their surroundings. There was only Rosie. They gravitated closer, but she caught herself at the last moment, before their bodies could touch, stooping down and starting the process of sliding tent poles through their nylon sleeves.

"We were pretty dramatic back then, weren't we?"

"We've still got some drama, honey girl," Dominic said gruffly, joining her in a crouch. They worked in silence for a few minutes, and normally that would have been fine for Dominic. Silence was where he lived. In studying Rosie surreptitiously, he could see she wasn't as comfortable with the lack of talking. *Words. She needs words.* "Tell me something about your day."

"I'm missing a Just Us League meeting tonight, and I'm a little itchy thinking of them eating soggy takeout tacos instead of something I made." Her head came up fast, before ducking back down. "Or did you mean something, like, work related?"

"Anything."

She blew out a breath, seeming uncertain. "I don't know how to talk to you anymore."

Without thinking, he reached over and took her hand, holding it tightly within his own. God. God, this situation had gotten so fucking far away from him. "You can tell me anything."

"I've been hiding Martha's Hot Pockets." Her expression was grave. "They explode all over the break-room microwave and she never cleans it up."

Dominic swallowed a laugh. "Where have you been hiding them?"

Her eyes widened. "In the trash."

He choked trying to keep his amusement buried, but it didn't work. Dominic's laugh boomed in the forest, sending birds flying out of the trees.

"She's going to find out," Rosie said, battling her own smile. "I'm going to be sampling Le Squirt Bon Bon for the rest of my life."

"What the hell is Le Squirt Bon Bon?"

"It's the nastiest perfume on the planet and it only exists so Martha has a power move." Rosie signaled him to stand up the tent and Dominic glanced down, realizing they were done stuffing it with poles. "What about you?" Looking kind of nervous, she rolled her lips inward. "Tell me something about your day."

Dominic handed her the stakes for two of the tent corners and they went about securing the shelter in place. Something about his day? Probably not the best idea to inform Rosie of how much time he'd spent lately staring at her clothes in the closet or sniffing her girlie soaps in the bathroom. "I've been doing some work in the basement at night. When I can't sleep." They traded a fleeting look and he wanted to kiss the guilt out of her eyes, but words were more important right now. "Found my framed commendations from the marines. The few pictures I took while overseas."

He raised his head to find Rosie looking at him.

"You should hang them up," she said.

"No, I . . ." Dominic left the tent area and moved to the nearby ring of rocks, squatting down to arrange them closer together. "I thought about it once, but I figured our house is already so small. Maybe one day if we had more room or a bigger place, I'd hang them up. They're not a big deal."

"Yes, they are," she breathed. "A bigger place. We haven't talked about that in a while."

Goddammit. Why had he brought up the house? Until now, it had been the silent secret between them, but with her innocent comment came a deceptive evasion—and he hated it. Lying to his wife was a sin, in his eyes. But when he opened his mouth to come clean, the truth only dug down deeper, further out of sight inside of him. "I've been thinking about it lately. Have you? Thought about a bigger place at all?"

She joined him at the stone circle, helping him move the rocks into a perfect ring. For the campfire their hippie therapist had requested, because that was normal. "I've thought of us moving to somewhere newer, with more space. Sure," she rasped.

"Would you . . . like that?"

Rosie's gaze flashed to meet his, danced away. "Maybe we should focus on the present right now and not the future, you know?" When Dominic made a grudging sound of agreement, she dusted her hands off on her jeans and stood, shifting in the crackle of forest-floor debris. "Um . . . what was the third thing? A hammock?"

He cleared his throat. "Yeah."

The tension remained between them as Dominic gathered wood for the campfire. When he returned, he helped Rosie hang the hammock between two trees. Despite the lurking strain in the air, working in tandem with Rosie felt natural . . . and long overdue. It had never been more obvious to Dominic that they'd been avoiding each other, except for their Tuesday-night sex marathons. Even the simple task of hanging the hammock felt intimate. In a way that wasn't physical. Like they were working in a partnership. He absorbed the feeling like a sponge.

"Okay," Rosie said, wiping her hands on her thighs. "What's next?"

"He said something about hanging a wind chime," Dominic responded drily. "Got to have those positive vibes, *man*."

"He's a free spirit." Rosie wrinkled her nose at him. "I think it's kind of sweet."

"Come on, honey girl. You would have rolled your eyes so hard at him back in the day."

She thought about that. "Probably. But I would have felt guilty about it afterward."

Something tugged in his middle over the accuracy of that. "So what has . . . changed about you? That you'd no longer roll your eyes at a stoned hippie who decorates with stuffed animals?"

Rosie's gaze traveled over him, as if she was startled that he'd asked something that deep. "Well, for one, last-ditch therapy was my idea and my pride is in the way of me admitting I went a little extreme." They traded a knowing smile. "But I wouldn't change the decision now. Lately I've learned that letting something feel crazy, not rejecting the unfamiliarity of a situation . . . can lead to something amazing."

"You're talking about the club?"

"Partly," she hedged. "Did you know me, Bethany, and Georgie formed the league because we all showed up for Zumba early? Really, it's Kristin's fault for being late." She smiled to herself. "Now, *Zumba.* That gets an eye roll. Who wants to watch themselves dance in a mirror?"

Dominic rolled a shoulder. "I could never mind watching you dance." They traded a ripple of heated eye contact, but he was enjoying talking to her too much to push it further. He didn't want to credit Armie, but something about being removed from their usual setting—being out there in nature—made him appreciate being with her, hearing her voice, even more than he normally did. "How the hell are we supposed to rig up this wind chime?"

"Oh." Rosie shook herself, obviously having forgotten their task. "I brought some string. Do you have your pocket-knife?"

"Always." He slipped the smooth object out of his back pocket and flipped open the narrowest cutting tool with his thumb. "What's your plan? Put holes in some sticks and hang them?"

"Yes. Maybe attach some pennies to the bottom so they clang?"

"Not bad."

Rosie laughed. "Not exactly good, either, but we'll get away with it." She pressed her lips together. "I think it goes against the hippie-cratic oath to give bad grades."

He slow-clapped. "Nicely done."

They spent a few minutes collecting sticks, Rosie retrieving them and Dominic whittling holes in the top.

"So . . . not rejecting something that feels crazy," Dominic said, calling back her earlier words while twisting metal into wood. "Does that also apply to the restaurant?"

"Yeah," she breathed, furrowing her brow. "Somewhere along the line, it did start to feel crazy. Taking that leap."

Regret slithered in Dominic's gut, knowing he'd been part of the reason opening her restaurant had become an unreachable goal. He could turn the tide now, though, couldn't he? Here they were, talking—*trying*—so it couldn't be too late.

"Sometimes when I was active duty," he said, "home seemed like a dream. Like it wasn't real and I'd never get back here again." He nudged her with his elbow. "I almost always thought of you frowning over a recipe or dancing from the stove to the sink. And I knew home had to be real. You cooking is not a leap. You . . . doing anything you set your mind to is not a leap."

"Thank you," she murmured, sounding almost surprised.

"I wish you'd do that more. Not . . . not encourage me, although that was really, *really* nice. But I mean talk about your time overseas. You've never talked to me about it."

A bolt turned in the side of Dominic's neck. The time he'd served with the military had been hard. It was hard for *every* soldier, being under the constant threat of attack, being so far removed from reality, you didn't know how you'd make it back. Vocalizing that meant exposing a weakness, however, and he didn't do that. Stiff upper lip. Be the strong one. He'd been raised with that mentality, and he worried that breaking that code might make him seem less dependable. Just . . . less. But he had to set aside those fears, because Rosie was watching him expectantly and—

A movement on Rosie's shoulder caught his attention.

"Shit, honey. Don't move."

Her face lost some color. "What is it?"

Knowing if he said the word "spider" she would freak the fuck out, Dominic reached out to slap the eight-legged creature off her shoulder, but it scuttled away, he cursed, and Rosie launched into the air like a torpedo, slapping at every inch of exposed skin on her body and shaking out her hair. "Oh my God. Is it still on me? Get it!"

"Honey girl," he said, biting down on a smile. "You have to stand still."

"What? *No!*"

He gripped her by the shoulders and turned her around. "You probably knocked it off."

"You're just saying that," she said miserably. "Oh my God. How big was it? Is it hairy?"

"You don't want to know," he said truthfully.

She screamed in her throat.

The spider reappeared on her arm, and Dominic smacked it off before she could become aware of it, watching as it hit the forest floor and disappeared beneath some leaves. "Gone. Got it." He gave up on suppressing his laughter. "It can't hurt you anymore."

"You *jerk*." Rosie threw herself into his arms, mouth pressed to his neck, her body shaking with mirth. "You enjoyed that."

"I don't like seeing you scared." He closed her in his arms and breathed in the coconut scent of her hair. "But I'm not going to pretend I mind this."

They melted against each other a little bit, Rosie's hand curling in the material of his shirt before she pushed away, both of them breathing heavily. As they continued making the wind chime, Dominic could feel her watching him. And he knew she could feel his attention coming her way, too. Every peek of her belly when she reached up to tie a stick to a low-hanging branch was catalogued in his mind. Every lip bite. Every elegant angle of her neck.

His own skin burned from the evidence of her interest, and just as he'd done that morning in the gym, he put himself on display for her. Fuck it. He'd use what he had. Rolling up his sleeves, he got to work lighting the fire, building it to a cluster of gentle flames. Night had fallen by the time they finished building the campsite and they wandered toward each other, right to the center of it, as if pushed by an unseen force.

"Earlier, you said you wanted to talk about the present?" Dominic said, nudging her chin up. "Let's do it."

Rosie's nipples peaked inside her shirt, accompanied by her shaky exhale. "Maybe I only said that because I was annoyed at you for bringing up our *Twilight* fight." She paused. "It happened in the past, but it's frustrating me in the present, so it's fair game to discuss."

"Good, talk about it. Get frustrated."

"You brought it up to make a point. That we're supposed to love each other through fights. Through all of it."

Dominic leaned in and breathed against her mouth. "Never mind why I brought it up. Call me every name in the book. Just don't act like we don't know every last thing about each other." His hand closed around the nape of her neck and the muscles turned to water, just like he'd expected. Just like always. "You know how to talk to me, Rosie. It . . ." Admitting a weakness was difficult, but he forced it out. "It fucked me up when you said you didn't."

"I'm sorry. It's so much easier to talk when you're talking back."

"Okay. Lay it on me." Dominic tightened his muscles, steeling himself for what was coming. "Tell me how hard it has been. How hard I've made it."

"I don't want to right now." Hesitantly, she raised her hands and conformed her palms to his cheeks. "You've been so sweet today."

"Please, Rosie. Get it all out so we can really start moving forward."

"It's been hard," she said softly. So softly. "It's like you left that final time . . . and never came back. I don't have my best friend."

"I'm here." He backed them toward a tree, pressing her up against it, knowing she could feel the chaotic pounding in his chest . . . and letting her. Not being the impenetrable fortress for once. They inhaled and exhaled against each other's mouth, his cock swelling with every tiny, feminine pant she let out against his lips. Christ, he would kill to give her one fucking orgasm. Just one. "Rosie." He brushed their lips together. "Honey girl, I'm right here."

She pulled him by the sleeves of his shirt. "Come closer," she breathed.

"Ah, would you look at this masterpiece!"

Armie's voice booming through the clearing was the equivalent of a brick wall slamming down between Rosie and Dominic. They jumped apart like guilty teenagers whose mothers had caught them making out in the family room. And something amazing happened. They both laughed. She fell into his chest and giggled—and hell, if Dominic didn't feel seven feet tall in that moment. Ignoring the incessant throbbing in his pants, he wrapped an arm around Rosie's shoulders and held her close.

"Busted," he said against her temple.

She looked up, smiling. "Feels like old times."

"Yeah," he said gruffly. "It does."

Rosie started to say more, but her jaw dropped at whatever was happening behind Dominic. He turned just in time to catch Armie ducking into the tent they'd erected, with not one but two women.

"Viva Team Vega!" called Armie as he zipped up the shelter, amid the squeals of his companions.

Rosie and Dominic were bursting at the seams as he hustled her back toward the parking lot, where they finally doubled over and gave in to tears of amusement.

"Did we just build a campsite so our therapist could have a threesome?" Dominic said.

"Officer, I swear, we were unwitting accomplices."

Dominic's laughter trailed off as he tucked a curl behind Rosie's ear. "Here's to not rejecting the crazy, huh?"

She regarded him in thoughtful silence. "Yeah."

Sending his wife to Bethany's that night knowing he wouldn't see her until their next therapy session was torture, but he couldn't help but hope they'd made some progress. Dammit, he would take it.

And someday soon, he would take his wife back.

CHAPTER THIRTEEN

A lot of people can throw together a decent meal," Rosie said, giving her friends a stern look across Georgie's dining room table. "But food should be about an experience. A *journey."*

In front of Rosie sat three covered dishes, and she didn't miss the ravenous looks Bethany and Georgie kept sending them. She'd asked them to refrain from eating today so they could participate in her first official taste test. It appeared they'd complied. And okay, she was being a little cruel making them wait to dig in, but she wanted to savor the moment. After building the campsite with Dominic yesterday, Rosie felt . . . exhilarated. Excited. New.

Ever since she'd reopened herself to the possibility of being a restaurant owner, she'd been struggling with imposter syndrome. Who did she think she was? Gordon Ramsay owned a restaurant. Did she think she was Gordon Ramsay? He might be a reality television star, too, but they would both be restaurant owners. How could she even put herself in the same category?

But while she cooked asado on Georgie's backyard barbeque, she hadn't felt like an imposter at all. Maybe that's why she was confident enough to revel in the suspense. Just a little longer.

Georgie propped her chin on the table and sniffed one of the covered plates. "You vicious woman. You're milking this."

"We never knew you were a sadist," Bethany commented, studying her nails.

Rosie hid her smile. "I just want you to really focus on how the food makes you feel, as opposed to what your mouth is telling you. It's going to taste good. That's a given. But tell me where the flavors transport you. That's what I'm after."

"Done."

"Got it."

Rosie whipped the napkin off the first plate with a flourish, outright giggling when both of her friends groaned in pleasure, leaning forward to inhale the steam coming off the meat. "Don't dig in yet. I'm going to help you craft the perfect bite."

Bethany picked up a fork and mimed jabbing it into her eye. "Rosie, you're evil."

"You'll take that back in a minute." Rosie took the napkin off the next dish. "This is an ensalada criolla. Tomato, lettuce, onion. Oil and white wine vinegar dressing. It's going to help counter the savory flavors of the meat. And . . ." She uncovered the final dish. "The pièce de résistance. My mother's chimichurri."

Georgie scooted closer to the table. "Okay, so a little bit of everything in one bite?"

Rosie nodded. "Correct. This would be the house dish. At my restaurant," she said, some shyness creeping into her tone. "I'd serve these three components together."

Bethany's face warmed with a smile. "Those words sound good on you."

Her cheeks heated. "Thanks." She waved her hands. "Okay. The time has come. Build your bite."

"Ooh." Georgie straightened. "Build your bite. Have you thought of putting that somewhere on your menu?"

"I am now," Rosie murmured, repeating the phrase under her breath. "Build your bite. Maybe we'll do appetizer combos and—" She cut herself off. "We'll talk about it later. *Eat.*"

She held her breath as she watched Bethany and Georgie carve off small pieces of asado, moving it to their plates before adding the chimichurri and a forkful of salad. Georgie shoved the bite into her mouth first, closing her eyes and sighing dramatically. "Okay. Oh my . . . Lord. How am I supposed to think straight when my taste buds are having a straight-up orgasm?" She hummed. "This flavor journey is taking me to a busy street. It's nighttime. Music is playing. People are dancing and making out in the alleys. There are lights strung overhead . . ."

Bethany popped in her own bite and groaned, her eyelids drooping. "Totally. I can totally see that. But I'm being transported to a backyard barbeque. I'm suntanned and half-drunk and there are bracelets clinking on my wrist and I'm so happy. This food just makes me happy."

Moisture—happy in its nature—sprung to Rosie's eyes.

"Wow. Both of those scenes are perfect," she murmured. "I couldn't ask for anything better."

"This is it," Georgie said, already carving another bite of asado. "This is your signature dish. I think your only problem is going to be convincing people to order anything else."

"Do I smell food?"

Travis strolled into the kitchen, shirtless, with a baseball bat slung over his shoulder. He looked so indecently male that Rosie had to look up at the ceiling.

"Uh, yeah . . . grab a fork. Let's get the male perspective."

"No way. No." Georgie shook her head. "If he eats this, he'll be forever unsatisfied with my cooking. Begone, fiancé. Forget what you witnessed this day."

"Ah, come on, baby girl." He laid a noisy kiss on her cheek. "No matter what, you'll always be my favorite meal."

"Oh, *come on*." Bethany shoved her future brother-in-law away. "I'm hanging on to my appetite by a thread here."

"Let him have one bite," Rosie cajoled, winking at Travis and cutting him off a slice of meat, preparing him a forkful, and handing it over. When his eyes widened at the taste and he staggered back a step, Rosie knew he was playing up his reaction and didn't mind in the slightest. "What do you think?"

"I think I'll have no problem convincing some of the Bombers players to make the trek to Long Island on opening night." He nodded at Rosie and set the fork down. "Once people taste your food, you won't need the extra help. But it won't hurt having a little star power on opening night, whenever you get to that point."

"Wow." Rosie searched for the right words and couldn't find them around the obstruction in her throat. "Thank you. I don't know what to say."

Hand on her throat, Georgie gave Travis a serious look over her shoulder. "You should be scared of how hard you're going to get laid tonight."

His laughter trailed behind him as he left the kitchen.

Bethany went to the fridge and took out three bottled beers, uncapping the brews and handing them out before falling back into her seat. "Totally unrelated to my little sister getting more action than a twenty-one-year-old on spring break in Cancun, I'm getting to the point where porn and my vibrator are losing their luster and I'm beginning to desire male company again." She took a brisk sip of her beer. "And, God, that's annoying."

Rosie drained half of her beer. "Amen to that."

Georgie visibly battled her smugness. "Sounds like things are . . . interesting . . . in the reconciliation department."

"You could say that." Rosie twisted her bottle on the table. "He's trying. Like, really, honestly trying to communicate better and that makes me hopeful. I'm *hopeful*. That's way more than I had two weeks ago. I think we might have a chance."

Bethany reached across the table and squeezed her wrist. "That's fantastic."

"Yeah. It is." Rosie wet her lips. "I can't help but feel like he's holding so much of himself back, though. I have this unsettled feeling in my belly sometimes, like I'm missing the bigger picture. The situation can't fix itself overnight, no matter how much I would like it to, you know? I have to keep reminding myself of that." She looked into the empathetic faces of her friends and decided to keep her paranoia to herself for now—the nitty-gritty was between her and Dominic. They'd pick it apart tomorrow in therapy. She'd just nailed down her signature dish and she wanted to enjoy that fact a little longer, so she searched for a way to lighten the mood without avoiding the topic of her husband completely. "Meanwhile, when Dominic and I are together, I can't go ten seconds without wanting to . . . to . . ."

Georgie waggled her eyebrows. "To what?"

"Yes, I need some specific imagery." Bethany clapped. "I've literally reached the end of internet porn. Spoiler, the only prize you win is shame."

"Fine." Rosie covered her face and lowered her voice to a whisper. "I want him to tie my hands behind my back while I . . . um . . . ride his face and tongue? You know that move?"

Bethany and Georgie stared at her in stunned silence, before Bethany drained her beer and rose to her feet. "Looks like I'm going back to the beginning of porn." She pushed out through the kitchen door. "I'll try and recover by the time Georgie's wedding rolls around."

In the wake of her sister's exit, Georgie shifted in her seat.

Rosie pressed her hands to her hot cheeks. "Go find your fiancé. I'll put this in Tupperware and head out."

"Thank you," she squeaked. "So see you at the next meeting . . . ?"

A laugh snuck out of Rosie's mouth. *"Go."*

Rosie and Dominic sat side by side on the couch in Armie's office. There was something in the air. Something that had been hanging in the atmosphere like sticky dewdrops since she'd arrived at the session, but Rosie couldn't quite put her finger on it. She only knew there was tension coiled between her shoulder blades and a sense of foreboding lingering in her belly. The first two sessions had been cathartic. They'd made progress, too. Hadn't they? So why did the issues between her and Dominic still feel totally unresolved?

"We've been presented with the river of Rosie's needs and we've crossed to the other side, as much as we can in our accelerated time together," Armie said, hopping up onto the edge of his desk. "We'll be using this session to discuss what Dominic needs."

Rosie's serene expression felt frozen on her face.

Armie had mentioned in passing during their first session that she and Dominic expressed appreciation and love in different ways. Rosie needed words to feel appreciated—that had now been established. She should have seen this moment coming. After all, she wasn't the only member of this marriage. Of course Dominic had needs as well. Wasn't that what Tuesday nights had been about?

An uncomfortable burn started in Rosie's sternum and traveled down to her belly, spreading. Tuesday nights hadn't been just for her husband. They'd been for her, too. In fact, Dominic was almost hyperfocused on her satisfaction when they had sex. None of this was relevant, anyway, because hadn't part of her reason for leaving been that their sex life had turned empty?

"Rosie?" Armie prompted. "You're quiet. Doing okay over there?"

"Yes," she rasped. "I think so."

"We don't need to do this," Dominic said, and she could feel him watching her intently. "She works all day, standing on her feet. Always makes sure I've got something home-made to heat up for dinner."

That unease in Rosie's stomach thinned the lining even more, and she could taste acid. When she'd walked into the office, she'd had the upper hand, and now it was slipping. The very fact that she'd *wanted* to have an upper hand when they were trying to get even footing increased her discomfort. Something didn't feel right, but she couldn't put a name to it yet.

"I think this is important, Dominic. The way you protect Rosie is a positive thing, but in this case, I think . . ." Armie's smile tightened. "I think you might need to quell that protective urge for the purposes of this discussion."

Dominic was silent for a few beats. "I don't know if I can."

"Try." Armie leaned forward, elbows propped on the knees of his ripped jeans. "Dominic, we know you express your appreciation for Rosie through deeds. Acts of service. We've been working on creating words, to go along with those actions." He paused. "It's important that you're not just giving, that you're also receiving. What is something that Rosie does that makes you feel appreciated?"

"I told you, the food in the fridge." Her husband shifted restlessly on the couch. Not Rosie. She couldn't move at all. "She contributes a well-earned paycheck."

"Okay. A paycheck is a contribution to the household, which is very important, but it's not meant to express love or appreciation specifically to you, Dominic," Armie said. "Let's talk about the food. What do you typically make, Rosie?"

"Um . . ." Her voice sounded rusted. "Sometimes I'll make a lasagna and just leave it there, so we can cut squares from it during the week."

"So the food isn't just for Dominic, it's for both of you?"

"Yes," she whispered, her pulse jumping in her wrists.

The cushions on the couch dipped as Dominic moved closer to her. "What is the point? She's not responsible for making me dinner. I'm a grown man."

"No, I would agree with that. But if you're claiming that's how she expresses—"

"If I'm not doing that, I'm doing nothing. I've been doing nothing." Rosie laid her ice-cold hands on the sides of her face. For the past week, she'd been feeling apprehensive, positive things were moving forward too easily with her and Dominic. Waiting for the other shoe to drop. Was this why? "Oh my God."

"That's enough of this," Dominic ground out, putting an arm around her shoulders. "Stop upsetting her."

Armie sighed. "Dominic, it's okay for you to be upset, too. Have you considered that maybe there are reasons this marriage hasn't been working for you, too? And not for just Rosie?"

"No, I haven't," he gritted.

She looked over in time to see his green eyes flash with

irritation. There was more happening in their depths, though. Uncertainty. Just a hint of it, but it was there, and it crumbled Rosie's house of cards. It took a lot to make Dominic uncertain of anything. Her husband was built out of conviction and duty.

"You should," Rosie whispered. "You should consider I haven't been good to you, either. I—I don't think I have—"

He scoffed. "Stop, Rosie. Just stop this."

"Look me in the eye for ten seconds. The way I couldn't do last time." She wasn't sure why it seemed vital to attempt that prolonged connection in that moment, only that it was. During their first session, she'd seen everything right there, visible in the windows to his soul. She'd seen frustration, apology, heat. She needed that reassurance right now more than she needed her next breath. "Look me in the eye and tell me you were happy in our marriage."

Dominic took her chin in his hand and leaned close, un-flinching as their gazes connected. This time, though, there was a barrier up. He was hiding. "I was . . . I was . . . happy."

Rosie made a sound and covered her mouth.

"If I wasn't completely happy, Rosie, it's only because you weren't."

It was hard to watch, her husband struggling to come to grips with his own lack of contentment, all the while desperate to reassure her. She'd had a shard of ice lodged right in the center of her chest ever since the night she'd given up on their marriage. This display of vulnerability from Dominic made it crack down the center and begin to thaw. God, she hadn't seen him like this in so long. Maybe ever. Thoughts raced behind his eyes faster than a major-league pitch. What went on in Dominic's mind?

"Dominic." Armie's voice brought her husband's head whipping around, his expression decidedly dazed. "Let's talk about what Rosie could do, instead of what she maybe hasn't done lately. I'm going to give you a few examples of expressions of love—you tell me which one appeals to you most."

Dominic shrugged a jerky shoulder.

"Rosie saying thank you for working hard." He let that option settle. "Rosie surprising you with a new pair of sunglasses. Rosie going with you to a movie. Rosie filling the gas tank of your truck without you asking . . ."

It was subtle, but she caught her husband's nod in her periphery.

"So you not only prefer to express your love through deeds, that's how you need love expressed to you in return."

"I don't know," Dominic said hoarsely.

The tip of her nose burning, Rosie slipped her hand beneath her husband's, threading their fingers together. "Try to talk through it, please?"

A muscle jumped in Dominic's cheek. "Not gas pumping," he said in a low voice. "I wouldn't want her to pump my gas—ever—and I don't care if that makes me a chauvinist. But I guess . . . I don't know. It would be nice to know she'd thought of me."

The unshed tears that had been poised behind Rosie's eyes lost the fight and cascaded down her cheeks. Her face felt freshly slapped. All this time, she'd blamed Dominic entirely for the decline of their relationship. But she'd been equally to blame. She might have fought in the beginning, trying to locate that old wildfire that had always burned between them, physically and emotionally. Somewhere along the way, she'd quit. At least Dominic had tried in his own secret ways to make her feel cared for. Protected. She'd done nothing.

When Dominic saw Rosie crying, his face paled. "No, honey. Please." He reached for her, hesitated, then caught her around the waist. Already throatily crooning comforting words, he dragged Rosie sideways onto his lap, wrapping his big arms around her body, as if he could ward off the icy realization that she'd been blaming him. And taken none of that blame herself.

Oh my God. This is my doing as much as his.

Every day, going through the motions and being so angry at him. How could she not have realized she was doing the exact same thing? How could she have been such a hypocrite?

Tears burned tracks down her cheeks, and Dominic watched them in horror, seeming as though he didn't have a clue what to do. For once. Finally, he leaned in and started to kiss them away.

"Shhh, Rosie. We're going to work this out. You're my wife and I wouldn't change that for any damn thing in the world. I'm your man." He exhaled roughly. "Details, right? Words? You need to know I'm always paying attention? Remember that time we took the ferry to Connecticut, the day before I was deployed? Your fingers and mouth tasted like the cranberry-orange muffin we split from the bakery, and I'd scour the mess tent for oranges every fucking day I was away, trying to get that taste back in my mouth." He turned her face, moved his head, and kissed the freckle behind her ear. Once, twice. "I missed you so bad. I miss you now."

That ice in her heart melted and dripped, halfway to vapor. "I miss you, too."

"Come home."

Lord, in that weak moment, she wanted nothing more than to do that. Go back to her husband and hope everything worked out. Hope that their new self-awareness would make all the difference. But she wasn't willing to gamble. She'd only learned a few minutes ago that she'd played an active role in getting them to this point. Separated. She needed time to get her head around that. To go back and comb through the past five years through an entirely different lens. They both needed to work on themselves—and their marriage—at the same time. They would never do that if they fell back into their old routine.

"Okay. Let's talk homework." Armie clapped his hands together. "Rosie, Dominic needs acts of service to feel appreciated. I will leave those up to you, but let me reiterate that—as your therapist—I feel strongly that sex should remain off the table."

Rosie bit down on her tongue and forced a smile.

Dominic dropped his face into her neck and groaned.

"Dominic, please continue exercising your vocal cords. Find ways to give Rosie the words she needs to hear. You did a tremendous job of that today." Armie's body fell bonelessly against the back of his chair. "It might not feel like it right now, but we've had a successful session, folks."

Even though it was insanely difficult, Rosie scooted off Dominic's lap, allowing him to keep her close with a protective arm around her shoulders. "Armie, you said you usually know by the fourth session if a couple is going to make it." She swallowed hard. "I know we still have one more session left, but do you know about us yet?"

His smile was apologetic. "Not yet."

CHAPTER FOURTEEN

A day after their rocky third therapy session, Dominic was grabbing a quick workout in the back bedroom—hoping to burn off some of his excess mental and sexual frustration—when he heard the sound of water running in the house and frowned. There was no one home, save himself—he couldn't be more painfully aware of that fact—and none of the appliances were turned on.

What gives?

He finished his set of forty pull-ups and let go of the metal bar, which he'd hung in the doorway of the guest room. He waited for his breathing to slow so he could listen again, double-checking that he indeed heard water running. With a frown, he walked barefoot and shirtless down the hallway, toward the kitchen, to investigate. His pulse started to race at the possibility that Rosie had come home, but there was no one there.

A sound from outside the house brought Dominic to the front door. He opened it—and found his wife in the driveway.

Washing his truck.

He was so stunned by the sight, all he could do was stare. His wife was in tight black yoga pants and an old sweatshirt, hair up in a bun. Gorgeous, so fucking gorgeous in the setting sun. Pink and orange streaked behind her in the sky and made her skin glow. Love ripped through him like a hurricane, forcing him to lean against the doorjamb. As much as he hated watching her perform any kind of manual labor, he couldn't help but be thankful just to have her there, whether it was temporary or permanent.

Hope rose up inside him, cramming his throat full as he searched the driveway for her things. Nothing was there, though. No suitcase. This visit was temporary—part of him had known that the second he opened the door. She'd made up her mind to go about their second chance the right way. He needed to try to respect that, which meant he wouldn't even lie to his parents about the situation, even though he'd been sorely tempted. When the phone rang for their bimonthly call, he'd almost answered and told them Rosie was great. That *everything* was great. Just to reassure himself. But he'd avoided the call instead, because next time he told his parents everything was great, he wanted it to be true. This visit was progress. At this point, he would take any increment of Rosie he could get, even though he wanted to devour her whole.

Their therapy session had knocked Dominic on his ass, although he still didn't believe Rosie was responsible for their situation. At all. Since returning from overseas, he hadn't taken her to Argentina, even though she'd always wanted to visit to honor her mother. Hadn't presented her with the dream house on the water, instead letting it languish untouched because he wasn't confident in it being good enough. Worst of all, he hadn't encouraged her to open the restaurant, even though she'd been talking about it for years. He was a quiet asshole who hadn't been giving her the words she needed. Of course she'd left. She'd done nothing wrong—and no one could convince him otherwise. Watching her cry over that bullshit yesterday had been pure torture.

Still. He could admit that Rosie giving him real, tangible evidence that she loved him . . . made the organ in his chest beat faster. Made it ache. And if it didn't make him feel like a punk, he might admit that watching Rosie clean his truck made him kind of breathless. When he and Rosie were in high school, she used to untangle his headphone cords. Sure, she did a lot of other things for him back then, like bake him brownies or put extra pens in his backpack before class . . . but there was something about the way she untangled his headphones and left them in a neat circle inside the cup holder of his truck that always got to him. Such a small thing, but he'd liked knowing she'd wanted to save him that minor frustration. He hadn't minded watching her fingers move, either. A couple of times he'd found himself tangling the headphones on purpose just so she'd fix them.

Growing up, he'd been shown love through unspoken acts. Having his lunch made for school, a new pair of shoes showing up just in time for the old ones to fall apart. Those actions made him feel cared for and he didn't have to *ask* for them, which saved him from feeling needy. Or like he needed to be taken care of. Men took care of their loved ones. Not the other way around. That's what he'd been taught from a young age and the belief was hard to shake, so he lived for the small acts of caring from Rosie. It meant she loved him enough to think about him.

So, yeah, while he wanted to strangle Armie for making his wife cry, he could also maybe admit he needed some evidence that this woman still loved him. He needed it bad. When he returned from Afghanistan, she'd shown him evidence of her love on a regular basis. Spontaneous hugs, elaborate date nights at home with candlelight, simply *telling* him she loved him. It was becoming obvious to him that she'd eventually stopped doing those things because he'd been showing her his love in a totally invisible way. How could she have known he'd been saving up for the house since the day he got back?

In those months after his return, he'd felt so inadequate compared to the men he'd left behind. His plans had seemed so trivial. So he'd set out to do better. Along the way, he'd forgotten to make damn sure Rosie knew she was the most important part of his life. He'd let the two of them drift. Now, having her show him she cared, that she'd thought about him, flooded him with gratitude and relief.

But he couldn't accept the gesture, could he? Not like this. In no world could he watch Rosie wash his truck in a rapidly dampening sweatshirt when it was fifty degrees outside.

Seriously, it might kill him.

"Okay, honey girl. Pack it in." Dominic came out of the house, letting the screen door slap against the doorjamb.

"Thank you for doing this, but you're going to get sick out here. Come in out of the cold, Rosie."

She pulled up the right sleeve of her sweatshirt to her elbow and dunked the sponge back into the bucket she'd filled, which explained the source of the running water. "I'll be done in fifteen minutes. Could you grab the grocery bags out of my backseat, please?"

"When you come inside."

There was a flash of something in her eyes that he'd seen at the therapy session. Regret. Heaviness. A little bit of panic. He didn't like it.

"I'm digging in my heels," she said.

"You've been doing a lot of that lately."

He instantly regretted his words when she broke their eye contact.

"I've got on two layers under this sweatshirt. Please just let me do this?" Her voice was laden with determination. "I need to do something for you."

Despite his fears over her falling ill, warmth rolled into his chest like clouds over the water, huge, blocking everything else out. "Will you stay for a while afterwards?"

She stopped soaping for a moment, looking at him over her shoulder. Blinking a couple of times. Slowly. "Yes."

That single word made anticipation sing over Dominic's skin, but his body needed to chill the fuck out. He was horny enough to read sexual intention into a brisk hello. If he'd learned anything by now, it was that his wife wasn't breaking the no-sex rule. And he hadn't caved on his promise, either. Next time he got relief, it would be inside Rosie, so help him God. Unfortunately, he was feeling the strain like nobody's business.

Dominic went inside to throw on a jacket, then headed back out to retrieve the bags from Rosie's backseat. While he was inside, she'd turned on the small vacuum cleaner they used for their cars, the loud hum absorbing the sounds of his footfalls. As he drew even with Rosie, she bent forward over the rear cab seat, leaving her tight, round ass on display.

Pure torture.

He itched to light up a cigarette, but he never smoked when Rosie was around. Only on the job site, while running errands, or after she'd fallen asleep. He'd come back from his deployment with the stress-reducing habit and she'd never asked him to stop, but he hated the idea of breathing tobacco breath anywhere in her vicinity and he damn well wasn't going to start now, possibly hurting his chances of winning her back even more.

By the time Dominic returned with the grocery bags in his arms, his dick was hard enough to jimmy a lock. Rosie was still leaning forward over the backseat, knees planted on the torn leather of his truck, hips tilted enough that he could see the stretch of Lycra over her pussy. Jesus Christ. Was it dark enough yet to hide them from passing neighborhood traffic if he climbed into the truck behind her and rocked his cock into her from behind?

She flipped off the vacuum. "Dominic?" Her eyes found him over her shoulder, then lit up with what looked like reluctant awareness. "Did you, um . . . get the bags?"

"Yeah," he rasped, hefting them up a little.

"Thank you," she returned, sounding breathless herself, that ripe ass still on display.

Dominic growled. "Goddammit, Rosie. Did you come here to torture me?"

"No." She quickly sat back on her heels. "No, I didn't."

"Just tell me what to expect here, Rosie. My body hurts. It wants yours."

"I know." She abandoned the vacuum and climbed out of the truck, hands wringing at her waist.

His heart picked up its pace so much at having her close—having her home—that he got dizzy.

"I'm really thrown off by what happened at our appointment, you know? Realizing we've both let this marriage get to this point . . . and I'm feeling kind of scattered. Like I've been seeing everything all wrong and I've just . . . I've fallen really hard off my high horse. And I don't know how or if we'll make this relationship work, but I know when I woke up feeling lost this morning, I wanted to be near you." She inhaled in a rush. "Can we just spend some time near each other for a little while tonight?"

"Yes," he said, voice resonating. His whole body resonating. "I want that."

"Me too." She wet her lips. "I'm going to finish up here. Can you go inside and preheat the oven for me? Three seventy-five."

Backing away from her when she'd just admitted to needing him, even in a small capacity, was fucking agony, but he did it. Anything to not screw up this chance to have her cross the threshold of their home, even if it was just for a few hours. He stopped to glance back at Rosie on his way into the house and found her watching him from beneath her lashes. Looking . . . in need of reassurance? He knew how to give it to her. By worshipping her, pleasuring her, communicating love with his body.

But that didn't work, did it? Not completely. Hadn't Rosie said she felt empty afterward? He had to find a way to offer more. Give more.

Tell that to the testosterone flowing through his veins. As soon as he got inside, Dominic dropped the groceries off on the counter and adjusted his hard cock through his sweatpants. He planted his hands on the edge of the kitchen counter and breathed in and out. "Okay, not jerking off for a week was a bad choice, bro. Admit it. But you can do this. You can be in the same room as your wife and not fuck her until she screams the town into a power outage."

Dominic visualized the same thing he'd been picturing all week, while trying to get his dick under control. One of his fellow marines had been bitten by a scorpion while on a perimeter check and the bite had gotten infected. Dominic pictured that mass of oozing flesh and started unpacking the contents of the grocery bags, teeth dug into his lower lip. Chicken stock, eggs, tomato paste, a green bell pepper.

His visualization exercise was working. He was halfway to losing his erection until Rosie walked in and immediately stripped off her sweatshirt at the door, carrying the T-shirt beneath it up to her breasts, showing off a hint of underboob before dropping back into place. She hung her sweatshirt on a hook and blew out a breath, glancing around the house as if she'd forgotten what it looked like, maybe even missed it—and Dominic's throat cinched tight.

"Your truck was already pretty clean," she said, tucking loose hair into her bun. "I feel like I cheated on my homework." Her laughter was kind of skittish, reminding him of those first few middle-school dates to the coffee shop, when they were just getting to know each other. "Wow. Why am I so nervous?"

"This is your home. I'm your husband. You shouldn't be . . ." Dominic heard the rote lines coming out of his mouth and dragged a hand down his face, laughing without a drop of humor. "I'm nervous, too, Rosie."

Her breath caught. "You are?"

"Yeah." Now that they'd returned to the scene of the crime, it became even more obvious how drastically their communication had dwindled. Their voices sounded almost foreign filling the kitchen together at the same time. "It doesn't make you see me as less of . . . a man? Knowing I'm nervous?"

"What?" She pressed a hand to the center of her chest. "God, no. It makes me feel like I'm not crazy. It puts us on the same team."

Surprise prickled up his spine. "I want to be strong for you at all times," he said hoarsely. "Isn't that my job?"

Her features softened as she regarded him. "Marriage isn't a job, Dom."

She hadn't called him by that nickname in so long, his insides jolted upon hearing it. All day long, it was shouted over the sound of hammering on the construction site, but it sounded different coming from his wife. It came from the past. The future. It held weight.

"Duty is something I understand. It's something I can't fuck up."

"I appreciate that. I appreciate what you do for us. For me." The hand dropped from the center of her chest and she crossed to the counter, close enough to Dominic that he could count the goose bumps on her neck. "It makes me feel closer to you when you let down your guard. Makes me feel like I can do the same."

Dominic was barely aware of moving closer. He found himself behind Rosie, zeroed in on the freckle behind her ear as she unloaded shopping bags. Fuck, she smelled good enough to take a bite out of. "You want me to put on your music?"

She shivered, fumbling a tub of sour cream and dropping it on the counter. "Yes, that would be nice. Thank you." Her pupils had bled completely into the brown of her eyes when she glanced back over her shoulder. "I'm making empanadas."

"Does that mean you're happy?"

"This time . . . it means I want you to be. Happy."

When he normally would have pressed his lap to her ass, kissed her smooth neck, and slid his hands up under the front of her T-shirt, Dominic backed away instead. God, it was unnatural to move away from the force field that drew him in so intensely. Like separating stuck magnets. Since she'd left, the kitchen had seemed so huge and empty; now it might as well be the size of a stand-up shower stall. His hands tingled with the need to run over her skin, and his mouth had definite acts of service in mind. Getting inside her head, however, was fulfilling a different part of him. The simple statement that she wanted him happy made his chest expand to the size of a marching band bass drum. Watching her prove it? Even better. Rosie had come over, cleaned his truck, and now she was making him a meal.

It was heaven on earth and nothing could ruin it. Not even his thwarted sex drive.

Dominic turned the knob of the old radio that sat on a perch in the kitchen window, salsa music crackling over the speakers. The device had belonged to her mother, and even though he'd bought her a new one several Christmases ago, she continued to use this one, static and all. Tradition. His wife loved tradition, but those little displays of it had been few and far between over the past few years. Or maybe she was just keeping them to herself.

Remembering how she used to dance in the kitchen while cooking made Dominic swallow hard as he watched her from his lean against the opposite counter. He catalogued every movement of her hands mixing the vegetables and meat in a bowl. Listened as she hummed along to the music as she spooned the filling into dough and forked the empanadas closed. When she turned to put them in the oven, Dominic took note of her shallow breathing and knew she'd been aware of him watching her the whole time. *Careful, man, you're letting the lifelong obsession with her show.*

"Those should be ready in thirty minutes," she breathed, fidgeting as she faced him. "Do you want to watch TV or—"

"Nah." Before he knew his own mind, Dominic stepped into the warmth of her space, capturing her left hand in his right. "Can we dance, Rosie?"

"Dance?"

Dominic came another inch closer, and Rosie's head fell back like a string had been cut, giving him her upturned face.

"I don't know i-if that's a good idea."

"You don't?" Hunger bloomed in his middle, but he kept his features schooled. "The therapist said we're allowed to kiss. Dancing must be on the hippie-approved list, right?"

"Whoa," she said unsteadily, her gaze dropping to his mouth. "First you want to dance and now . . . kissing. You can't just throw all of that out there."

Dominic grinned and rubbed his right thumb in a circle around the palm of her hand. "Didn't ask to kiss. I said I wanted to dance." He slipped his left hand around the small of her back and eased their bodies together. "You made that leap, honey girl."

Rosie sputtered for a moment, but if she noticed Dominic swaying her into the low, slow beat of the music, she didn't show it. "So I did."

"I forgive you for sexualizing me."

"Shut up," she said on a giggle, then cut herself off with a gasp when she realized they were dancing. "Oh, you think you're slick?"

"Did you seriously forget how much game I have, Rosie?" He brought her tighter to his body, groaning inwardly over the tits that poked into his stomach, the press of their thighs. "Maybe you need a reminder."

"Maybe I do," she whispered, her breath fanning over his mouth. "Just remember the rules, okay?"

Dominic made a sound in his throat that somehow spoke of misery and contentment at the same time. It was amazing to simply hold his wife again. For the last five years, whenever they touched, he got impatient almost immediately to satisfy her. Please her. Now he wondered if he'd been trying to overcompensate for not giving her what she really needed. Words. Intimacy without sex. Dominic dragged his tongue across the seam of his lips, noticing the flutter of her eyelids. What was he supposed to be doing again? Oh, right. Reminding her he still had a modicum of game left. "Mmm, girl. Your hands really worked that empanada meat."

She burst out laughing into his chest, her whole body shaking.

Dominic's deep rumble joined hers and tension ebbed from his shoulders. Damn, he loved making her laugh, and those instances had been too few and far between. For way too long. "What?" He nudged her forehead with his chin. "You saying my game is rusty?"

"Those are your words, not mine."

"All right. Take two." They grinned at each other for a moment, but Dominic felt himself sober. "When you were standing at the counter, the sunset was coming in through the window. All around you, turning these little curls near your ears to gold. I was thinking, I wish I was a painter or a photographer because keeping something that beautiful to myself makes me a selfish bastard. Even though I want you that way. All for me." He closed his eyes and breathed in roughly through his nose. "Every perfect fucking inch."

As he spoke, her fingertips twisted in the neckline of his shirt, her body going pliant against his. Somehow they continued to turn in a slow circle in the center of the kitchen, but Dominic didn't have a clue how, when his body felt stiff and aching all over.

"Just kidding," she murmured, going up on her tiptoes, sucking in a breath when Dominic dragged her higher against his body. "Your game is still tight."

The word "tight" on her lips almost broke him. Almost made Dominic rip the yoga pants right off her. Two steps and he could boost her onto the counter, lick that sweet pussy he'd been missing like hell. *No. For the love of God, don't fuck this up.* If he pushed and she backed off and left, he would hate himself for ruining this moment.

"Talk to me about something, honey girl," he rasped. "You made an appointment to see the old diner space. You haven't gone yet, right?"

"Nuh-uh. No," she said too quickly, still on her toes, clinging to his collar, letting him turn her around the rapidly darkening kitchen. "No, but I tested my signature dish out on Georgie and Bethany. They loved it."

"Sure they did. That's amazing." He pressed his lips together. "Was it the asado?"

She breathed a laugh and it slipped over his collarbone.

"Of course it was. You'll taste it someday soon, I hope." A beat passed. "What have you been doing without me around? Do you cook?"

"God no. I've been eating at Grumpy Tom's mostly. After work. Beer and a burger or whatever is easiest." He stretched his fingers across the small of her back, trying to reach as much of her as possible. "Been sleeping with the television on. I know you hate that, but it's too quiet otherwise."

"Surely you're not implying I usually fill the silence with snoring."

"I wouldn't dare." He chuckled. "Nah, you don't snore, but you . . . murmur things."

She looked up at him, her mouth close. So close. "I do?"

Dominic nodded. "Mostly about the spice rub needing more paprika." Briefly, he brushed their foreheads together, even though he was dying to linger. "Sometimes you ask for me."

The kitchen seemed to close in around them.

"What do you do when I ask for you?"

It was getting hard to swallow. "Kiss your shoulder, hold your hand."

"You do?"

Dominic just looked at her, suspecting his heart—as well as the truth—was evident in his eyes.

"My appointment to look at the commercial space is on Friday. Do you . . . want to come?"

"Really?" His heart knocked in his chest. "Yes. Yes, I want to come."

The double meaning of those words wasn't lost on either of them. Their fleeting dose of eye contact was proof of that.

This was it. She was moving forward with the restaurant. Even as he pulled her closer, he couldn't help but get the sense his wife was slipping away . . . and he couldn't figure out why. That reality made him want to claim her, own her, the way he'd grown accustomed to doing.

Dominic wet his lips and focused on not thrusting his hips. Not an easy feat, considering he was packing enough wood to build a deck and both of them were well aware. No way she couldn't feel his erection with their hips pressed together, snug and restless. Any minute now, he was going to screw this up. Break the rules. Push too hard. So it hurt like hell, but Dominic settled Rosie on the flats of her feet and stepped back, swiping the back of his wrist across his sweating upper lip.

Talk. Talk. Make words.

Words. That thought shook something loose and Dominic gripped the lifeline before he could reach for Rosie again where she stood trembling under the dim pendant light. "Earlier I was thinking about how much you love tradition. I, uh . . ." He swallowed hard, begging blood to return to his brain. "I was trying to distract myself this week, so I cleaned out the basement and found one of your mother's boxes. There are some recipes on notecards banded together." He turned away from her beauty out of pure necessity, opening the drawer where he'd stashed the notecards. There was a ring box wedged in beside the notecards, but he didn't want Rosie to see that. Somehow her mother's wedding ring had ended up in their basement storage area and he'd opened the box to reveal it was missing stones and needed to be cleaned. He wanted to have it polished and the stones replaced, so he could give it to her when she came home. Which was the definition of *getting ahead of himself.* No help for it, though. A man could dream.

"The notecards were stuck together, but I peeled most of them apart without damaging any . . ."

Dominic trailed off when Rosie's hands went sliding up his back. They stopped at his shoulders and he fell forward with a groan, catching himself on the counter at the last second.

"Turn around and kiss me."

"I can't. I can't do it. I'm all fucked up."

"Please? I miss kissing you so much."

"Miss it?" That made him turn around, a frown dragging his eyebrows together. "I devour that mouth when we're . . . when . . ." *When we're fucking.*

Christ. Was that really the only time he kissed her?

Regret gripped Dominic around the throat and he shot forward, capturing his wife's mouth with a growl. She sobbed against his lips and everything inside him sped up, slowed down, sped up again. He couldn't stop to get a good breath because that split second of time would allow him to think, realize he never kissed his wife just for the hell of it. Just to be close to her. What the hell was wrong with him?

It was a full-on attack—and there was nothing he could do to slow himself down. Especially not when she moaned like she'd been waiting for this, for a kiss in the kitchen, for years.

Jesus Christ, had she?

Dominic bent her backward over his forearm and plowed his tongue into her mouth, once, twice, three times, his eyes flying open when Rosie's joined his, brushing tentatively at first, then with more and more confidence. She ripped at the shoulders of his T-shirt until he eased back enough to let her tear it off over his head, leaving him shirtless.

"Rules, rules," she whimpered against his mouth. "I—I just wanted to touch your skin."

"You want your man's clothes off, you fucking take them off." He pulled her upright again and backed her up until she hit the counter. "Anytime." His mouth moved over her face, neck, and throat, raining openmouthed kisses. "Anywhere."

Rosie's expression was dazed, her hands running up and over his pecs. "God, you look so good. I didn't . . ." She bit her lip and laughed in that beautiful, exhilarated way he hadn't heard in a long time. "Until I saw you in the gym the other day, I just assumed you got this way on the construction site."

Dominic licked into her mouth and felt her body go boneless, her thighs restless against his. "I've got a motherfucking ten at home," he growled against her swollen lips. "You think I'm stupid enough to let myself go soft?"

Her head fell back, and Dominic trailed his tongue up the center of her throat, sliding it into her mouth when he drew even with her lips. Kissing her and knowing he wasn't allowed to be inside of her heightened every one of his senses to a fifteen. The rasp of her pussy every time her yoga pants moved against his sweatpants. The drag of their wet tongues, the smell of coconut on her skin. He grew wild absorbing every nuance without crossing the point of no return, but the deprivation threatened to rob him of sanity.

"Rosie," he said thickly, sampling her mouth with slow bites. "I want to kiss you for another ten hours straight, but I can't." He gave in and ground their hips together once, moaning into her neck, listening to her echo the sound. "A little more of that mouth and I'm going to finish."

"Do it," she whispered in his ear, trying to wrap her legs around his hips. "I want you to."

Not for the first time in his life, Dominic wished he wasn't stubborn to the fucking bone. "No." He pounded the kitchen counter with a fist. "Told you. Inside my wife or nowhere at all."

Rosie made a frustrated sound, and he cut her off with a kiss, because he didn't have a choice. His mouth was drawn back to hers with such intensity, he wondered how she'd ever walked through the house without him luring her into a make-out session. By the time they came up for air and dove back into another damp, writhing dance of tongues and teeth, pre-come was beginning to bead on the head of Dominic's cock and nothing, nothing could stop him from rubbing that swollen flesh between her welcoming thighs.

"Please," he slurred into her neck. "Please."

"Do you trust me?"

"Yes. Yes."

Dominic watched under half-mast eyelids as Rosie splayed her hands on his chest and pushed. He allowed himself to stumble back a step—and she pushed him again, bringing the backs of his legs up against the edge of a dining room chair. "Sit down, husband."

He was always the one to dominate, but that power had been taken out of his hands. All he could do was sit back, hips shifting, wincing over the discomfort trapped in his briefs. "Wife."

She pressed a finger to her lips. "Shhh. Trust me."

Rosie started to strip, right there in their kitchen, like a fucking goddess, backlit only by the weak kitchen bulb. Her T-shirt came off slowly and was dropped to the floor, leaving her braless, those aroused bronze-tipped tits making Dominic's breath wheeze in and out of his mouth.

"Touch them. Play with them, you gorgeous little cock tease."

"Soon . . ."

When she turned around and slowly peeled the yoga pants down her thighs, Dominic gripped himself through his sweatpants, massaging the stiffness, making it worse, with no way to stop.

"I know that thong," he gritted out, watching her reveal the strip of red that ran through the center of her high ass cheeks. "I've tied you to the bedpost with it, ridden you with it wrapped around my fist, shoved it in your mouth to keep you quiet. I own it as much as you do, don't I?"

Rosie kicked aside her pants and nodded, coming toward him in nothing but a red triangle of material between her legs. "That's right," she whispered, stepping between Dominic's outstretched legs and giving him a slow, hypnotic kiss. His hands climbed over her hips and kneaded her tits, mouth swallowing her gasps. "You know how to own everything you're touching," she said, flickering her tongue against his. "But I want to own you right now."

Dominic's groan was full of pain, his right hand returning to squeeze the bulge between his thighs. "Tell me what I have to do to stop hurting."

Keeping their mouths locked together, Rosie straddled Dominic's legs and sat. His stance was so wide, however, it left her core spread open for him to see, the red thong stretching over her pussy, unable to cover all of it. Dominic had no choice but to yank down the waistband of his sweats and furiously jack himself off, the end already approaching. There was no other outcome with his sexy-as-hell wife 99 percent naked on his lap and purring at him like a seductress.

"Are we breaking the rules?" he managed through clenched teeth, his chest heaving. "Say yes, honey girl. Say yes and I'll fill you full."

Rosie shook her head, a secret smile curving her lips. And then her fingers slipped down between her spread thighs to massage the drenched flesh beneath her panties. "I'm already so close, just from kissing you," she said unevenly. "Tell me when you're close."

Dominic threw back his head and roared at the ceiling. "Goddammit, I told you—"

"Inside me or nowhere at all." Her body started to tremble,

her nipples turning to tight peaks. She scooted closer on his lap, the points of her nipples sliding through the sweat on his chest. "Remember sophomore year of high school?" Rosie murmured brokenly at his lips. "All those times in your bedroom when we were supposed to be studying."

"I haven't forgotten a single second with you."

Tenderness flashed in her eyes, before it was once again overrun with lust. "We'd only make it about fifteen minutes before you had my skirt off and you were rocking, grinding against me . . ."

Dominic groaned. "Are we still pretending you didn't scoot your hips all over the bed until I could see your panties . . . all wet and tucked between those tight ass cheeks?"

"You caught me," she breathed, her eyes closed, and the fingers between her thighs started to move faster, producing another bead of semen on Dominic's cock.

He was losing it. Losing it. Hearing her reminisce about those sweaty afternoons was going to push him over the edge and there was nothing he could do about it. Fuck.

"We took it as far as we could without going all the way." Her eyelashes fluttered. "And we finally decided just the tip didn't count, didn't we?"

Dominic lunged forward off the chair, dropping to his knees, carrying Rosie with him. No sooner had her back landed on the floor of their kitchen did Dominic nudge his wife's panties to one side and sink the head of his erection inside her pussy. Not driving it the entire damn way made him crazed, but the tight pressure of her entrance around his tip was incredible. Perfect. His fist squeezed along his inches, top to bottom, jerking off into the warmth between Rosie's thighs.

"Such a wet girl, aren't you? Got soaked teasing me with those pretty legs spread, didn't you?" The bottom of his spine twisted and he groaned, knowing the end was coming fast. Now. "Keep playing with your clit. Do it. Get off with me."

"Yes," she whimpered, two fingers busy rubbing that button of flesh.

His tongue wanted to play with it so bad, he was salivating, but that would break the rules, wouldn't it? He didn't have a clue anymore. Just knew he was going to die if he didn't get relief.

"I'm coming, Dominic. Please. Yes."

Dominic gripped himself hard, feeling the release in his balls, a trapdoor opening for him to fall through. He pushed his mouth up against his wife's ear and spoke through gritted teeth. "Listen closely. If I can play 'just the tip' with your virgin pussy for a fucking year, I can play the long game to get my wife back. I'm getting you back. Don't you think for a second that I won't kill to make us right again." He swallowed the rising emotion in his throat and let the orgasm break over him. "I love you."

It was agony to say those words knowing he wasn't getting them back. It ripped something open inside his chest, and he fell on the only anchor he'd ever known, kissing her neck while his body emptied of pressure. Rosie's did the same, shaking beneath him, her hips and heels moving restlessly on the floor, seeking purchase.

Something was different this time. Something had changed.

He wasn't exulting in the proof that he'd satisfied her. Maybe to a mild degree—he was a man, after all. Her thoughts weren't a total mystery right now and he loved that. He looked into her eyes, that contact holding, and for that moment, there wasn't a single mystery between them. Just honesty. They were in this struggle together.

Honesty.

The house. He needed to tell her about the house.

Dominic pressed a kiss to Rosie's forehead and helped her sit up, unable to stop his hand from running over the curve of her shoulder, up the column of her neck to cup her cheek. "Hey. Tell me you don't regret that." He cleared his throat. "Please?"

Rosie shook her head. "I don't regret it . . ."

She seemed as if she wanted to say more, but couldn't. There was still too much holding her back.

It was on the tip of his tongue to tell her about the house he'd bought them, but that hesitation on her part made him swallow the revelation down. Lock it back up.

The light in her eyes dimmed a little at his own hesitancy.

The timer on the stove went off.

As Rosie stood to take the empanadas out of the oven, Dominic's head dropped forward on a curse. He couldn't help but feel like he'd missed the buzzer-beater shot. She'd been right there in front of him, as vulnerable as he'd seen her in a long time, and he'd missed another chance to reach deep inside her mind. To grab on to their connection and twist his fist, strengthen it until they had no choice but to be together again. By the time he lifted his head, she'd put the empanadas on a cooling rack and started dressing herself. "So once they're cool, you can—"

"I owe you a date," he said, not wanting to hear the awkwardness in her tone. Wanting that conspiratorial tone back she'd had earlier when they were dancing. "I want to take you out on a date, Rosie."

She smoothed her hands down the front of her T-shirt. "When?"

"Tomorrow night." Dominic stood and pulled up his sweats, never taking his attention off of her. "I'll pick you up at six."

"I can do that." Her hands met at her waist, fingers tangling. Finally, she dropped them and crossed to the door. "I'll see you then."

"Wait." Dominic stayed her hand on the knob and waited until she met his eyes. "Thank you for all of this. The truck, dinner . . ."

"You're welcome." She glanced back at the kitchen. "It felt like going back in time." Her voice dropped to a whisper as she lifted onto her toes and laid a soft kiss on his mouth. "I missed you. I missed how we were. Just . . . stay with me, okay?"

He cradled the back of her head and kissed her hard. "I'm not going *anywhere*."

Dominic stood at the door long after she'd gone, wishing he'd been honest about the house. Wishing she would have stayed. He had to be honest with himself first, though. And he knew those impulses to keep his feelings and insecurities to himself, those beliefs that providing for their small family should be done in silence . . . they had to be dealt with. Maintaining his stiff upper lip hadn't worked. It was time to show Rosie that every single day of his life had been about giving her a dream he'd thought was most important to her. To them.

Right or wrong about that, tomorrow night he would bring her to the house.

Tomorrow he would lay it all on the line.

CHAPTER FIFTEEN

Rosie was nervous. For a date with her own husband.

There wasn't a woman alive who could blame her, right? She'd known for a while that her husband was majorly hot. Some time and distance had really brought that fact home to roost, though. When she'd taken off his shirt in their kitchen, that feast of muscles and tattoos had almost made her cry happy tears.

I've got a motherfucking ten at home. You think I'm stupid enough to let myself go soft?

Standing in front of the guest bathroom mirror, Rosie fanned her flaming cheeks. She'd never seen Dominic as desperate as that moment he threw her on the floor. He was always rough, but he'd been an animal. One who'd managed to restrain himself for the good of their marriage . . . and that might have been the sexiest part of all.

Rosie picked up the new bottle of curl treatment she'd bought during the week, spritzing it on her tresses to keep them tamed before squeezing the strands in her palms, the practiced action making her feel sensual. Tight in some places, loose in others. God, it had taken all her willpower to leave Dominic last night. Not because of his touch, although that alone was a powerful enough aphrodisiac. No, it was the effort. He was *trying.*

She closed her eyes and swayed, a smile curling her lips as she replayed their dance in the kitchen. That was the man she'd fallen in love with. It would have been so easy to stay the night. Move back in. Trust that everything would get better.

Rosie opened her eyes and watched her smile vanish.

But she knew. She'd been down a winding road with Dominic and she knew there was so much more to work through. The man still had secrets behind his every glance, every word. As much as his walls came down when they were kissing and giving each other pleasure, she could almost sense that dam inside him, holding back a whole host of important things. Lord, he was getting so much better at saying what was on his mind, but she was fighting for the future they'd envisioned. She would stay true, she would wage a war for their survival, but she owed it to them—and the young people they'd once been—to see this through.

After one final glance in the mirror, Rosie padded into the bedroom and regarded the deep magenta dress. She'd bought it that afternoon at the store before clocking in, and the tags were still on, dangling from the armpit. With a low neckline and satin material, it wasn't practical at all. When was the last time she'd purchased something frivolous like this?

The day Dominic had come home from overseas. Her mother was still alive then and they'd gone outlet shopping and she'd found a summer dress covered in little stars that cupped her breasts just right, but allowed her to maintain enough modesty for the airport in the middle of the day. She'd smoothed lotion on every inch of her skin and sat at the kitchen table while her mother fashioned two braids and piled them on top of her head. Anticipation had been running laps around her stomach for weeks, waiting for Dominic to come home to stay. He'd grown increasingly quiet every time he was on leave, but she'd chalked it up to the knowledge that being home was temporary. Things would be different now.

She'd never felt more beautiful than she had when Dominic spotted her from the top of the airport escalator. His eyes widened and he seemed almost winded. But the optimism she'd plied herself with had faded the closer he got to the bottom. She couldn't hold on to it. Not when he'd visibly steeled himself against her happiness to see him. And that stoic countenance—that mask—had never completely gone away.

Rosie slipped the dress over her head and reached back to tug the zipper into place. Not for the first time, she wondered what had happened during Dominic's stints overseas. Sure, she'd asked him. Trying to pry information out of her husband had been a lot easier in those early days. She'd even tried to tickle it out of him. The more he'd resisted, the more Rosie had realized he would carry the burden of those years alone. Now, though . . . she wondered if she should try again. It wouldn't be fair to use their separation as a means to coerce information out of him, especially if he didn't want to

share, but she couldn't help wondering if convincing Dominic to open up about that time would be the key to bringing
them close again.

The front door of the house closed downstairs and Rosie
took a deep breath, enjoying the butterflies in her stomach.
That would be Bethany coming home from work. Wouldn't
it be fun to show off her new dress to a girlfriend? She hadn't
done that in so long.

Minutes later, a knock on the guest room door had Rosie
turning around, fingers fluttering at the hem of her dress.
"Oh God. Okay. Come in."

Bethany was frowning when she opened the door, but
then a smile cleared her face. "What?" She stomped her foot.
"You are so hot in that dress. I am attracted to you right now.
No joke. Go through with the divorce so we can get married." She squealed and clapped her hands. "Sorry, I took
that too far, but you look insane."

"I feel insane." Rosie twisted her hips side to side. "It
wasn't on sale, either. I splurged. I'm not even sorry!"

"You shouldn't be! Sorry is for suckers!" Bethany took
Rosie's wrists and held them out to her sides. "Do you have
shoes?"

"I was just going to wear my work heels—"

"Nope." Bethany made a ninety-degree turn and marched
out the door. "Follow me."

They were sitting on the luxurious white carpeting in
Bethany's walk-in closet when Georgie appeared in the
doorframe. Dressed in a clown suit. "Hey. I wasn't invited
to the shoe party?"

"It was an impromptu affair. Rosie is going on a date with her husband."

Georgie dropped into a cross-legged position. "Where?"

"I don't know." Nerves flickered in her fingertips. "He just said he'd pick me up at six."

"Ooh. Mysterious."

Rosie hummed and slipped on a pair of matte gold stilettos. "These?"

"God, yes, that gold complements the color of the dress beautifully," Bethany breathed, waving a hand at Rosie's feet. "Make sure you bring along some flats in your purse, though. I once ditched a date in Manhattan and opened nine blisters on my feet trying to catch a cab in those things. They're not made for walking."

"Ah yes," Georgie said. "The classic sitting-only shoe. Extremely practical."

Rosie chuckled and stood up, taking a runway strut out of the closet and back. "Practical or not, they're designed to put impure thoughts in a man's head."

"Any inanimate object puts impure thoughts in a man's head." Bethany made a disgusted sound. "Box of cereal. Boner. Ice-cube tray. Boner."

Georgie pursed her lips. "Still haven't ended your man sabbatical, Bethany?"

"Nope. Worked out my urges with some quality internet time and I'm back on track." The blonde tipped her chin in Rosie's direction. "So . . . are we interested in putting impure thoughts in Dominic's head? I thought that was a no-no."

Rosie squared her shoulders. "It's inevitable. We're just . . ."

Georgie made an explosion sound, accompanied by hand gestures.

"Yes. That." Rosie smoothed some imaginary wrinkles out of her dress. "We're still following the rules, but there might have been some . . . toeing of the line."

Bethany wiggled her eyebrows. "Is that what the kids are calling it nowadays?"

"Travis calls it adult naptime." Georgie slapped both hands over her face. "Oh my God, he's so cute. I can't even deal with it."

Rosie smiled. "Sounds like you resolved the wedding-venue issue?"

"Totally resolved. We're really getting married in my mom and dad's backyard." She dropped her hands from her face to reveal a bright pink blush. "I'm going to have his babies all over the place. I can't believe this is life."

I used to feel that way. Rosie could remember it clear as day, that floating, rapturous sensation where the future stretched out in front of her like a red carpet. Thing was, last night dancing in the kitchen with Dominic, she'd been back in that place. Right up until she'd walked out the door, actually, the years of silence and uncertainty had been stripped away—and there'd just been floating. God, she wanted to be back there so bad. Back there to stay.

"You're quiet, Rosie." Bethany nudged her with a wedge heel. "What's up?"

"Nothing." She pressed a hand to her belly. "I'm excited, that's all. It feels like a first date and I haven't had one of those since middle school. And I'm pretty sure I wore cropped cargo pants and a fashion scarf then, so hello, improvement."

"Hell yeah," Georgie said, reaching up to give her a high five. "How often did you and Dominic go out before you vamoosed?"

Rosie let out a breath. "Hmm, let's see. Never? We started off our marriage staying home alone, and we never broke the habit."

"Why do you think that is?"

She didn't need a moment to consider the question, since Dominic's possessive nature had been on her mind for a while. "Dominic liked having me to himself. And I loved being with him, so we kind of fell into a pattern of avoiding social situations, except for the odd visit to his family in the Bronx. By the time my mother passed and I needed a friend, I guess it kind of felt too late to try. Dominic's mother is so sweet to me when we go to visit. She tries to fix me up on friend dates with her nieces, but they've already got their inside jokes and . . . I kind of feel like an intruder." She split a look between the sisters. "For the last couple years, every time I spoke to you two at the Brick and Morty company picnic, I hoped we'd get to spend more time together, but . . ."

"I'm really glad we finally are," Bethany murmured.

"Me too." Brows pulling together, Rosie smoothed the material of her dress. "If Dominic and I can make this work, he'll have to get used to sharing me. I wonder if he realizes that." They sat in silence for a moment until Rosie started to fidget, needing a distraction from her first-date nerves. "Sidetrack me. How was everyone else's day?"

Georgie made a sound. "I hate to bring this super-fun, girly mood down, but . . . I worked a birthday party this afternoon—I don't know if you can tell from my elaborate face paint. Anyway, there was a discussion at the adult table. You know that woman Becky, who worked in the supermarket?"

Bethany hummed. "I get my groceries delivered."

"I know her." Rosie frowned. "Haven't seen her in a while, come to think of it."

"Yeah." Georgie's swallow was audible. "Her marriage was rocky, from what people can tell. And one morning, she just . . . took off. Left her kid with the husband. But . . . he wasn't really interested in being a single father. So Supermarket Becky's brother is in town now. He's taken over raising the little girl, but he's not having the easiest time. She's seven."

A shoe dangled, seemingly forgotten, from Bethany's index finger. "Oh my God."

"I know."

Remembering how close she'd been to her mother at that age—at every age—Rosie felt her stomach twist. But an idea occurred to her. "We should help. The Just Us League." Rosie wet her lips. "We could start a schedule. Meals and babysitting? I can't imagine everyone wouldn't want to help."

Bethany was slowly nodding. "Great idea. We've got, like, nine empty nesters in the league who would kill to have a little one running around once in a while. Not to mention Georgie, who is like foaming at the fucking mouth to put her ovaries to use—"

"True dat," Georgie said, raising the roof.

"And, Rosie, you could create a meal schedule . . . that's your department." Bethany sniffed. "Of course, I'll bully everyone into staying on track. Because obviously."

"This feels like an emergency, right? Should we get started now?" Georgie jumped to her feet and whipped out her phone, her fingers flying over the screen. "I've alerted the league phone tree. If this brother is anything like Dad, he's probably in the fetal position by now. We could head over, drop off some dinner, give him a breather . . ."

Bethany chewed her bottom lip. "Rosie has her date."

As if on cue, the doorbell rang downstairs.

A few beats of silence passed.

"Sorry, Rosie." Georgie dropped her hand holding the phone down by her side. "I didn't mean to put a damper on things."

"Don't be silly. I'll just go let him in," Rosie said, leaving the closet. Bird wings flapped in her throat with every step as she descended toward the front door. Amazing that she could get this nervous and excited about seeing her husband of almost a decade, but there it was. Her mind was definitely preoccupied with the little girl and overwhelmed man across town, but nothing could stop the hot, delicious, butter-like melt that slid between her thighs when she answered the door and Dominic—dressed like he was playing to win—stared back.

The rich scent of his aftershave reached her first and plucked her senses like fingers on a harp. He wore a black sweater and dark gray chinos that molded to him almost indecently, drawing her eye to every ripple of muscle on the man. His knuckle tattoos were the only ones visible, reminding her that the sharp-dressed man was also a badass marine to the core.

When she finally managed to drag her attention to his face, the breath caught in her throat at the way he looked at her, like he was savoring every inch his eyes climbed, starting at the tip of her shoes and steadily ascending, definitely not in a rush.

"Goddamn."

"You look great, too." Based on his lack of reaction, she wasn't sure he'd heard her compliment.

"I haven't seen you in that dress before. It's new."

Rosie tried to pull sufficient oxygen into her lungs, but it was almost impossible when his voice was nothing more than a rough scrape. "Um . . ." She tucked a curl behind her ear. "Do you want to come in?"

Finally, he met her eyes, and the heat there backed Rosie up a pace. "Sure." He stepped over the threshold and kept coming, reminding her of a panther stalking its prey—and she liked it way too much. "Back in the day when you invited me in, your mom would put out a plate of alfajores. She'd make me eat at least nine before she was satisfied."

"I remember," Rosie managed, emotion clinging to the sides of her throat. "She loved you."

"Maybe." One corner of his mouth lifted. "Or she was

trying to clog my arteries and kill me so I wouldn't take her baby girl away."

Rosie huffed a laugh. "She did have an evil streak."

"Is that where you got it from?" He licked his bottom lip and perused her neckline. "Because that dress is damn sure trying to kill me."

"Don't look now, but your game is improving," Rosie whispered.

When had they reached the kitchen? She wasn't even aware they'd moved until her back met the kitchen counter, and Dominic planted his hands on the edges, leaning in to take a deep inhale of the air near her neck. "Our bed doesn't smell like you anymore."

"If you're planning on taking me there tonight to fix the problem, think again."

"Give me some credit." His lips trailed across her cheek and locked their mouths together in a kiss that drew moans from them both. "I was just going to ask to borrow your perfume so I could spray a little on the pillow."

"Oh," she murmured. "That can be arranged."

Bethany and Georgie chose that moment to burst into the kitchen, talking animatedly. They obviously thought Rosie and Dominic had already left because they both performed a double take upon discovering them in the kitchen. Georgie tried to go back up the stairs, but she ran into Bethany instead, and they both jolted, stumbling.

"Sorry!" Georgie called. "I didn't . . . We thought you guys were gone."

Bethany was staring at them like the cat who'd caught the

canary. "Look at you two. You read about raw, primal urges in books, but you never see it—"

"Bethany." Georgie elbowed her sister. "Are you drunk?"

Rosie hid her face in Dominic's shoulder. The man had made zero move to free her from the trap he'd made with his body.

"When is her curfew?" he said, winking at the sisters. "I'll try to have her back on time."

Before they could answer, there was a knock on the door. Several, actually. Footsteps sounded on the porch and voices reached the interior of the house. With a wince, Georgie crossed to the entrance and opened the door—allowing at least half a dozen Just Us League members to pile in, a good number of them holding covered plates of food and casserole dishes.

"Where is the child?"

"Where is this poor man?"

Variations of the same question were asked while Georgie, Bethany, Rosie, and Dominic gaped at the intrusion. It wasn't over, either. At least five more women walked in bearing aromatic offerings before Bethany spoke up.

"Seriously, everyone?" Bethany sputtered. "Georgie texted you less than ten minutes ago. How did you get here so fast?"

"We were all at a church potluck down the street."

The women—young and old—traded nods.

"We received your text at the same time, collected our dishes, and piled into our cars."

"Swiped this green-bean casserole right out from under

the pastor's nose," one of them said, setting off a chain of laughter. "The poor man was mid-scoop."

"This is more important," said Candy, the woman who ran an artisanal-cheese-and-wine shop in town, making her a local favorite among, well, everyone. "We want to help."

"Rosie," called an older woman with a green wool cap— Melinda, if Rosie wasn't mistaken. "Are you going to kiss that man or not?"

"We already—" Rosie squeezed her eyes shut. "Oh God."

"What's going on?" Dominic asked, his breath tickling her ear. "Fill me in."

Forming coherent sentences when Dominic's powerful body was heating her like a furnace was not exactly easy, but she forced the words out. "There's a new man in town. His sister ran off, her husband followed . . . and he's been left to care for their child."

Dominic's brows drew together. "You said he's new in town?" Rosie didn't have a chance to question the dawning realization in her husband's expression before he spoke again. "Everyone is heading over there to help out, huh?"

Rosie nodded.

"Including you."

"No." She shook her head. "This is supposed to be our night."

"That's why I'm coming along." He leaned in and kissed her forehead. "I'll push the reservation a couple of hours and we'll eat afterward."

"Really?"

His exhale bathed her mouth. "Not going to lie, I want

you alone," he said. "But I can tell you're only going to be half with me. I'd rather wait until you're all here."

"How dare you show up looking this good. Saying things like that."

He opened his mouth to respond and closed it, his forehead wrinkling. "Should I stop?"

She lifted up and kissed him softly, heat radiating from her face when a cheer went up from just beyond the kitchen. "Does that answer your question?"

"Rosie," Candy called, turning Rosie's head. "My two dishes were already reheated once. Are they safe to freeze and heat up again?"

Rosie surveyed the offerings. "Is there meat in that lasagna?"

"No, ma'am. I wish there was," Candy replied. "Those damn *vegetarians* have infiltrated the church and—"

"Yes, you can reheat the lasagna. No on the pork dish, though."

Rosie started to turn back to Dominic, but Melinda tapped her arm. "How would you portion this? I'd say there's enough for three nights, if we stretched . . ."

"Um. We can mix and match a little, but we should use the more perishable items first. Here, let me get something to take notes. Everyone, line up your dishes." Rosie was torn between wanting to leave and feeling really amazing that the women seemed dependent on her advice. Her . . . leadership. For a woman who'd been ignored on the cosmetics floor of the mall for *years*, being seen as relevant was like a breath of fresh air. One she couldn't help but suck down, letting it stretch her fingers as she picked up something to write with. "We'll need kid-friendly meals, ladies. Who makes the meanest macaroni and cheese?"

Several hands went up.

Rosie smiled and clicked her pen.

CHAPTER SIXTEEN

*C*hrist, could these women put away booze. Dominic had been allowed entry into a secret society where women swore like sailors and objectified men. It was goddamn enlightening, to say the least. Every once in a while, Rosie threw an apologetic glance over her shoulder at him, but it was completely unnecessary. He could have stood there all night and watched her run the show. Even as he marveled over the woman he'd married, however, he couldn't help but feel distinctly out of place. Not only because he was the proverbial fox in the hen house and stood out like a red ink blot on a white shirt. But because, for the first time, he was seeing his wife through a different set of eyes and realizing . . . she'd grown. Without him.

He'd had nothing to do with it.

Dominic opened Bethany's fridge and took out a bottle of water, uncapping it and drinking deeply. He would have much preferred a beer, but he wouldn't have even one knowing Rosie would be in the passenger seat of his truck. Rosie, who was now writing out a recipe for chicken Parmesan with one hand, tracing out a new spreadsheet with the other—all while having a full conversation. This was the same woman he'd passed in their silent house, day after day. All the while, she'd had these amazing capabilities.

She should have been running that restaurant years ago.

God, maybe . . . she should have left him years ago.

"Hey." His wife turned to him, her eyes bright with exhilaration. "Hey, um . . . there's a big Tupperware container of carbonada in the fridge. Oh, and some alfajores on a plate on top of the microwave. Could you help me put them in the truck?"

"On it."

"Thank you."

She started to say something else, but several people began talking to her at once, hijacking her attention. On the way out of the house, with his arms full of food, he couldn't help but pause in the doorframe and take in a wide shot of the scene. Everyone was getting ready to pack up and move out, and Rosie was doing the same, Bethany and Georgie helping her pile supplies like napkins, paper plates, and plastic forks into a bag. He could easily see her doing the same thing in a bustling restaurant, knowing exactly what everyone needed to make their dining experience fluid, better, because it was second nature.

This. This is what made her happy. Not warming up her car in the morning or breaking his back on a construction site. She wanted to feed people. When she hadn't gotten enough encouragement at home, she'd gone and found it elsewhere. The worst part was, he'd known she wanted to own her own place. From the time they were in high school, her dream had been front and center in conversations with him. With her mother. Instead of buying her a restaurant, however, he'd been selfish and spent money on a house. A house he thought she'd love as much as him. A house they'd spent their youth designing like spun sugar, over the phone, under the stars. If he'd talked to her more as an adult—or *listened*, rather—he wouldn't have buried the importance of Rosie owning her own restaurant beneath his selfish desire to be her provider. He'd *needed* that role, and a house was something he could give her all on his own. Maybe he'd even done it on purpose, subconsciously, trying to be the proverbial breadwinner.

But a restaurant . . . that would be all her. And none of him. None of *them*.

Still, if he'd known how happy it would make her, he would have used the money he'd saved to buy her a place. Somewhere she could shine. Except that opportunity was no longer available.

Had he actually planned on showing her that house tonight? Was he insane?

Dominic walked out into the cold with a lump the size of a fist in his throat. Since the day Rosie left him, he'd been asking her to come home. She'd been hesitant, and while he knew they had problems, he'd thought she was being stubborn. Unreasonable. But as he slid the tray of alfajores and pot of stew into the back cab of his truck, he finally admitted to himself that therapy was exactly where they belonged.

Rosie spreading her wings and flying was a beautiful sight to witness, but would it mean she flew away from him? How selfish was he to be worried about that kind of thing?

Dominic closed the rear door of the truck with a curse, turned, and came face-to-face with Rosie. She looked so familiar and beautiful in her red coat, he wanted to get on his knees and ask her forgiveness for being a selfish bastard. *I'm sorry, honey girl.*

"Are you okay?"

"Yeah," he rasped, avoiding her eyes. "Ready to go?"

She nodded slowly and crossed to the passenger side. Dominic followed, opening the door for Rosie and boosting her onto the seat, his groin tightening at the flash of thigh as she buckled up and crossed her incredible legs. Apparently not even guilt could keep him from lusting after his wife. He wanted nothing more than to wait for the rest of the cars to leave, then drag her back inside and give her a nice, hard quickie up against the door in that tight dress.

And it would solve nothing except his incessant hunger for her. Momentarily.

Ignoring the curious look from Rosie, Dominic closed the passenger door and skirted around to the driver's side, starting the truck engine a second later. Rosie read him directions off her phone, but apart from that, there was no conversation. Dominic wanted to ask her when she'd cooked the carbonada and if she'd used her mother's recipe for the hearty soup, but everything sounded disingenuous in his head after he'd finally admitted to himself he'd let her dreams hang in limbo for so long. She'd been pining for something in secret while he'd worked toward an entirely different goal. All of which could have been avoided if he'd *talked to his wife.* Kept her close instead of at arm's length where she could never suspect he wasn't invincible.

"I think this is it," Rosie murmured, prompting Dominic to set aside his thoughts and pull to a stop at the curb. After putting the truck in park, he leaned toward Rosie and they looked at the modest two-story home. It was lit up like Christmas.

She laid a hand on his arm and a current ran through his body. "We'll get everyone organized and then we'll go have dinner. Okay?"

"You'll get everyone organized." He cleared his throat hard and dislodged her hand, missing her touch the second it was gone. "You were impressive, honey girl. Back there. You like being a leader, don't you?"

Dominic hardened his jaw and waited for her answer, even though he already knew what it was. *Is this really who I am?* A man who'd created an image of his wife that suited him and never noticed she had more inside of her, dying to get out?

"I think . . . maybe I've always had the ability to be one."

He looked over to find her watching him with uncertainty.

"Do you think so?"

"Yes." He wanted to take her hand back, to kiss her palm, but his own hands felt frozen. "Yes, Rosie. I think you have the ability to do anything."

Her shoulders relaxed.

"Thanks," she whispered.

Outside the truck, car doors closed, the Just Us League

arriving en masse. Rosie gave him one final searching look before climbing out. Dominic carried the heavy stew toward the front door and Rosie held the baked goods. They were flanked by two dozen women with intention in their strides, and Dominic had to admit, they were pretty damn impressive. Next time someone on the construction site wanted to talk shit about the local women's club, he was going to damn well set them straight.

Bethany reached the door first and knocked briskly, flipping back her blond hair and adjusting the collar of her long white coat. She had the kind of confidence Rosie deserved. The kind his wife might have if he'd taken the time to encourage her, to show he had faith in her.

The door opened to reveal a man Dominic recognized, confirming his earlier theory. Port Jefferson didn't exactly appeal to tons of single men. It was too coincidental that the single man who had just opened the door was the same one who had recently started working for Brick & Morty.

Wes Daniels took off his cowboy hat and slapped it against his thigh, utter consternation written on his face at seeing the horde of people outside his door.

He swept over them with a suspicious glance and focused in on Bethany. "You."

"You?" Bethany sucked in a breath. "You're the one? Taking care of a little girl?"

"That's right." He positioned the hat back on his head. "Who are all these women? Is this your coven?"

"Oh, I don't believe this," Bethany hissed, turning on a heel to face the crowd. "Someone take over. I can't be the ambassador of this mission. There's a conflict of interest."

"What's that?" Dominic asked.

"We hate each other," Bethany responded with a tight smile.

"'Hate' is a strong word," Wes drawled, propping a forearm on the doorjamb. "Unless you're referring to the clear fact that you hate being attracted to me."

"Oh my God," Bethany sputtered. "My head is going to explode."

Wes gestured at their enthralled audience. "What's all this?"

Bethany sighed. "Food. We brought food."

"I don't want charity," Wes said after a beat. "If that's what this is, I'll thank you kindly to take it on home."

Rosie stepped forward and her soft voice was like a balm over the whole situation. The tension ebbed immediately when she joined Wes on the porch, laying a hand on his arm. "Let's start over. I'm Rosie. This is . . . everyone." Smiles and murmurs followed. Wes spotted Dominic standing among the women and nodded in recognition. "We're a tight-knit community here and I think we might have been a little overzealous. We're not here to deliver charity, we're just excited for the chance to be good neighbors. Everyone here has been the recipient of the same at some point."

Transferring his attention from Rosie to Bethany, Wes started to say something when a little girl bounded out the door, stopping in front of Bethany.

"Oh," Bethany said, sweeping the hem of her coat back. "Hi down there."

"I'm Laura. You look like Elsa."

Bethany blinked. "Who's that?"

"Elsa in the movie *Frozen*," the girl replied, bouncing on the balls of her feet.

"Ah, come on. You must know, Bethy," Wes said, a grin spreading across his face. "She's the ice princess."

A moment passed. "Let's not call me Bethy."

Wes chuckled on his way into the house. "Come on in, ladies. And gentleman. Don't worry about taking your shoes off."

Dominic and Rosie traded an amused glance when the little girl took hold of Bethany's hand and dragged her into the house. "Let's go. I'll show you Elsa. I have the doll."

"Oh. Um . . . sure."

Dominic put his hand on the small of Rosie's back and guided her into the house. The whole place whipped into chaos within seconds, women piling coats onto the couch, rooting through the fridge to make a spot for their offerings. A doll in a blue dress sang about letting it go loud enough to drown out conversation. In the midst of it all was Rosie. She toed off her gold heels and directed traffic, taping a meal schedule to the fridge. She bit off strips of tape and slapped them on dishes, writing expiration dates in Sharpie.

Again, Dominic found himself struck dumb by her talent. How she moved so gracefully, answering questions as she worked. When Laura was finished playing with the shrieking doll, she danced into the kitchen, poking foil-covered trays with a finger. "Are there—"

Rosie handed her a cookie.

Dominic found himself backing toward the door. As much as he wanted to stand there and absorb the light and warmth from his wife all night, he couldn't. Witnessing the proof of how much Rosie's giving nature had been stifled was too much. He could almost feel his heart growing to accommodate these new parts of her. Another part of him warned it was too late, though. He'd hurt the woman he loved—and without the benefit of a time machine, he didn't know how to repair the damage he'd done.

Dominic curled a hand around the doorknob, but Georgie's voice stopped him.

"Where are you going?"

A silent breath left him. "Will you just tell her I'm proud of her?"

"Dominic—"

He walked out of the house before Georgie could try to convince him to stay. He couldn't. Couldn't let another minute pass wherein he was the roadblock standing between his wife and what she wanted most.

As soon as he reached the bottom of the porch, Dominic dialed Stephen's number and held the phone to his ear. "Hey," he said, when his friend answered. "That realtor we used to buy the house. Mine and . . . Rosie's new house." He swallowed hard. "You think she could help us put it back on the market? Priced to sell."

Rosie had no idea how much time had passed between walking into Wes's house and looking up to find Dominic gone from his post beside the door. It could have been twenty minutes or two hours. God, she *hoped* it wasn't two hours. She'd only meant to get everything put inside the refrigerator and give out meal assignments, but the questions kept coming, and before she knew it, she wasn't merely planning cuisine for the household, she was commiserating with Just Us League members about their kitchen disasters and giving them tips to avoid catastrophes in the future. Every time she thought, *Okay, now on with the date portion of the evening*, a new situation arose.

Dominic must be . . .

Where *was* Dominic?

Rosie's attention shifted over to Georgie, who—come to think of it—had been hovering around for the last half an hour, nervously eating way too many cookies. "Hey." Rosie caught her friend by the elbow. "Did you happen to see where my husband went?"

"Oh, that."

She raised an eyebrow at Georgie, who promptly deflated.

"I'm not sure what happened. He looked a little out of place so I went over to make small talk and he wasn't feeling it. He left, Rosie. And . . . he wanted me to tell you he's proud of you."

Her throat muscles cinched up tight. "Why would that make him want to leave?"

Georgie sighed miserably and handed Rosie a cookie. "I don't know."

The cookie was inserted whole into Rosie's mouth. "You know what? I just . . ." Her frazzled nerves spoke up, demanding to be heard. "I don't even want to pick it apart. Actions speak louder than words, anyway, don't they?"

She'd been *excited* about the date, bought a new dress, and . . . yes, she felt extremely crappy for letting Wes's situation get in the way of her night with Dominic, but he'd seemed to understand. Had even wanted to help. And right now, his disappearance was just another in the long line of confusing and hurtful moves her husband had made. At that very moment, she wasn't even interested in the *why*.

Rosie spoke around the hurt occupying her throat. "Should we crack open some wine?"

"On it."

But the next morning had been a different story. Rosie most certainly had been interested in the *why* when it came to her husband's disappearance. She'd picked up her cell phone off the bedside table, hesitating only a moment before group-texting Armie and Dominic.

Can we fit in a session this morning?

Both men had agreed with one-word answers, as if they sensed anything more elaborate might make her scream, which wasn't altogether inaccurate. And the Dominic who'd showed up at the therapy appointment? Oh yeah. This was the Dominic she knew well.

The one who gave away nothing as he held the door open

so she could pass through into Armie's office. He'd been waiting in the parking lot when she arrived and hadn't said a word beyond a gruff hello. No explanation as to why he'd left Wes's house early. Left their date early. Nothing. He was back to being an impenetrable concrete wall.

The sudden change in him carved a chunk out of her middle. Or it started to, anyway. She was well versed in shutting down, too, it seemed. Closing herself off wasn't as easy as it used to be, but she yanked on the switch until her inner electricity went off.

With her back ramrod straight, Rosie dropped into the cluster of pillows indicated by a too-observant Armie, refusing to look at Dominic as he sat down beside her.

They'd tried to make it work. It hadn't.

Simple as that.

She'd called this emergency therapy session this morning because she desperately needed an outcome. Good or bad. Either she walked out of there with the missing piece to her husband's puzzle or they completed the sessions and moved on with their lives.

Her mouth turned arid at the possibility the latter might happen. Was she prepared for that eventuality? On the drive over, she'd been rife with frustration and determined to either force progress or call it quits. As always, though, when Dominic was in the same room, nothing was cut-and-dried. Even now, when she wanted to shake him like a snow globe, she also wanted to crawl onto his lap and beg him to talk to her.

Armie fell into a sideways pose across from them. "Well,

I hope this is important. I was in the middle of making my own blackberry preserves."

Dominic sighed. "Is that code for an orgy in the woods?"

Rosie gasped and elbowed her husband in the side. "Dominic."

Armie released a hearty laugh. "It's not a code, but I am planning to share the preserves with my female friends, and there's always a possibility it might lead to—"

"Sorry I brought it up," Dominic said, tight-lipped.

"Obviously there is a great big elephant in the room, but I can't read minds, so someone needs to start talking." The therapist split a bemused look between the two of them. "Both of your auras are edged in gray and extremely murky."

"Really?" Dominic drawled. "You wait until the fourth session to break out the aura talk?"

"Ah, that's right," Armie said, unaffected by her husband's continued assholery. "This is the fourth and final session." His twinkling gaze ticked over to Rosie. "You called for the early meeting. What would you like to say, Rosie?"

She swallowed hard, the sudden spotlight making her question her decision. "W-well, everything was going fine. At least, I thought so. I understand now that I was part of the problem, so I was trying to communicate with Dominic—"

"Say it to him," Armie urged with a flick of his wrist.

"Oh. Okay." Rosie turned toward Dominic and her heart started to beat faster, now that she was actually looking at him for the first time that day. No shave. Circles under his eyes. A wrinkled shirt. He looked how she felt. Why wouldn't he look at her? "Um. I tried to show you my appreciation by cleaning your truck and making you dinner. And I thought we were . . . I—I guess I thought we were getting somewhere—"

"You weren't part of the problem."

Dominic still wasn't looking at her so it took her a moment to realize he was speaking to her. "What?"

"I said," he rasped, "you weren't part of the problem in this marriage. Stop saying that."

"I was."

His jaw bunched and he shook his head.

Exasperation clogged her throat. "If I've done nothing wrong and I'm so perfectly perfect, why did you ditch our date?"

Armie let out a low whistle from across the pillows. "Ouch, man."

"It wasn't like that," Dominic said.

"What was it like?" Armie prompted.

Dominic opened his mouth and closed it. Said nothing.

"Please," Rosie whispered, bringing her husband's head around. "It hurt me."

He made a gruff sound into his fist, pressing against his mouth for long moments. "I was watching you kick ass with those women, Rosie. Doing what you were born to do. And it was so fucking obvious that I've been holding you back for a long time." He shook his head. "I didn't realize how much."

"So you left because you felt . . . guilty?"

A muscle jumped in his cheek. "You don't know the half of it."

Rosie waited for him to say more, turning to face him when it was obvious he was committed to being silent. "If this is about the restaurant, Dominic . . . I let the years pass without trying to achieve that goal. Without going after the restaurant. I could have pursued my dream harder, too. This isn't a blame game."

His eyes closed. "It should be."

Armie scooted closer, eagerness in every line of his body. "Tell her why. Right now."

Dominic stared at some invisible spot on the wall. Minutes ticked by, but nothing came out of his mouth, and with every second that passed, Rosie encountered more and more dread. He really wasn't going to offer an explanation. The expression "hitting a wall" had never made more sense than it did at that moment.

Eventually, Armie stood and paced to his desk, while Dominic and Rosie remained unmoving on the pillows. He scratched a few notes onto a legal pad and moseyed over to the office door, opening it.

"I hate to be the bearer of bad news, Team Vega," he said briskly. "But we've arrived at the end of our fourth session and I'm afraid your marriage isn't going to make it."

A lead weight dropped in Rosie's stomach. Her limbs lost feeling.

Dominic leapt to his feet, his broad shoulders riddled with tension. "Excuse me?" He laughed without humor, but Rosie could see the panic in his eyes. "That's bullshit."

"I'm rarely wrong about these things." Armie let out a weary breath. "Like I said, I've been doing last-chance couples counseling for thirty years and I get a pretty accurate read by the fourth and final session." He drummed his fingers on the door. "We gave it the old college try, folks, but a resolution is simply not in the cards."

Rosie took her first breath in what felt like hours, her body remaining winded even though she hadn't moved a muscle. "A-are you sure?"

Armie nodded sadly and the pillows beneath her turned to spikes.

"Rosie!" Dominic near-shouted, demanding her attention. "We're not going to take one person's opinion as fact. Let's go." He held out his hand to her, but she couldn't lift an arm to take it. "Rosie," he said raggedly. "Come on. Please."

God, she wanted so badly to take his hand and forget everything Armie had said. Dominic was right. Taking one person's opinion and running with it didn't make the best sense. If only she hadn't witnessed her husband shutting down so resolutely. Refusing to give her a full explanation as to why he'd left their date. Okay, he'd unintentionally held her back. He felt guilty about it. If that was the source of their problems, she was prepared to work on it. But there was more. So much more that he'd left unsaid. And so she couldn't leave with Dominic. Not when she couldn't trust him.

Oh God, is it over?

For real this time?

When she continued to leave Dominic's hand suspended in air, her husband went very still. Still as stone. Finally, a muscle slid up and down in his throat, and he backed toward the door, never taking his eyes off her until he was gone. The utter disbelief and horror she'd seen in his expression lingered long after his truck roared out of the parking lot.

CHAPTER SEVENTEEN

For the first time in Rosie's life, she was considering getting drunk at work.

In the perfume-sampling business, there were customers called puff princesses. They went down the entire line of little glass bottles, spraying each of them into the air and sniffing as the particles fell around them in a fine mist. Puff princesses were the worst. They made a mess, they stunk the place up, and they never, ever bought anything.

Usually during a shift, Rosie came across one or two of these types of customers, but today would land itself in the record books, because she'd had to endure no fewer than a dozen puff princesses. Someone had to be playing a practical joke on her. It wasn't even dinnertime and she'd already lost her sense of smell. Rosie could vouch for the science that suggested a person's other senses were heightened when one of them stopped working. Because there she stood in her uncomfortable heels, bottle in hand, smile plastered to her face—and she could count every speck of gray in the marble floor. Could hear every conversation taking place among the maze of glass cosmetics cases so clearly, the browsers might as well be hissing in her ears. If she squeezed the green bottle in her hands any tighter, it was going to shatter.

Her marriage was over.

For a second time.

Friday evening was darkening the sky outside the department store and Rosie hadn't heard from her husband since yesterday's ill-fated therapy session. All day, she'd been expecting him to show up and demand she cut the shit and come home. But he hadn't.

He wasn't going to, was he? Lord, that possibility terrified her.

Out of the corner of her eye, Rosie caught sight of Joe the security guard making his rounds. Without thinking, she set down the bottle of perfume and clicked on high heels in his direction. Rosie's expression must have matched her mood, because when she called Joe's name, he turned to her with wariness etched into his craggy features.

"Hey there, Rosie."

"Hi, Joe." She forced a smile, but it felt fractured. "I'm just curious. When was the last time you saw my husband?"

He shifted. "Now, Rosie . . ."

She crossed her arms and raised an eyebrow.

"This morning." Joe coughed into his fist. "He came by this morning to drop off my envelope. Looked like hell, as a matter of fact. Are you two having a spat?"

"Something like that," Rosie muttered, spinning on a heel and returning to her post only to find two puff princesses in hoodies going to town. Her husband was still conducting his protective measures behind the scenes, but he wouldn't just call her. The last thing she needed to deal with, on top of her twice-broken heart, was a couple of lookie-loos. "Excuse me, ladies. Do you need—"

They jump-turned and flipped off their hoods.

"Surprise!"

It was Bethany and Georgie.

Rosie exhaled a laugh, even though her shoulders remained full of tension that wouldn't quit. "What are you guys doing here?"

"I have the shopping bug," Georgie said with a wince, setting down the pink bustier-shaped perfume bottle in her hand. "Ever since I got the makeover, I'm no longer satisfied with overalls and baseball caps. It's very inconvenient. I have to wear the right bras . . ."

"And wash your hair . . ." Bethany added.

The sisters wrinkled their noses at each other.

"Anyway," Georgie enunciated, giving Bethany her back. "We thought we'd pop in and say hello. We have a proposition for you."

Rosie couldn't have been happier to find her friends in the store. She needed the mental break and definitely required the laugh to maintain what sanity she was clinging to, but any minute now, Martha would stomp around the corner—

"I'm not paying you to socialize, Mrs. Vega."

Pressure bloomed behind her right eye and started to pound. The voice of her supervisor was obnoxious any day of the week, but with Rosie's diminished sense of smell, Martha's syllables and vowels worked their way under her skin like thumbtacks.

"We're customers," Bethany said sweetly, picking up a random bottle without looking and handing it to Rosie. "This one, please. It'll bring all the boys to the yard."

Georgie buried her face in the crook of her elbow.

Rosie bit down on her lower lip to trap a laugh, but a snort escaped. And that's when the avalanche effect happened. That show of mirth gave way to the beginning of hysteria. She'd just been spoken to—again—by her power-tripping supervisor, her marriage had gone from fractured to broken, her feet were killing her, and she'd inhaled enough scents to make her nose-blind.

On top of everything, she'd canceled the appointment to view the space on Cove Street with the realtor that morning. Dominic had said he'd come with her, but upon waking to no missed calls or texts, she'd been too afraid to find out if he'd show up or not. And God, that made her so mad. He was the one who'd asked for a second chance. Not her. She'd been prepared to move on and he'd come barreling back in, claiming they could fix what was broken. Well, he'd broken it all over again, and she was done.

Matter of fact, she wasn't simply done with her husband. She was done with this job.

She hated this job.

It made her feel like scenery. And even though her confidence was shaky—it was so damn shaky—she needed to pick up and move on before she let herself drop back to that level of complacency she'd been in before leaving Dominic. She might even end up *more* comfortable with doing something she hated, unable to imagine a better situation. She could barely imagine one right now and that scared her.

A bubbling laugh escaped her mouth. "I quit."

Martha reared back with a gasp.

Bethany's and Georgie's mouths dropped open.

Rosie exhaled in a rush and unclipped her name tag. She started to hand it over to Martha, but the woman crossed her arms, lifting her chin and refusing to take it. So Rosie dropped it on the ground and stomped it into a half-dozen pieces, little shards of plastic scattering on the marble floor of the cosmetics section.

"I'm sure you'll have no problem finding someone to replace me. Everyone is looking for extra cash around the holidays," Rosie said, putting some steel into her spine. "But you will have a problem keeping them. Especially if you keep reheating fish in the break room. That should be illegal. You, Martha, are the Le Squirt Bon Bon of bosses." She tucked an escaped curl back into her bun. "Shall we, ladies?"

Rosie set down the perfume Bethany had handed her and swept down the aisle of glass cases, flanked by her two friends. At several of the registers, her coworkers stopped what they were doing to give her golf claps and respectful nods. By the time Rosie reached the exit, she'd grown several inches. Next time she came to this department store, it would be to splurge on another dress. No more perfume. No more puff princesses.

God, she was scared knowing she'd receive only one more paycheck and then she'd have to rely on her modest bank balance, but so be it. You couldn't put a price on self-respect, and she desperately needed to take some back.

The cold October air reached right through her clothes upon hitting the sidewalk.

"Oh my God," Rosie said, covering her cheeks with both hands. "I can't believe I did that."

"I can," Georgie said, laying a sympathetic cheek on her shoulder. "After what happened with Dominic yesterday, you earned the right to stomp a name tag or eight. Martha is lucky it wasn't her face, as far as I'm concerned."

Bethany took Rosie by the shoulders. "Look, that was completely badass, but it was a big, bold move that's going to come with changes. Are you okay?"

"Yes." Rosie shook her head, nerve endings snapping in her wrists and fingertips. "No. No, I feel like I'm going to jump out of my skin. But tomorrow I'm going to come back better than ever. I have to believe that. I just don't want to think for a while, you know?"

"Girls' night out," Georgie piped up, breathing warm air into her hands and rubbing them together. "It's the only solution."

Bethany's mouth curved into a smile. "Fair warning, ladies. I don't do any half-assed girls' nights out. If we're doing this, we're swinging for the fucking fences."

Her sister whooped.

"Manhattan, here we come," Bethany murmured, eyes sparkling.

A fire built in Rosie's belly as she listened to Bethany

formulate plans. How long had it been since she'd really cut loose? Tonight she'd make up for lost time.

Dominic had just ordered his second beer when Travis and Stephen walked in looking like someone had pissed in their Cheerios.

"Whatever it is," Dominic said, taking a pull from his fresh Heineken, "I don't want to know."

Travis snorted and kicked out a stool, signaling the bartender as he sat down. "Shot, please. Whiskey."

"One for me, too," Stephen said, choosing to pace instead of sit down. "Make it a double."

That gave Dominic pause. Stephen's idea of partying was adding a second scoop of protein powder to his morning smoothie. His wife, Kristin, ran a tight ship, and since Stephen was trying to prove he was wholesome-family-man enough for her to start popping out babies, he didn't drink beyond the casual beer. Whiskey meant the world was falling down.

Dominic knew a thing or two about that. He'd gotten shitfaced after the impromptu therapy appointment that had ended in disaster—and he was well on his way there again tonight. Every minute he spent sober, he replayed the moment Armie had told them his marriage to Rosie wouldn't work. That it was really over. Deep in his bones, he knew that was impossible. But he had no goddamn clue how to prove that to his wife. Worse, if he could go back in time and relive that therapy appointment, he still wasn't sure he'd come clean about the house. So there he sat. Flawed beyond belief and missing his wife like hell.

The bartender set down two shot glasses and sloshed whiskey into them from a pour spout, taking the twenty-dollar bill Travis slid across the bar. Travis tossed his back, the ex–professional baseball player swiping a hand across his mouth.

"You want to know," Travis said.

"No, I don't."

Stephen leaned against the bar, holding his semi-full shot glass.

"Let me paint the scene for you," Travis continued.

Dominic frowned. "Are you sipping that shot, Stephen?"

"I like to savor the taste." To drive his words home, he took another dainty sip, visibly trying not to gag. "S'good."

"Jesus, man. Just order a Coke."

"A soda won't erase the memory of my wife in ice-pick heels and a miniskirt trotting off down the driveway."

"Christ. I knew this was woman-related." Dominic eased back from the bar. "Look, I've got my own problems."

"Yeah, you do." Travis leaned an elbow on the bar and faced Dominic. "Again, let me paint the scene for you. I'm standing in my kitchen, minding my own business. Georgie is in the bedroom and I'm getting ready to . . . you know, go see her there—"

Stephen dragged his hands down his face. "That can't be relevant to the story, you asshole."

"It is." Travis seemed to be fighting back a smile. "I was carrying her a glass of wine to the bedroom—*our* bedroom,

Stephen—when she comes out . . ." His skin paled and he seemed to be having a hard time swallowing. "She's in this dress I've never seen. It's pure white. White." He got off the stool and turned, looking back at Dominic and Stephen over his shoulder, one hand indicating his ass. "I could see the shadow between her—"

"Enough." Stephen held out a stern finger. "Don't say another word."

"I've never seen those shoes, either," Travis muttered, sitting back down and burying his face in his hands. "I can't believe this is happening."

Dominic split a look between his friends, a growing sense of doom starting to mount in his chest. "Okay, so both of your women are dressed up. Where are they going?"

"Out," Travis and Stephen stage-whispered, twin looks of horror on their faces. "Bethany showed up to both of our houses hanging out of the top of a limousine, drinking champagne straight from the bottle."

The door to Grumpy Tom's flew open and Wes walked in, tipped his cowboy hat to the bartender, and ordered a Budweiser. When he saw Dominic, Travis, and Stephen gathered at the bar, he nodded a greeting and made his way over. "You three look like your mamas told you to stop playing video games and take out the garbage."

Travis slumped back on his stool. "Worse. Our women are on their way to Manhattan in stripper heels."

Wes slapped a hand on the bar, but cut his laugh off midway out of his mouth. "Hold on a second, is, uh . . . is Bethany with them?"

"She's the goddamn ringleader!" Stephen shot back. "You know what song she was blasting in the limousine when she showed up? 'Like a Virgin.' I'm going to hear it in my sleep tonight."

Travis snorted. "Who's sleeping?"

Dominic was barely able to hear his friends over the increasing tempo of his heartbeat. The beating spread to every inch of his body until he was one giant pulse. "My . . . wife wasn't in that limousine. Was she?"

Travis threw up his hands. "Yes. She was. That's what I've been trying to tell you."

Wes inserted himself between them, a look of concern marring his brow. "Was Bethany wearing the stripper heels, too?"

Acid rose in Dominic's stomach like a geyser, and he leaned forward on the stool, forcing breath in and out through his nose. He didn't like this. He didn't like it at all. Rosie was supposed to be home safe at Bethany's. She wasn't supposed to be leaving town, going to an unfamiliar place. Especially not when their marriage had been declared unsalvageable. Was this a sign that she was ready to shed him like a layer of old skin and move on?

A vein popped behind his eye and throbbed sharply.

All four men were silent for a good minute, none of them watching the ball game that was playing on the screen above their heads. When the bartender poured them a shot on the house and walked away, they each tossed the golden liquid back without hesitation or a countdown.

"Well, boys. I'll leave you to it. There's a church lady babysitting Laura for the night," Wes said, sniffing. "Might go get some grocery shopping done."

Travis snorted. "You're going into the city, aren't you?"

Wes nodded about ten times and sighed. "Yeah."

"Hold on," Stephen said. "Is this an option? How come no one said going to Manhattan was an option?"

"I can't just go chasing Georgie into the city and dragging her home," Travis said, his expression incredulous. "You know how hypocritical that makes me? I partied for years before I found her and settled down. She's never had a chance to cut loose. Besides." Travis crossed his arms over his chest. "I trust her. She even gave me the address where they were going. Wrote it with little smiley-face o's."

"I trust Rosie, too." Dominic's voice emerged in a scrape. "It's men I don't trust."

All four men growled. The bartender poured them another shot.

Wes sighed as he downed his whiskey. "Guess we're taking a cab."

Dominic was in mental hell, wondering where Rosie was, what she was wearing, what she was thinking, whether the night out was just the girls having fun . . . or if she'd needed it. They hadn't spoken since he'd walked out of Armie's office and that distance had been harder than a motherfucker. How hard had it been on Rosie?

Christ. He just wanted to give her good news the next time they met. If he was going to come clean about being a selfish prick, he wanted to have a solution to go along with his apology. *I'm sorry I fucked up, honey girl. Here's the money you need for the restaurant. You're going to do amazing things.* He'd been rehearsing those words in his head since officially putting the house up for sale.

Travis dropped a hand onto his shoulder. "Listen, man. You know how I get the inside scoop on the ladies now that I'm going to marry Stephen's little sister and give her babies?"

"Fuck you," Stephen muttered.

"Yeah," said the other two men in unison.

Sensing something bad on the horizon, Dominic's heart lodged in his throat. "What?"

"I think I know why they're blowing off some steam." Travis blew out a breath. "Rosie quit her job this afternoon. Like, told her manager to go jump in a lake and stomped her name tag to smithereens. That kind of quitting."

Dominic couldn't manage a decent breath. Panic seized him at the thought of her being harassed or upset. "Did something happen at the store?"

"No," Travis said quickly. "Bethany and Georgie were there. Apart from her supervisor giving her some attitude, nothing happened. She's fine. Georgie just said a girls' night was in order." He took his time pointing at each of the men. "That's why we're going to let them have it."

Wes sniffed and drained his beer. "Fuck that."

They all threw some bills onto the bar and walked out.

CHAPTER EIGHTEEN

Rosie watched the lights of Manhattan pass by in a blur. Some of that blur was thanks to the champagne she'd downed on their limo ride into the city. Mostly, though, it was just the nature of tonight. The breathless pace of it, the freshness of the experience. She was dressed in silver sequins—straight from Bethany's closet—her hair was in glossy spirals around her face, and she'd been decorated with dark, cherry-red lipstick. She barely recognized the woman looking back at her from the opposite window's reflection.

Good. She wanted to be a different kind of Rosie tonight. A Rosie who took risks and made decisions for herself, for better or worse. Tomorrow morning, when she woke up, she wanted to be someone who wasn't afraid to try new things. Maybe getting drunk and dancing with her girlfriends was a far cry from opening a restaurant, but she had to start somewhere.

She couldn't blame Dominic for the sheltered life she'd been living. As much as she wanted to blame him for the fact that she never went out, never cultivated friendships or had fun, she had to take ownership. Once upon a time, she'd wanted nothing more than to be home with him. Just the two of them. But toward the end, staying home meant staying in silence. Bobbing around feeling like a disconnected spare part.

She refused to feel that way tonight.

With the expensive leather rubbing the bare backs of her thighs and the sounds of the city drifting in through the open moonroof, Rosie might as well have been living on a different planet. The lack of familiarity excited and scared her at the same time. With her axis already tilted, she was getting ready to tip it even more. Before the night she'd gone to stay at Bethany's house, she never would have believed she'd leave her husband. This morning, she never would have believed she'd quit her job. Something was changing inside her. Throwing herself outside her comfort zone when everything was already in flux made her pulse race.

Bethany scooted closer on the leather seat. "Hey. You okay?"

"Yes." Despite her answer, Rosie shook her head no. "I've never gone out dancing and drinking like this. Not without Dominic."

Her blond bestie sipped from her champagne flute and tilted her head thoughtfully. "What are you worried about?"

"We're not even in the club yet and I feel unfaithful," Rosie admitted, cupping her knees in her hands. "I'm in this weird place where I'm not sure if I'm afraid to piss off Dominic or if that's exactly what I want. And I would never look at another man while we're still married—that's not what I mean. Maybe . . . maybe I'll never be able to look at another man. But this dress and this situation where he can't confirm my safety would be enough to drive him crazy."

Bethany sighed. "I'm sorry it's so complicated right now," she said. "Look at it this way—if going out in a sexy dress is enough to make him lose his shit, the deed is done. The shit has been lost. But you're here. Might as well relax and enjoy yourself." They both glanced toward the other end of the limousine where Kristin was trying to fix Georgie's hair and getting her hand slapped away. "We didn't come here to meet men, Rosie. It's just going to be us girls dancing and curating hangovers. There's nothing wrong with that."

Rosie's spine straightened. "You're right." She blew out a breath. "I deserve this."

"You're damn right you do," Bethany drawled, tossing back the rest of her champagne.

"I'm going to dance until I get blisters."

"Ouch, but yes. Who says fun can't be bloody?"

The limousine started to bump along the cobblestones that signaled their arrival in the Meatpacking District. Their destination appeared in the window, and Rosie's excitement level rose, eclipsing her trepidation. While they'd been getting ready earlier that evening, Bethany had regaled her with stories of nights out at the Gansevoort Hotel. It was a sleek black building, looming high above the packed Friday-night street. After their driver helped them out of the limousine, the women linked arms and clicked on their heels toward the entrance.

As soon as the seemingly identical doormen swung open

the double doors, sexy, earthy music rode over Rosie's bare skin and she inhaled the myriad scents of expensive perfume, cologne, and the rich, polished tones of the hotel lobby. It was darker inside the hotel than on the street, the staff almost intimidatingly good-looking in all-black uniforms.

The women piled into an elevator with several strangers and hit the button labeled Lelie Rooftop. It took them to the penthouse club in three seconds flat, letting them out into one of the most decadent spaces Rosie had ever seen. Just like downstairs, the atmosphere was dark, lit up tastefully with modern chandeliers and muted red candlelight. The club took up the entire rooftop of the building, sprawling in every direction with lounge areas and a dance floor, with a bar in the center of it all. Every side of the club afforded a different view of the twinkling New York City skyline and the Hudson River beyond. It was luxurious and magical.

"Wow," Georgie breathed, getting off the elevator beside her. "And I thought the Waterfront was lit," she said, referring to Port Jefferson's favorite date-night spot. "I should have practiced dancing before we came. I'm going to look like a tawdry chicken out there."

Rosie giggle-snorted. "No, you're not."

Bethany signaled a passing waitress, said a few words to her, and they were led through the undulating masses of people, through another set of glass doors, only to be seated in the very corner of the closed-in terrace on a collection of low leather couches. Around them, the avenues stretched out in between the tall buildings like arms wrapped in Christmas lights. They were high up enough to see the downtown sprawl that made up Lower Manhattan and uptown toward the Empire State Building, which was lit orange and yellow for fall.

"You weren't kidding when you said this wouldn't be a half-assed girls' night out," Rosie murmured when Bethany came up beside her to look out over the city. "I would have been happy with fancy sushi and a rom-com."

Her friend was visibly trying not to look smug. And failing. "The club owner owed me a little favor. We were in a bidding war over some lighting fixtures online. I let him win in exchange for the VIP treatment next time I ventured into Manhattan." She threw her arms out wide. "Witness the spoils of décor war."

They high-fived.

"But wait, there's more." Bethany slipped something that looked like a credit card out of her clutch purse and pressed it into Rosie's hand. "He hooked me up with a free room in the hotel. I thought you could use a night to clear your head."

"I'm staying here?" Rosie took the shiny gold card, turning it over in her palm with a puffed laugh. "I didn't bring my pajamas."

"Don't you know by now I think of everything?"

Rosie wanted to ask for more details, but Bethany left her standing at the railing and went to sit down. After taking in another deep breath of the city, she followed.

"They don't have many places like this in Georgia," Kristin said, as they all sunk down into the lush leather couches.

"This is the type of establishment churches sign petitions against in my hometown. I bet my mama senses my proximity to the devil right this second. She's probably itching up a storm."

"Way to perpetuate the sexy vibe, Kristin," Georgie said, patting her sister-in-law on the shoulder. "So do we order drinks at the bar or—" Just then, a giant bottle of vodka was plunked down into an ice bucket at the center of the table, along with a selection of fruit-juice mixers. "Oh, okay. I can get behind this."

"I bet Stephen is beside himself right now," Kristin breathed, her expression gleeful. "He about died when I told him his dinner was in the microwave. I blew out of the house like a turkey trying to escape Thanksgiving. His face. I'll never forget it."

Georgie turned to Kristin. "Why do you like torturing our brother so much?" she asked. "Don't get me wrong. I know he's a natural target because everything gets under his skin. But you seem to take particular joy in inflicting misery."

"If there's one thing that has been passed down between the women in my family—besides our recipe for sweet potato pie—it's the knowledge that a man must be kept on his toes at all times. The second he gets comfortable, the magic fades." She shifted around in her seat with a sniff. "I plan on being chased and placated until I've got both feet in the grave."

"How very uplifting." Bethany golf-clapped. "I plan to enjoy watching that from the sidelines."

"Oh no you won't," Kristin shot back. "You'll be getting chased yourself."

"By who?"

Kristin worked her neck like a strutting pigeon. "You know who."

"Uh-oh," Rosie muttered, fishing the bottle of vodka out of the ice and beginning to pour drinks for everyone. "At least let her get a buzz before bringing up Wes."

"Wes?" Bethany uncrossed her legs and doubled over, laughing loud enough to draw attention from the surrounding patrons. "You can't be serious. You think Wes is going to chase me? If he tried, I would slap the ego out of him with both hands."

Georgie raised an eyebrow. "You've given this some thought."

"I've given him no thought. None whatsoever."

"Now, Bethany," Kristin said slowly. "There were enough sparks shooting between the two of you the other night to start a fire. Don't piddle on my leg and tell me it's raining."

Bethany's mouth fell open and then snapped shut. "Maybe that kind of antagonism between a man and woman is normal for you, Kristin, seeing as how you terrorize my brother for sport. But it's not normal. Me and Wes actually dislike each other."

"Antagonism is fun. Makes him work harder between the sheets." Kristin ignored the groans from everyone, throwing an elbow at Georgie. "You and Travis had your fair share of spats and it only made him work harder to earn your favor. Tell me I'm wrong."

Georgie's drink remained suspended in the air for several beats. "Oh God, she's right."

Rosie could sense Bethany staring at her profile. "Rosie, lend some much-needed sanity to this conversation. You don't actually think Wes and I . . ." She trailed off with a shudder. "You can't actually believe there's something there. Do you?"

"Um . . ." Rosie pursed her lips and pretended to consider the question. "I mean . . ."

Bethany gasped.

"Hear me out," Rosie rushed to say, laying a hand on her friend's forearm. "You know your own mind and how you feel toward Wes. But. Well, I think if you do decide to enter into a long-term relationship with someone, he needs to be a certain way. Strong. Capable of . . ."

"Putting up with my shit?"

"That's not what I was going to say."

"Yes, it is," Georgie piped in, sucking down half her drink with relish. "Oh my God, this is already shaping up to be an amazing night."

Bethany wrinkled her nose at her sister. "You're all dead wrong on this one. Sorry." She shook around the ice cubes in her tumbler. "I'll admit there might be a certain unfortunate sexual . . ."

"Synergy," Georgie supplied.

"Ooh!" Kristin danced in her seat. "Magnetism."

Rosie tilted her head. "Connection?"

"Scourge." Bethany pushed her fall of blond hair back over her shoulder. "It's an affliction. An annoyance."

"Only one way to get rid of it," Kristin singsonged.

Bethany smiled sweetly. "Drop it or I'll tell Stephen you're pregnant."

Georgie did a spit take. "What?"

Rosie covered her mouth with both hands and tried not to laugh.

"How did you know?" Kristin gasped, hands flying to her stomach to feel around. "I'm not even showing yet."

"The level of your drink never goes down. You're just pretending to sip." Bethany shook her head. "How are you planning on using this to make my brother insane?"

"I'm not revealing my secrets." Kristin huffed for a few seconds. "You're really taking the wind out of my sails here. Is a surprise pregnancy-announcement-slash-gender-reveal soiree with a Venetian theme really so much to ask?"

"Yes," Bethany and Georgie said at the same time.

Rosie needed to get out of there before she burst into a fit of laughter. "I'll go to the bar and get you a ginger ale, Kristin," she said. "We're all going to keep your secret, aren't we?"

"Yes," the sisters grumbled.

A moment later, Rosie breezed back into the even busier club, the dark, anticipatory vibe swallowing her whole. Since being seated outside, the music had grown louder, the lights dimming even more. The bar was packed with people trying to get the attention of the bartenders, but she didn't mind waiting and soaking up the atmosphere. The later hour had turned people more amorous. There wasn't a hint of air between the dancing couples. As Rosie watched, a man's hand slid down his dance partner's back and massaged her bottom, making the woman's mouth open against his neck. Rosie could almost hear the heavy breathing, the groaning, the whisper of clothing rasping together.

As she got closer to an open space at the bar, Rosie's pulse rippled in time with the bass. Heat slithered around in her belly and pressed her thighs together. Dominic would know what was happening below her waist at a single glance. What would he do? She'd always done her best to keep her arousal hidden on days that weren't Tuesday, but on that scheduled night, she would finally let the veil drop. He'd strip her naked and press her facedown on the couch, bring her to a blistering orgasm to take the edge off, then embark on a slower, more deliberate round two.

Rosie's nipples beaded inside her dress, her shaky inhales loud in her ears.

God, she needed to be touched so badly. Kissed, stroked, embraced. All of it. She and Dominic might have been relying too much on sex to bolster their marriage, but it had been satisfying in the moment. A fleeting connection during which she could feel the pull of a deeper one. One they'd neglected for years. After what happened in therapy yesterday, she couldn't sense his dependable presence at her back anymore. The rug had been pulled out from under her feet and she was in a continuous freefall. She might be mad as hell at Dominic for several things, but she would never stop wanting those arms to wrap around her. To catch her.

The bartender appeared in front of Rosie with a tight smile. "What can I get you?"

"A ginger ale, please. Thanks," she managed over the music—and then realized she'd forgotten her purse outside. "Oh, shoot," she muttered at the ceiling, torn between explaining the situation to the bartender or running back outside and attempting to retrieve her purse before he came back . . .

Dominic saw Rosie the second he stepped off the elevator. He came to an abrupt halt, blocking everyone's exit behind him.

Jesus. It wasn't news to Dominic that his wife was fine as hell, but that fact wasn't usually on display quite so fucking clearly. She could have walked out onstage at the Grammys to accept an award in all those sequins. And with those legs. And that ass.

Even in the dark club, her skin glowed. What little light there was flocked to her, highlighting the smooth curve of her calves, the plump side of her breast—which definitely should not be showing. Not here in this public place with hundreds of men. He could feel the primal tug of possessiveness in his gut, his throat, his clenching fists.

My wife. No one looks at my Rosie but me.

It was written in his DNA to charge over like a bull and demand to know what the hell she was thinking. He wanted to rip off his shirt and wrap it around her, hiding every delicious inch of skin from anyone who might want a taste. Taking her home was a given.

Christ, more than anything, though—more than anything—he wanted to throw himself down at her feet and worship her. *Look at you, honey girl.* The hottest thing in the fucking club.

As if he'd spoken to her out loud, Rosie's head turned in his direction and the incessant motion around him slowed. So beautiful. She was so goddamn beautiful. Not just her face or her body or the clothes. Looking at her through a sea of strangers, the years of their lives were right there between them, rushing like a river. The excitement of falling in love, the hormonal lust of their teens, the trust they'd built while he was away, the millions of hours they'd logged talking on the phone or in her backyard, the silence that had fallen when they stopped trying.

Hearing their marriage was over.

Dominic made a sound halfway between clearing his throat and choking.

On the way into Manhattan, he'd been determined to come collect his wife, and the more miles they'd eaten up, the more his head of steam had built. *I'm going to remind her where she belongs,* he'd thought. With their eyes locked and the reality of their situation sitting on his shoulders like a ton of bricks, that shit seemed so juvenile. *I've lost my wife. She's going to move on without me unless I man the fuck up and work on myself. On us.* Dragging her out of the bar like a caveman wouldn't win her back. And he was fresh out of tries. Mistakes were no longer an option. There was only one direction left to go and that was forward.

Dominic was only vaguely aware of Travis asking the hostess where he might find a girl with "bangs, freckles, an adorable laugh, and a rock on her finger the size of a base-ball" as he cut toward Rosie where she stood at the bar, still looking at him like a deer in headlights.

"Miss," the bartender was saying when Dominic reached her. "Six dollars for the ginger ale, please."

Without taking his eyes off his wife, Dominic slid a ten out of his wallet and handed it to the bartender. "Keep it." Now that they were close, Dominic had to once again check the impulse to carry her to a dark corner and snarl at anyone who dared glance in her direction. Instead, he leaned in and spoke near her ear. "I'm Dominic. What's your name?"

He heard Rosie's breath catch and prayed he was doing the right thing. The past would always be there, but she needed to know he could change. That they could be differ-ent. Better. "I'm Rosie," she said finally, her gaze dropping away to land on the ginger ale. "I'm supposed to bring this to my friend."

"You mean I just paid six dollars for a soda and it's not even for you?"

She pressed her painted lips together to hide a smile. "You didn't ask."

Dominic eased the drink out of her hand and set it back on the bar. "Let the waitress bring her what she wants. I'm more interested in what you want."

"I was just trying to figure that out."

"Meaning?"

There was no space at the bar. There was no space in the whole damn club—and it was loud as hell, music and voices creating a din. In order to talk, Dominic had to get close and Rosie did the same, stepping into his space and pressing her tits to his chest slowly, so slowly, and, needing an anchor, his palm splayed over her hip.

"Meaning I can't decide if I want to hide with my girl-friends all night or if I want to dance." She shrugged a grace-ful shoulder. "Cut loose a little."

Dominic's hand rode over her hip and slipped around to her back. Which was very much bare, all the way down to the swell of her ass. He ground his back teeth together, her eyes challenging him, and his voice emerged strangled. "Do you cut loose very often?"

"No." Her answer puffed against his lips. "Never."

She was telling him something. It was there in the sudden somberness of her eyes as she searched his face. Her lack of a smile.

"If you have a man, he's . . ." Dominic swallowed hard. "If you have a man, he's probably spent a long time assum-ing you need security instead of excitement. Dreams. Maybe he's always known you're the most exciting woman in the world, but he's not sure you feel that way about him. So he works and provides. He can control that."

Fuck. Had he just said that out loud? A gash was open and oozing on his chest after voicing those words to the world. He had a hard enough time admitting these things to him-self. But here he stood with the woman of his dreams and their future hanging in the balance, so if a second chance meant opening wounds, so be it. He'd open every last one.

"Not sure if she thinks he's exciting," Rosie breathed, confusion knitting her brow together. "How . . . long has he thought this way? Why?"

Dominic forced a casual smile. "You're asking the wrong guy," he said, his fingertips drawing patterns on her smooth back. "If I had to guess, though, I'd say it started a long time ago and got worse after he saw other parts of the world, met new people. Got some perspective. After that, the only thing he felt confident in giving was stability. Maybe after being raised to believe that was a man's job, it was easy to fall into it."

Damn, he was grateful he'd pretended to be someone else. Every time he took a shaky step forward, the pretense was something to fall back on. The role-playing made talking easier.

"Look at you. You know? You're the most incredible woman I've ever seen. So beautiful you make me ache. And you've got a heart to match. You're patient and loyal and dedicated and kind. A man who never worried about doing enough to earn you? That man would be an idiot."

The yearning in Dominic's chest gave him no choice but to pull her close, tight enough against his body that Rosie's back bowed.

"You probably came out tonight to get away from him. When I walked in here, I could see that. You've been missing this chance to shine. And God, you shine so fucking bright." His mouth found her ear and opened just beneath it, taking a small bite as her hips pressed forward, cradling his growing cock. "If your heart is set on having this night to yourself . . . I'll go. If that's what you need. But I'd love to stay and learn everything about you."

Rosie turned her head and kissed his jaw. "I'd love that." Their eyes met. "And I think there's a lot I need to learn about you, too."

With that, she took his hand and led him out onto the dance floor.

CHAPTER NINETEEN

Was this a dream?

It felt like a dream.

She was leading her husband of almost a decade onto the dance floor of a swanky bar, the city spread out around them like a bedazzled Christmas-tree skirt—and he'd just surprised the hell out of her. Dominic could definitely be classified as the strong, silent type, but his temper had a trip switch. And Rosie putting herself out there or in jeopardy was most definitely the trigger. When he'd stepped off the elevator, she'd fully expected to be carried out of there like a sack of potatoes.

But . . . no. That hadn't happened, and her equilibrium hadn't recovered.

Apparently Dominic had no intention of letting that happen anytime soon, either.

Her nerve endings were just beginning to zap in anticipation of being pressed up against her husband when he shocked her again. They reached an open spot in the center of the dance floor and despite the upbeat tempo of the music,

Rosie assumed he would pull her close. Claim her, like he'd always done when they danced in the past.

That's not what happened.

Rosie held her breath at the sight of him as he turned, his strong teeth sinking into that sculpted lower lip. His mouth was curved in the beginnings of a smile, but his eyes were blazing hot as they tracked up her body and back down. Heat was already a living, breathing thing inside her, but fire shot straight to her loins now. Down the insides of her thighs. She was wet. So wet she almost couldn't bear it. Her desire was so prepared to pop like a firecracker that when Dominic snagged her hand and pressed his thumb into the small of her wrist, she moaned and swayed toward him.

She caught his wink a second before he spun her in a full circle and dipped her back so far the ends of her hair almost reached the floor. Laughter bubbled from her lips as he pulled her upright again. Their foreheads found each other, their lips ticking up into smiles.

"We going to show these kids how to dance, or what?"

"Yes," she said breathlessly, finding it hard to speak at all while an awakening took place inside her. She'd been here before. With Dominic. A long time ago. This side of him was so familiar. It reached into her and found the counterpart she'd buried. The piece of her that embraced fun because she had a partner in crime. His smile coaxed it back into existence, spreading confidence and joy to her darkest corners.

The change inside Rosie must have shown on her face because Dominic seemed transfixed, his hand tightening in what felt like an unconscious move on her wrist.

"Dance for me," Dominic said, his gaze running over every inch of her face. "Dance for yourself."

Excitement bit at her ankles, her hips, encouraging them to move. Dominic's hands found Rosie's waist and squeezed it tight, allowing her to raise her arms up in the air and lean back, just a little, rolling her body and watching with racing breath as Dominic enjoyed the show. She could see how desperately he wanted to tug her close, feel that writhing motion on his lap, but he dragged his hands down to her hips instead, helping her move them in a figure eight. His own hips slowly began to do the same, and finally he eased his arms back, disconnecting Rosie and him physically, though their eyes remained locked tight.

They moved in perfect rhythm with each other and the music, lower bodies ticking to the right, then left, his circled back and Rosie's cinched forward, mimicking sex, creating a flush on both of their necks, high on their cheekbones. Dominic licked his lips and trailed his attention down to her breasts as they picked up the pace of the dance.

Wow. She'd almost forgotten how he could move. He'd proven his abilities at that very first middle-school dance and had only improved during high school, but this was different. He was a man. She was a woman. And there was more at stake.

Their marriage hadn't worked. Was this his way of fighting for it?

Maybe it was the vodka. Or the champagne. Or the dress, the club, her sexual frustration, or the situation as a whole. Take your pick. But her rebellious streak from earlier that day was back, and she had the sudden urge to push. She knew Dominic better than anyone and this wasn't easy for him. Having her on display. Encouraging her to do it. What would it take to break him? The tiniest nudge? Or had he really shown up wanting to change?

A new song pumped through the club, and she closed her eyes. She twisted a tight curl around her index finger and swayed her hips provocatively. Her fingers left her hair and trailed down the front of her dress, narrowly avoiding the tips of her breasts, coasting down to her thighs. She cracked her eyelids to find Dominic watching her intently, his big chest rising and falling with fast, deep breaths. But he didn't stop her as she threw her hair back and turned in a circle, her lower body bumping to the music—and then she took it down to the floor, grinding her hips in a circle on the way back up.

Dominic's fists clenched, then loosened. Looking her in the eye, he snagged her wrist and yanked her close, up against his chest.

This is it. He's going to hustle me out of here.

"You're incredible with or without me," he rasped beside her ear. "I can do my best to learn to live with both if it means I get to keep your heart."

His mouth skated down the side of her neck to her clavicle, openmouthed kissing her there, before he pulled away and spun her in another circle. Dizziness wrapped itself around her mind, and she couldn't get her rhythm back. Not with the waves of emotion crashing inside of her. Thank God for the music. It swallowed the small sounds she made while gasping for air. And her husband must have sensed she was ready to be held, anchored, because one second she was mentally free-falling—and the next? He'd pulled her up against his strong body and tucked one muscular thigh between her two, leaving a strategic ridge of muscle right there.

"Oh my God," she whimpered, sliding her arms around his neck to keep her balance. Her need had been burning bright since Dominic had approached her at the bar looking so rough and ready among the polished boys in the club. Jeans, boots, and a relaxed-fit, long-sleeved shirt that was lived in. Worked in. This was the man who turned her on. He always would. There was no question about that. With his words echoing in her ears and his body so sturdy and solid against hers, that need skyrocketed now.

Should she be perched on Dominic's thick thigh when their marriage had been declared unsalvageable? The jury was out. But he'd revealed something at the bar. A genuine revelation when she knew he wanted to react differently. He'd tried, even though exposing a weakness was difficult for him. Really tried. And that meant something. It hadn't been easy for him—he was used to keeping it inside—and now he was checking his possessive urges to let her shine.

What else was there? If she could still wait with bated breath for another admission or more progress from Dominic, maybe . . . maybe it wasn't the end?

Was that too much to hope for?

"If I'm going too far too fast, let me know," he rasped, his hand trailing roughly down her spine, fingers spreading right above the beginning of her bottom. "But I think you need this as much as I do. Am I right?"

"Yes," Rosie said before she could stop the admission.

Here in the dark club, the lines were blurred. Some rule laid out by a therapist seemed silly and arbitrary up against the heat their bodies were generating. What he'd shared. The past. The future that hung in the balance. Their attraction was an elemental thing and it was roaring down on them like a category five storm. Was it any wonder she was scared to jump in headfirst, though? Every time they took a step forward, something seemed to knock them off course. He'd handed her a way to maintain a small barrier, hadn't he? She grasped onto it now.

"I know we just met, but . . ." she whispered, twisting her fingers in the material of his shirt. "Can you hold me tighter?"

His arms turned to steel, his nose moving to her hair, inhaling roughly. "I'll do anything you ask me to do," he said in a gravelly voice. "Except walk away."

Rosie slid higher on Dominic's thigh, pressing her hip to his erection and listening to him hiss a breath through his teeth. "I've got a room downstairs for the night." She dragged her fingernails down the center of his chest, stopping just above his belt, tracing the leather with a pinkie. "Convince me to bring you with me, Dominic."

The muscles in his arms flexed hard at the revelation that she had a room in the hotel, but instead of commenting, he stooped down a little and came up between her thighs in a hard grind, loosing a curse in her ear. Getting that friction exactly where she needed it made Rosie's eyes roll back in her head, and she couldn't stop, couldn't keep her hand from sliding between them to palm his erection.

"Rosie," he growled, sinking his teeth into her neck. "I need to fuck you. I'm going out of my mind here. The way you move. The way you smell." He thrust his hips against her center once, gripping her backside to hold her still while he did it again, again, again, his breath turning shallow in her ear. "I could come just like this after watching you dance. Don't let me. Bring me to your room and I'll stay hard, stay fucking until you're ready to tap out. You should know that's how I do it. It's never over until you stop screaming for more. Convinced?"

Her nod was uneven, her blood turbulent with lust. "Th-the key. It's at our table—"

Dominic cut her off with his mouth. His hold on her bottom urged her against his huge arousal, his tongue dipping into the deepest recesses of her mouth and retreating in a slow, sensual drag. A kiss that was pure worship.

"I'd offer to go get your purse for you, but this is what you've done to my cock." Another thorough kiss that had her thighs scrambling against his, gasps building in her throat. "Go get the key before I find a dark corner of this club, hike up that dress, and do something illegal." His right hand dropped from her backside, his fingertips brushing the back of her bare thigh. "After seeing how those hips move, you better believe I'd risk getting arrested to be nine inches deep next time you dance."

Rosie's inner walls contracted with such intensity, she fell against him, letting her mouth be caught up in another furious kiss, Dominic's calloused palms scraping over her exposed back, her hips. She broke the contact out of necessity and stepped away, because the unmistakable tightening of an orgasm had begun and she didn't want it that way. Every ounce of her being required all. The whole experience, not just temporary relief.

"Meet you at the elevator?"

Dominic nodded, his dark gaze gobbling up her hips and breasts. She couldn't tear her attention off of him, no matter how loudly her brain commanded her to go get the key. So when someone pressed her purse into her hand, smacked her on the butt, and said, "Get out of here, you're making everyone jealous," she breathed a sigh of relief.

"Thanks, Bethany," she called over the music. "I owe you."

The blonde turned and saluted her, then waded into the fray surrounding the bar. Before Rosie could fully turn back around, Dominic had her tucked into his side, guiding her toward the elevator with long strides.

Rosie's pulse was on a roller-coaster ride, except it was stuck in the upside-down portion, sending her on continual, gravity-defying loops. The man breathing on the back of her neck as she unlocked the hotel room door was her husband. She shouldn't feel like a virgin about to lose it on prom night, but she did. Oh Lord, she did.

Dominic's hands gripped the doorframe on either side of her as she fumbled the card, trying to see the instructional arrows in the muted interior of the hallway.

"Don't they believe in lights at this hotel?" Rosie murmured choppily.

Her husband plucked the card out of her hand, shoved it in the slot, and yanked it out. And her vagina reacted as if he'd just thrust in and out of her, contracting and growing damper by the second. They'd boarded a packed elevator; otherwise, she was pretty sure they wouldn't have made it to the room without consummating the evening. The way he looked at her on the way down had had her knees shaking. They still shook, her belly hollowing when the green light flashed on the card reader, and Dominic shoved open the door.

Even in her state of hormonal upheaval, the luxuriousness of the room made Rosie catch her breath. "Oh, wow."

It was large, even by New York City standards. A king-sized bed with a fluffy white comforter took up the entire left side of the room, and a pair of silk pajamas were folded on the chrome side table, courtesy of Bethany. There was a flat screen and a modern fireplace on the right. Straight ahead was a floor-to-ceiling window that overlooked downtown Manhattan, buildings looming close and far, like a 3-D painting.

Dominic's hand closed firmly around the nape of Rosie's neck, and she dropped her purse, whimpering into the silence of the room. The zipper of her dress came down and the heavy, sequined material dropped, pooling at her feet, leaving her in a black thong, a matching strapless bra, and a pair of five-inch gold heels. The air didn't move a whisper. Nothing moved for several moments as she stood there, shivering as her husband's eyes roamed over her body.

This. This was why keeping their hands off each other was practically impossible. Rosie craved the act of being overwhelmed by his strength. Dominic needed to quench Rosie's thirst and claim her in the process. Their passion, at least, was the perfect partnership.

One afternoon during their senior year of high school would forever be etched on her memory. Alone in Dominic's house while his parents were visiting his aunt in the Bronx. She'd been struggling with an odd impulse for weeks, and he'd coaxed it out of her with long, drugging kisses on his couch that led to hands stroking inside each other's pants, moans filling the air. With her face hidden in Dominic's neck, she'd quietly asked him to pin her wrists over her head—and he'd gone almost limp with relief, before obliging. The rigid fly of his jeans had dragged over her clit and she'd orgasmed on the spot.

Now Dominic's palm drifted from her nape, traveling slowly down her spine and over the swell of her bottom. His finger tucked into the low waistband and peeled the panties inch by painstaking inch down her thighs. Her bra came off next, snapped free in the back, tumbling to the floor forgotten. Rosie struggled to fill her lungs, her aroused nipples rising and falling on harsh breaths.

"Please," she whispered.

Dominic swept her up in his arms and strode across the room. She frowned when they bypassed the bed, but excitement coursed through her veins when Dominic set her down on the modern circular table arranged in front of the huge window. Her naked back to the city, Rosie shook with anticipation. What was coming? What was he going to do with her?

Dominic came into view, his mouth ghosting over hers. He touched his tongue to hers lightly, teasingly, then eased back to strip off his shirt, tossing it aside. Filter obliterated, Rosie could only hum in appreciation of his ripped physique, the city lights illuminating every valley, sinew, and riot of ink. Her hips moved restlessly on the table as he undid his belt and the fly of his pants, taking out his huge erection in a clenched fist. Rosie sobbed at the sight of it.

His tongue licked along the seam of her lips. "This would have convinced you without words to bring me back to your room, isn't that right?"

Rosie squeezed her eyes shut and nodded.

"Rubbing your pussy all over it in public. You must want it pretty goddamn bad."

The table grew slippery beneath her and she tried to move her thighs together to hide the evidence of how needy she was, but Dominic blocked her with his hips.

"You have no idea how bad I want to cram you full of this cock. I'm fucking starving for my wi—for you."

"Yes," Rosie whimpered, sliding her legs apart. "Please—"

"Oh no. Not yet." Her back landed firmly on the table, Dominic's hand on the center of her chest. "The city is going to watch me eat my fill."

It wasn't a large table by any stretch, so Rosie's head tipped over the other side, affording her an upside-down view of Manhattan. Buildings as close as across the street, windows with their lights on and off. People moving in their depths.

Could they see her? She had no idea. Would she mind if they did? The excitement spinning all across her skin like pinwheels said no. No, she definitely didn't mind. Just like on the dance floor, she welcomed the hint of rebellion. Welcomed the chance to stretch her wings and measure the span.

Dominic circled around the table at an unhurried pace. His finger slipped down the folds between her legs, making her cry out, but he only trailed the moisture he collected around her belly button, her nipples. And then he was even with her face, dragging the thick head of his erection across her panting mouth.

"I want one good, deep push inside that beautiful mouth. Just to get me wet for stroking. Don't think I'll be able to stop myself from beating off while I tongue your little clit."

Rosie's hips twisted on the table, the body part in question desiring friction. Relief. Now now now. At the same time, her mouth was starved for the taste of Dominic, so she parted her lips and let him sink in a couple inches. She moaned around his flesh, and his progress halted.

"Shhh. Relax and take it deeper." He eased his hips forward, stretching her lips around his girth, air escaping him in growling bursts. "More?"

Incapable of vocalizing that yes, yes, she wanted every inch of him, she reached back and buried her fingernails into his backside, urging him closer, deeper.

"Fuck," he roared, gripping the base of his arousal and drawing it back out, leaving it perched on her lips as his belly heaved. "You feel so good. So good. One more push. I need it."

He drove back into her mouth cautiously, but still faster than last time, stopping when he hit resistance and the salt of him traveled down her throat. The sound and feel of his pleasure were an instantaneous addiction and she needed more. It had been so long since they'd fulfilled each other the way they needed. The way they required.

"Look at you, enjoying the shit out of it," he gritted, tapping his hard flesh against her lips a few times. "Tell me to stop, Rosie."

"One more," she whispered, the second word cut off by her husband entering her mouth on a groan, his thickness taking up every corner, his belly hair tickling her chin.

"Jesus Christ," he panted, freeing himself and rounding the table in one long step. He fell to his knees and pressed her legs open, diving in for a devastating lick that exploited her swollen clit and brought Rosie's back off the table in a violent arch.

"Dominic. Oh my God. Yes. Yes." His thumbs massaged their way from her knees, down her inner thighs, where they met at her juncture. Gently, those same thumbs took turns rubbing her clit, one after the other, before his tongue took over and flickered against her nub, not stopping, never stopping until she was slapping the table with the flats of her hands and sobbing his name. "Suck. Please."

It shouldn't have made her even hotter when he laughed and changed the pattern of his tongue's soft jabs, but it did. Her hips wouldn't stay still, and a low, carnal twist started in the lowest part of her belly and wrapped around her limbs like tentacles. She threw her head back over the edge of the table and felt herself soaring over the city, unstoppable and strong—and when Dominic's lips closed around her clit and applied just the right amount of suction, the buildings splintered in front of her eyes, light fragmenting in every direction. Of their own accord, her thighs wrapped around his head and she screamed.

That scream was still echoing in the room when she was dragged off the table onto the floor, onto her hands and knees. A shaking hand pressed her cheek into the carpet and jerked her hips up. No amount of preparation could make her ready for Dominic's invasion of her body. It was forceful and glorious, his hard length entering her so quickly and with such ferocity, her knees left the ground and plummeted back down, wider than before, shoved that way by masculine hands. A working man's hands. Her husband's hands.

"I loved you dancing in that dress. Looking so free. Like you could do anything. You can, honey girl." He reared back with his hips and reentered her with a savage thrust, his muscular chest slapping down on her back so he could talk directly into her ear. "But you knew this was coming. You knew looking like a jack-off fantasy in front of other men would cost you."

Did he speak the truth? Yes. Yes, the anticipation of Dominic's reaction was part of the reason for tonight's excitement. She couldn't help it. She didn't want to help it. This attraction between them had a nature all its own. One of those rare things in life where the frustration and strife were always worth the payoff. Taking her husband inside her body always sent her on a thrill ride, but she wasn't trying to hold back her enjoyment this time in anticipation of the loneliness that usually came after. There was understanding and broken-down barriers between them now. She'd been honest with him, and in turn, her body did the same.

Rosie pushed a moan through her bared teeth, dropping her head forward to watch her breasts bounce again and again as Dominic pounded into her from behind. She watched his substantial length enter between the upside-down V of their legs. Could have gone on watching it forever, especially when the fingers of his left hand started massaging her clit, his drives turning hard and punishing, his tunneling shaft finding that secret spot deep inside her and teaching it a lesson. Owning it. Her.

"What are you looking at down there, huh?" Dominic panted, putting his middle finger on her clit and jiggling it until the motion blurred. "I'll tell you. You're looking at the inevitable, Rosie. Me inside you. Is inevitable. Us fucking like animals on the floor is inevitable. That's how it's always going to be, because you own my urges. You created them and you satisfy them."

"Yes, yes, yes," she chanted, her open mouth moving just above the carpet. "I want to satisfy you. I need to."

He slid his fingers into her hair, gripping, tilting her head back until she was looking at the ceiling. "You'll satisfy me by proving I fuck you right." His thrusts slowed but didn't lose an ounce of effectiveness as he continued to enter her, grinding deep with powerful circles of his hips. "We both know you're not done for the night. You might hold out for a week every time, but once those panties drop, you can ride me until morning. Isn't that right, honey girl?"

His words tightened the bolts in her middle, cranked them until her thighs were jelly, shaking, another release sailing toward her on a tumultuous sea.

"You really have to wonder why I stay jacked? I got my wife's greedy little pussy to satisfy—wouldn't trade it for anything on this earth, either. I handle my business."

When Dominic let go of her hair and continued to rub her clit in perfect strokes, she broke. Couldn't hold on any longer. Her body jolted and shuddered, the rush of sensations heightening when Dominic's tongue licked up her spine, his erection pressing deep inside her, giving her inner walls that delicious flesh to seize on. "Dominic."

"Don't worry," he growled, cinching his hips back and punching them forward, wrapping a forearm around her waist to hold her steady. "I'm taking my turn."

Sobbing, dizzy, Rosie nonetheless planted her hands and knees, wanting to give Dominic the same relief he'd given her. Craving the chance to be the instrument that got him there. Instead, she was hauled off the ground, dangling in her husband's arms for one step, two, before being tossed onto the bed. He grabbed her ankles and flipped her over and—*God. My God.* She almost had her third orgasm simply from watching Dominic fist his engorged arousal and position his bulky body between her thighs, panting, sweat shining on his brow, falling forward on a curse, and pressing the tip inside her.

"Fuck yes, Rosie, that's how I love it." He plunged his

erection inside her halfway, then drew it out, smacking himself against the seam of her private flesh. "You know I love it all soft and satisfied. Don't have to worry about waiting until you get comfortable with every fat inch." He thrust deep to the soundtrack of her scream and gathered her wrists above her head, ramming his hips forward. "I can just ride my woman and listen to that slick slide of my cock taking her higher. And you are going higher again, aren't you, honey girl? Can't help it after coming twice. A couple of strokes of that sensitive clit and you'll tighten up like a fucking dream. Again and again."

This was her heaven. No denying it. Having her hands pinned, being filled by Dominic, nowhere to go. No way to escape the quickening of her body. She could only spread her legs and absorb the weight of him traveling up and back on top of her. A vessel on the water, cresting the waves and plunging back down. Rising and slamming. Her husband's hips bucked, his teeth leaving marks on her neck, his thumbs pressing into the insides of her wrists, as if searching for her pulse so he could match it. And she swore he did. As her heartbeat kicked into a sprint, the slap of Dominic's manhood against her happened in faster succession. Without cease or time to prepare, his flesh tunneled into her again and again, hungry grunts coming from his chest, his mouth. Delivered into her neck, they vibrated through her, and she gloried in the using of her body. In that moment, she was this man's mate, and he was in need, and it was as simple as that.

"Christ. Oh Christ." He raked his teeth over her shoulder,

his hands frantically gripping her knees and pushing them up to her shoulders, pressing down with his entire muscular frame and sending euphoria coursing through Rosie. "Ten years later and I still can't believe what a tight little fuck you are. My tight fuck," he groaned, angling his hips and—

"Ohhh. Yes." Her vision went black, then sparkly, as the base of his driving erection journeyed over her clit. Her fingers flexed in his grip, back arching. "Dominic, don't stop. Right there. Please."

"I got you. I've always got you."

"Please."

Jaw clenching, he bore down with his lower body, and she screamed, a climax tearing through her like teeth one moment, utter bliss the next. "God. Oh my God. Oh my God!"

His forehead dropped to hers. "Mine. You are mine. You are my fucking life."

"I'm yours," she sobbed, moisture leaking from her eyes, body on fire, heart under attack. "Yours, Dominic. Come inside me. Show me who I belong to."

A choked sound fell from his mouth and his body tensed. Rosie clenched him with her intimate muscles for everything she was worth, moaning at the incredible vision above her. This beautiful man floating on the edges of another plane. One they could only travel to when they touched. His flesh jerked inside her, his mouth falling open, hissing her name, big body trembling enough to shake the bed.

"Rosie. Rosie. Fuuuuuuck. So good, honey. So sweet and tight." He thrust one more time and fell on top of her, muttering brokenly into her hair, his hips rolling like they couldn't help it. "Mine. Need my wife. Need her."

Rosie was already halfway to losing consciousness, the tumult of emotions and physical satisfaction leaving her a pile of mush. The last thing she remembered was Dominic kissing her cheeks, her forehead, her mouth, then turning her onto one side and tucking her into the warmth of his body.

What do we do in the morning?

That was her final thought before everything faded to dark.

CHAPTER TWENTY

Dominic woke up to the sound of his phone vibrating. His eyes cracked open and blinked back closed against the early-morning light. His phone wasn't on the bedside table of the hotel room, and he resented the idea of getting up to find it, because for the first time in . . . he couldn't remember how long, his wife was naked and wrapped around him, breathing evenly against his shoulder. His arm was asleep and it could stay that way, for all he cared.

They didn't do this anymore. Cuddling. Unconscious or conscious. When they touched, it was an explosion of lust. Greedy. When it was over, they went about their regularly scheduled program. Rosie went to shower. Not wanting to admit he needed the comfort and intimacy afterward, Dominic went out to the shed and fixed something or simply went to sleep. They hadn't gravitated toward each other in the dark and clung like this since those months before he'd been deployed.

How had he survived for years without this?

Rosie hummed drowsily in her sleep and the vibration went through him, tumbling end over end in his stomach.

His cock stirred against the soft sheets, and he tucked his hips back, not wanting to wake her up just yet. She was too beautiful like this. There wasn't a time when she wasn't, but the trust it took to surrender to his protection in sleep was humbling. That trust had been missing—no way around it now. Rosie might have trusted him to provide, to be faithful, to protect her with his life, but she'd been keeping her heart guarded.

Regret clogged his throat. Why hadn't he recognized sooner that his contribution to their marriage wasn't enough? At what point had he forgotten the moments like this? They should have been placed ahead of all others. Holding her in the expensive bed with dawn breaking over the skyscrapers in the distance, he was on the verge of being . . . enough. This was what she needed. Affection. Words. Maybe that was the only answer and he didn't have to search any further.

His wife rolled closer and snuggled into his side, resting a closed fist in the center of his chest. God almighty. Dominic breathed through his nose and closed his eyes. This was heaven on earth. She was soft and sweet and he never wanted to move. Words. Encouragement. He could learn to give his wife those things on a regular basis and this would be his. Last night was proof that he could earn her trust by letting her fly, by supporting her. By being there to lift her up when she needed it. And she did need it. He'd learned from the mistake of his silence and would never let that need go unfulfilled again.

Dominic reached under the fluffy down comforter and trailed a hand over the curve of her hip, smiling softly when her lips popped open and a breath shook out. Not awake, but definitely getting there. He should wake her up, drive her home, and tell her she'd have the rest of the money for her restaurant soon. It was Saturday and neither of them was working. Maybe he could convince her to test her signature asado dish out on him.

Jesus, last night she'd called herself *his* out loud. Something had shifted between them. So while his gut was screaming at him to tell Rosie about the house he'd bought in secret—the sale of which would fund her restaurant—the absolute last thing he wanted when they'd just risen from the ashes was to crumble them into dust again. Unable to draw a decent breath around the panic, Dominic buried his nose in her hair and inhaled.

Rosie wanted the restaurant. He would give that to her. He had to.

His conscience spoke from the back of his brain, urging him to wake up his wife and just be honest. Lay everything out there. How much he loved her and wanted to make her happy. How he'd put her restaurant aspirations on the back burner and selfishly pursued the dream he'd thought *they* shared—a house. How he'd been taught to equate showing emotions with weakness, so he'd pushed her away, instead of keeping his walls down, the way they'd been when he was younger. Before he'd looked around and decided his only offering to Rosie was hard work. Reliability. Instead of confiding in her that he didn't feel like *enough*, he'd fallen into the pattern he'd been shown his whole life. Head down, work hard, don't reveal a single chink in the armor. If he just opened his mouth right here and now, they could walk out of this room with no secrets between them.

Do it.

Or he could never tell her about the house and stay on track. Follow the plan. Fix this.

Needing to get his head straight, Dominic carefully laid Rosie among the pillows and got out of bed, already missing her soft curves against him. Missing her breath, her scent, and her sounds.

I'll be a better husband to you, honey girl. I promise.

Dominic ran a hand over his shaved head and stooped down to retrieve the phone from his jeans pocket. There was one missed call and one text message from Stephen. Since he'd essentially abandoned his friends last night, it was probably a good idea to call Stephen and let him know he was more than fine. Sending one final glance at Rosie where she lay in the bed, Dominic dressed quickly, pocketed Rosie's room key, and stepped into the hallway. He fell into a green velvet chair in the elevator area and hit call.

"Oh! Well, if it isn't the phantom menace. Thanks for letting me know you're alive."

"Christ." Dominic dragged a hand down his face and laughed. "Calm down, Mom."

There was some shuffling around in the background and a door closed. "You did the right thing disappearing. What a scene. They're probably going to ban Long Islanders from the club and call it the Castle Law."

"Shit. What happened?"

"Wes and Bethany happened, mainly. Which really pissed

off my wife, because she likes being the center of attention. It's been a great night slash morning for me."

"Sorry to hear that," Dominic said, realizing his chest felt lighter than it had in years. How long had he been living with an anvil on his chest? "What do you mean, Wes and Bethany happened?"

"I mean," Stephen said, drawing out the word, "Bethany went inside after Rosie to see what was keeping her and apparently handed off a room key?"

"Yeah, I might know something about that."

"How nice for you. My wife isn't even speaking to me." His friend blew out a harried breath. "Anyway, after you two left, my sister let some dude at the bar buy her a drink. Before she could take a sip, Wes showed up and drank it—a pink martini, too, so remind me to give him shit about that—and paid the dude back."

"What did Bethany do?"

"What do you think?"

"Raised hell."

"Ding, ding, ding. Good thing the music was loud, because she tore a strip off his ass." Stephen's laugh was kind of bemused. "To be fair, I'm pretty sure he did the same to her. I think I really like this guy."

"Yeah, he's all right. Not bad on the job site, either." Dominic stood up so he could look down the hallway toward Rosie's room. Logically, he knew she couldn't have left without getting on an elevator, but he was . . . lovesick. Might as well call it what it was. Having Rosie out of his sight was causing him physical discomfort. "What happened with Travis and Georgie—"

"Don't. Don't bring it up. I just ate breakfast."

"They did the opposite of Wes and Bethany, huh?"

Stephen made a disgusted sound. "Let's just say you're not the only ones that needed to get a room. You'd think they hadn't seen each other in a year."

"Gotcha." Dominic chuckled. Normally, he hated relationship talk of any kind. Why? Because it forced him to reflect on his own shortcomings? Yeah, that must have been it. He'd convinced himself his marriage was normal, if not perfect. In reality, so much had been broken, there almost hadn't been enough glue to put it back together. "Thank God we came here last night," Dominic said, not realizing right away that he'd spoken out loud.

"It sounds like things are getting better, man. I'm glad." Stephen cleared his throat. "Speaking of you and Rosie. There's another reason I called."

Dominic lowered himself back into the chair. "What?"

"The realtor called. There's a cash offer on the house."

His heart kicked into a gallop inside his chest. "Yeah? A good one?"

"Well, you did price it to sell. This offer is slightly lower, but it's in the neighborhood of what you were hoping for." He paused. "I made a call to the commercial realtor selling the building on Cove. Along with the money she made through the GoFundMe, it's more than enough to lock down the restaurant space for Rosie. A cash sale for the owner, some capital for her if she wants to give it a face-lift—"

"Yeah, I would want her to have enough to do whatever she wants." Restless, he leaned forward, then pushed to his feet, pacing once again to the end of the hallway and staring at the door. The love of his life slept on the other side. They were so close to getting back on track. He had the answers, he was just . . . weighed down with one final question. Would his honesty be enough? He had the power in his hands to give her the thing she'd always wanted. A simple signature and he'd make up for everything.

"Dom," Stephen said, sighing. "You know I'll help you do whatever you think is right. But I'm going to be the voice of reason one more time. Just talk to Rosie. Make the decision together."

Dominic swallowed, taking a step toward the room, then turning back around. He thought of the woman who'd danced last night with total abandon, the woman who'd taken command of those women in Wes's kitchen and filled needs before they'd arisen. The woman who loved cooking so much, she used to dance in their kitchen. She'd rediscovered that passion on her own, without him, because he'd neglected to give her that support. Right now, he could make up for it. Make up for everything and watch her succeed.

"Accept the offer."

Rosie stared at her hand curled on the pillow, listening to her measured breathing.

Dominic was coming back.

They'd turned a huge corner last night, against all odds, and her husband had *not* just crept out of the room like she was a one-night stand. Forcing herself to relax and be patient wasn't easy to do—yet. She'd grown accustomed to parting ways with Dominic after sex, mentally and physically. But after last night, she expected more. Would she get it?

"Yes," she whispered, rolling over onto her back and stretching her sore muscles, arms extended over her head, toes pointed. "Definitely yes."

She couldn't believe it. Yesterday at this time, she'd thought her marriage was over for real. Kaput. For good. But she'd just spent the night wrapped in Dominic's arms and it had been like visiting heaven. He'd made a comeback and she wasn't going to doubt him. Her heart implored her to trust the only man she'd ever loved—and she could do nothing but comply.

When she heard the room key slide into the lock, the corners of her mouth ticked up into a smile. Instead of giving in to the modest urge to cover her naked body with the fluffy comforter, she made no move to satisfy the impulse. She crossed one leg over the other and arched her back a little, putting herself on display.

Dominic walked in and came to an immediate stop, his throat muscles moving in a slow, thick lift and fall. "You're really trying to make us miss that eleven o'clock checkout time," he said in a gravelly voice. "I'm not complaining."

Her nipples beaded at his abrasive tone. "I didn't think so."

After a brief pause, he tipped his chin toward the door. "That was Stephen on the phone. I didn't want to answer and wake you up."

"Work stuff?"

"Yeah." Tongue resting on his lower lip, Dominic stripped off his T-shirt, dangling it from his fingertips for a moment before letting it drop. "Feels good. Coming in here and knowing I can just get in bed with you. Talk to you. Touch you." He shook his head. "Can't believe I haven't been doing it all along."

"We better get started making up for lost time—"

A growl interrupted Rosie. It was coming from her stomach.

A beat of silence passed before they both broke into laughter. Dominic unfastened his jeans and shucked them off with zero fanfare, leaving him in a tight pair of black boxer briefs. Rosie was granted only a glimpse of his inked, honed muscle glory before he planted a knee on the mattress and dove onto the covers beside her. "Would you rather . . ."

Laughing, Rosie turned to her husband and buried her face in his chest. "I remember this game."

"You should." He slipped his fingers into her curls and cradled her head. "We used to play it constantly."

Rosie gave an exaggerated sigh. "We must have stopped because I won all the time."

Dominic snorted. "You must still be half-asleep, because you're dreaming."

"There's only one way to settle this." She bit his nipple lightly and felt his sex thicken against her thigh. "Fire away."

He caught her mouth in a quick, groaning kiss. "I'll throw

you a softball to start. Would you rather get room service for breakfast, or should we get dressed and go out?"

She fingered the waistband of his boxers. "Is that even a question?"

"Room service," he rasped, rolling his hips forward. "Got it."

"My turn." She took a moment to think, her lips curling at the memory of how they used to play this game for hours at a stretch, trying to outdo each other by coming up with the most outlandish scenarios. "Would you rather walk through the lobby of this hotel without your pants on, or . . . with a face full of shaving cream?"

"Shaving cream."

"Really? Why?"

"My legs are too sexy, honey girl," he teased against her lips. "I'm not going to be responsible for inciting a riot."

Rosie dug her fingers into his ribs and tickled him, resulting in Dominic flipping her over onto her back and pinning her wrists above her head. "Your turn," she breathed.

He dropped his head to the crook of her neck and laid a hot, openmouthed kiss on her sensitive skin. "Would you rather take a bath in refried beans, or . . . with an iguana?"

"Oh *God.*" A shiver passed through her. "Beans. One thousand percent."

His mouth spread into an amused smile. "I had a feeling you might say that."

"I'm trying to get sexy here and now all I can feel is a scaly green body scampering around all nervous and shifty-eyed—"

"Christ. Maybe you're right and my game is slipping."

Rosie hummed and passed him a little side eye. In truth, she was having no problem getting sexy. *At all.* With her husband's hips wedged up tight between her thighs and his erection at the ready, she was growing wetter by the second. God, he smelled like faded aftershave, sex, and man. But the best part of the moment was the ease between them that was returning. The time they'd spent together since she'd left had started off stilted, but this was the furthest thing from stilted. She looked up into Dominic's eyes and saw her husband again.

He pressed his thumbs to the pulses of her wrists and gave her a cajoling look. "Can I get a redo?"

Her shoulder shrug was prim, as if she was in control and not at the mercy of her powerful husband. "I'll allow it this once."

"Thank you," he murmured drily, before his expression turned thoughtful. "Would you rather spend the day in the city, or head back to Port Jeff and call the realtor so she can show you that building on Cove?"

In the space of a second, she was breathless, her heart fluttering wildly. "Go back to Port Jeff and look at the building."

Dominic nodded, his gaze running over every inch of her face. "Good. Let's call her."

Rosie made a sound of agreement, positive she might explode into a million tiny pieces. Not only did she seem to have her marriage back and improved, but the silver lining she'd been reaching for was now closer than ever. And with her husband on her side, she felt as if she could do anything. "Yes, we'll call. After."

He tucked his tongue into his cheek. "After what?"

Rosie spread her legs wide and watched Dominic's jaw slacken as gravity ground his hips down into the juncture of her thighs. "Would you rather . . ." she whispered, forcing him to lean closer to hear her, "finish with my ankles around your neck, or lay back and watch me ride?"

His breath released in a rush, warming the side of her face. "You're right. You always did win this game."

Their low laughter was warm, intimate. "I see your memory has been jogged."

"Thoroughly."

She freed her wrists from where he'd been keeping them stationary above her head. She slipped her hands down his back, into his briefs, and dug her fingernails into his rock-solid ass. "How do you want me?"

Before she could finish phrasing the question, Dominic rolled them over, his brown, tattooed skin beneath her on the crisp, white sheets, forming the most beautiful contrast. His pupils were dilated, his breath coming in short pants that shuddered in and out of his huge chest. While he shoved down the waistband of his briefs and took out his arousal, Rosie captured handfuls of her curls and lifted her breasts, making him moan in the quiet hotel room. She bumped her hips side to side, dancing seductively in the morning light, before leaning down and bracing her weight on his shoulders. Letting their sexes mold together and dragging her wetness up and down his length, glorying in the sight of his clenched teeth, his strained neck muscles.

"*Fuck* me, Rosie."

Her nails speared into his shoulders. "Oh, I plan on it." She reached back and took his thickness in her fist, guiding it home and impaling herself inch by painstaking inch. Enjoying the rare occasion of having Dominic underneath her, Rosie savored it, taking him deep, grinding lightly, and teasing herself back up to the tip. "Do you like that?"

His punctuated laugh was rife with frustration. "You know I fucking live for it." Their eyes met. "That I live for you."

With an emotional tide rising in her chest, Rosie reached up and gripped the headboard and rode her husband *hard*. His mouth fell open, hands flying to her hips and gripping tight. Yanking, pushing, shoving, bruising. After a handful of minutes, her thighs started to burn, but she didn't cease the rough marriage of their lower bodies, even when the wet, smacking sounds blurred together and he shouted her name, his abdomen knitting in that telltale way. "Come with me, Rosie."

She was close. So close. *So close—*

"Changed my mind," Dominic said hoarsely, flipping Rosie onto her back, her head at the foot of the bed, his body covered in a sheen of sweat. "Your husband knows what gets you off. Get those ankles around my neck."

"*Yes.*" One brutal drive of his hips and Rosie screamed, Dominic swooping down to eat the sound with a filthy kiss, his lower body pounding down again, again, until his face screwed up and he came apart along with her, holding his hardness in the deepest recess of her body and shuddering violently.

They collapsed side by side into the bedsheets a moment later, their heads turning at the same time, eyes locking. Their hands slid toward each other, fingers locking. And they smiled.

CHAPTER TWENTY-ONE

Rosie checked her appearance for the tenth time in the store window. Smart jacket. Boots. Skinny black jeans. Did she look the part of a restaurateur? Or even an aspiring one?

She rolled her shoulders back and exhaled, a small smile curving her lips.

Yes. She did.

Fine, she was about to make a seriously lowball offer on this restaurant, but she watched enough HGTV to know that people did it all the time. It was practically expected. She just wanted her offer to be considered seriously enough to make it to the negotiation stage—and it would. What would her mother say if she were here, witnessing Rosie doubt herself?

Not much, probably. But she'd convey a well-meaning rebuke with a raised eyebrow that said, *They should be nervous about meeting us, Rosie.*

Rosie closed her eyes a moment and breathed. She was here, she wasn't an imposter, and her faith in herself was intact.

Grateful for the ride on a bubble of confidence her

mother's memory gave her, Rosie looked at the time on her cell phone and refused to panic. The realtor was late to show her the commercial space, but that didn't mean she'd found her unprofessional over the phone or didn't take her seriously. Briefly, she'd entertained the nightmare that the realtor and Martha belonged to the same knitting circle and had ruined Rosie's chances of buying the space—it wouldn't be so far-fetched in the small town—but she remained optimistic.

And wasn't that nice?

Rosie tilted her head to one side and let the cool October breeze sweep along her neck. It was Saturday afternoon and she could still feel the Friday-night whisker burn there from Dominic's unshaven jaw. A pulse fluttered between her legs and she took a shaky breath. Rosie wasn't an expert on marriage or sex. She wasn't an expert on anything, really, except maybe the amount of garlic to put in her chimichurri sauce. However. She was reasonably sure married couples didn't usually have the best sex of their lives ten years after the wedding. Just a hunch.

Even now, standing outside the space where she dreamed of opening her restaurant, the legs keeping her upright were nothing more than holograms. She'd left the real ones back in the Gansevoort Hotel. Apparently her brain had been left behind, too, because mush had made up the contents of her head for the past few hours. If she licked her lips, she could almost feel Dominic's good-bye kiss.

After calling the realtor and having beignets for breakfast, they'd shared an Uber SUV with Travis and Georgie from Manhattan to Port Jefferson. For once, Rosie and Dominic hadn't been uncomfortable with the PDA taking place in their vicinity. Dominic had sat beside Rosie in the middle row, stroking her palm in circles with his thumb, his hot attention on her thighs enough to make her squirm in the leather seat. After they'd dropped off Travis and Georgie, her stop had been next. She'd had butterflies in her stomach as Dominic walked her to Bethany's front door, kissing her before letting her inside. Kissing her. Sure. If that's what you called utterly and completely claiming her mouth. Another brush of his tongue and she would have dragged him inside and hung a sock on Bethany's guest room door.

Do not enter. Ravishment by husband in progress.

Rosie unbuttoned her jacket and waved some cool air toward her cleavage and underarms. Great. Now she was going to meet the realtor with sweat stains. Real professional and dignified.

It wasn't only their lovemaking that continued to replay itself over and over in her mind. No, her thoughts were occupied by so many moments from Friday night. The things he'd said. How . . . capable and incredible he'd made her feel.

I loved you dancing in that dress. Looking so free. Like you could do anything. You can, honey girl.

Those sentiments were like echoes from the past. From Dominic before. And he'd meant what he said. Meant every word. The intensity in his touch, his stare, his kiss had been enough to make her believe . . . and now here she was. Ready to buy this space. She and Dominic were solid. And *she*, as her own woman, was solid.

She and her husband were entwined, and being separated from him had been hard as hell. On the ride from Manhattan, she'd decided to move back into their home. Really, she couldn't imagine spending another night without him after the breakthrough they'd made. Even now, she had so much love blooming in her chest, she could break into a spontaneous dance at any moment. But she couldn't regret her decision to leave in the first place. By following her gut and refusing to continue with the status quo, she'd learned a lot about her own strength. What she was willing to accept. She held on to that lesson now as she stood waiting.

While the afternoon clouds passed above, drifting in front of the sun and moving on, Rosie couldn't help but replay Dominic's words from the night before. *After that, the only thing he felt confident in giving was stability. Maybe after being raised to believe that was a man's job, it was easy to fall into it.* She'd found her confidence, but did Dominic still lack his own when it came to being a good husband?

If they'd tackled those insecurities in therapy, she wasn't certain they'd been resolved. Not if she still didn't have a clear idea of the worries plaguing her husband. She only knew one thing for certain: he was making a real, concerted effort to give Rosie what she needed, and she had to do the same. What secrets lurked behind those beautiful green eyes of his? She tapped her cell phone against her leg for a few seconds, then lifted it to call him. He'd promised to meet her here after running a few errands—

"Mrs. Vega? I'm Emma. Hi."

Rosie pushed the cell into her purse and faced the

woman approaching on the sidewalk. She was around the same age as Rosie. Not a local face, but she nonetheless smiled warmly as if they already knew each other. They shook hands.

"Please call me Rosie. Thanks for coming to show me the space."

The realtor pulled out a handful of keys and squinted down at the dangling white circles, each of which had a different address written in a scrawl. "Thank you for not giving me a hard time over being late. It has been a *morning*."

"I hear that." Rosie shifted in her boots and tried not to betray how anxious she was to see the empty space and visualize her own décor on every blank surface. "So . . . have you—"

"Shown this property to anyone else?" Emma winked at her as they pushed into the dark commercial space. "Two other people have been interested, although I have no current offers. That's the good news."

Rosie followed her inside. "What's the bad news?"

Emma heaved a sigh and fumbled for the light switch, finally flipping it on and illuminating the room. Rosie swallowed hard, rapidly blinking back the moisture that sprung to her eyes.

My God, it's perfect.

Last time she'd stood inside these four walls, there had been people and noise and slapdash decorating. Without those trappings to impede her creative process, her restaurant took shape around her. One wall would be a spicy, textured gold. They would need bold white accents, maybe some antique sconces. Bethany could help with that. No tablecloths on the tables—she wanted the candlelight to bounce off the gleaming wood surfaces and make the dark interior sparkle like stars in the sky. She would leave the rest of the walls in their natural exposed-brick state, and Dominic could repaint them, make them look beautiful. Cinnamon and cloves and orange—those scents would remind people of her place. An *experience*.

". . . kind of finicky, truth be told . . ."

Rosie tuned back in to what the realtor was saying. "I'm sorry," she said, shaking loose the gorgeous illusion in her head. "Can you repeat that?"

Emma smiled knowingly and toed aside some left-behind debris, advancing toward Rosie. "They got some early interest in the building. Some credit issues popped up for the first applicant or it would already be sold. Nevertheless, after those bites we received right off the bat, the owner decided to increase the price." She gave Rosie a commiserating eye roll that said she didn't agree with the decision, but couldn't do anything about it, either.

And then she rattled off a new number that made Rosie inwardly blanch.

"I see," Rosie croaked. "I'm afraid that's out of my—"

"She'll take it," came a gruff voice at the front door.

Rosie sucked in a breath and turned to find Dominic leaning against the wall, arms crossed. A badass hiding in the shadows, watching her. "When did you get here?" She shook her head. "What do you mean, I'll take it?"

He pushed off the wall and came closer, hitting her with

enough heat in one look to rival the power of a thousand suns. "You want it?"

"Yes," she whispered, turning her back so they could have something that resembled a private conversation. "It's . . . perfect. It's everything I've been seeing in my dreams." When his features softened and pure, unfiltered adoration stared back at her, she stepped closer, sighing over the welcoming embrace of his heat. "It's too expensive. We can find someplace else. Maybe they'll even come down on the price at some point."

Dominic tipped her chin up. "Rosie, look at me."

She searched his face, her heart racing faster at the amused tilt of his lips.

"We got this. Okay? This is your place."

Call her naive. Call her greedy. Call her whatever you wanted. She needed to hear those words, to live in that reality so badly in that moment, that she didn't question her husband. If Dominic, a careful planner to the extreme, told her they could afford the building, then she believed him.

"Oh my God." She leapt into his arms and released a watery laugh, feeling so amazingly whole when he laughed, too, free and unrestrained. "Oh my God, is this happening?"

Dominic stroked a hand down her back, taking a deep inhale near her temple. "Cash sale. Where do we sign?"

Emma sputtered a little. "W-well, there's an application process, but I ran Mrs. Vega's credit before driving here and I can say with confidence that . . . well, you're paying cash and her credit is outstanding, so I'll just make a quick call to the owner and—"

The front door of the restaurant burst open and Stephen stomped in with a long piece of plywood over his shoulder. Travis took up the rear, winking at Rosie as he passed.

"We're just going to get a head start patching those floorboards in back," Stephen explained to the realtor. "Water damage, you know. It will only get worse if not handled immediately, and then we'd have to renegotiate the sale, right? No one wants to buy a property with that kind of hassle attached."

Before Emma could answer, Bethany danced in surrounded by a cloud of dust motes, already flipping through a book of paint samples. "I'm seeing textured gold and pops of white," Bethany mused, throwing Rosie a wink. "Congrats, big shot."

Wes filled the doorframe. After sending a long look at Bethany's back, he tipped his cowboy hat at Rosie. "Obliged to return the favor, Mrs. Vega."

Georgie ducked under Wes's arm and entered with a bright smile. "I'm just here to entertain. Construction karaoke! Who's with me?"

So many emotions coursed through Rosie—disbelief and gratitude, to start—that it took every ounce of willpower to remain upright. It helped that Dominic's arms were banded around her like steel beams and he wasn't showing signs of letting go anytime soon.

"You're going to kill it, Rosie," Dominic murmured into her ear. "They might be our friends, but they wouldn't be here unless they knew what you're capable of."

She eased back a little, letting him kiss the tears from her face. "And you?" Rosie whispered. "More than anyone, I need to hear that you think I'm capable."

His thumb smoothed over the arch of her eyebrow, his gaze running a lap around her face. "You're going to rule this world, just like you rule mine."

There was so much quiet confidence in his voice, she must have imagined the flicker of trepidation there. Still, she started to question if he needed to talk, to tell her something, but hard rock started blaring in the space, interspersed with the sound of a hammer, and Dominic's quick grin chased her worries away.

"This is my restaurant," she breathed.

He planted a kiss on her forehead. "This is your restaurant."

CHAPTER TWENTY-TWO

Dominic couldn't stop staring at Rosie.

All seven of them—Dominic, Rosie, Travis, Georgie, Bethany, Stephen, and Wes—sat in a circle in the middle of the empty restaurant scarfing down pizza like it might be their last. Rosie had disappeared twenty minutes ago and returned with boxed wine, to the resounding cheers of everyone who'd spent the day laboring. She was already playing hostess, and, damn, it suited her. Cross-legged on the floor, dust in her hair, jacket long since discarded, she lit up the whole place. Forget decorating, *she* was going to be the attraction.

Dominic ignored the churn in his stomach that had been there since the morning. When he'd walked back into the hotel room, he'd hovered between two choices. Tell her about the house or keep it to himself. Seeing her this happy, it was hard to believe he'd made the wrong decision, but his conscience seemed hell-bent on making him question himself. He finished his Solo cup of cheap wine, setting it down in between himself and Rosie. The action caught her eye and she raised an eyebrow, asking without words if he wanted more. Dominic shook his head slowly and reached over to thread their fingers together.

"You're celebrating. Have another," Dominic said, leaning over to speak in her ear and press a lingering kiss on her cheek. "I'll make sure you get back to Bethany's safe."

"Thanks," she replied after a moment, her eyelids significantly droopier. There might be an animated conversation taking place all around them, but they could have been the only two people in the room. As much as he appreciated the support their friends had shown his wife today, he wouldn't mind being alone with Rosie. No, he sure as hell wouldn't mind that.

Wouldn't be long before he'd have to share her every night. That thought made his shoulder perform a jerky roll, but he disguised the motion by refilling Rosie's cup.

A lull in the conversation had the group taking a collective breath.

"So, Rosie," Stephen said around pizza crust. "Do you have a name for the place yet?"

Dominic held his breath as Rosie pressed her lips together, hands folding and unfolding in her lap.

"I'm not totally settled yet, but I was thinking . . . Buena Onda. The rough translation of that is 'good vibes.'" She smiled over at Dominic, almost shyly, like he didn't worship every word out of her mouth, every idea in her head. "The kind I want this place to have."

"Buena Onda," Dominic said involuntarily. Maybe he just wanted to be the first one. "Perfect, Rosie."

They didn't break eye contact until Bethany spoke. "I love

it, too. It sounds comforting. Welcoming. Like a neighborhood family place, with flair." She twirled a finger in the air,
closed her eyes, and breathed deeply through her nose. "I'm
envisioning a big scripty *O* on the awning . . ."

Eyes trained on the blonde, Wes cleared his throat into his
Solo cup. "Sounds like you're thinking of a totally different
kind of big *O*."

Bethany cooed at the man to her left. "Awww, poor thing.
Need instructions on how to deliver one?"

"Like hell I do."

They smiled at each other through gritted teeth and everyone tried not to laugh.

Everyone except Stephen, who appeared to have lost all
interest in his pizza. "One day I woke up and everyone was
talking about my sisters like sexual objects."

"Eww, Stephen," Georgie complained from her position
in Travis's lap. "Gross."

"Oh, it's only gross when I point it out?"

Travis's hearty laugh echoed off the walls. "Come on,
baby," he said, standing and hoisting his fiancée up against
his chest. "Let's spare your poor brother his misery."

"Thank you." Stephen heaved himself forward, reaching
for another piece of pizza.

"Yeah." Travis strode for the door. "Let's go home and get
into our pajamas." He winked at the group. "And straight
back out of them."

Stephen dropped the slice like it was on fire. "Okay. I've
hit my limit." The foreman stood and dusted off his jeans,
turning to a chuckling Rosie. "I'm happy for you, Rosie.

You're going to add something really special to this town." He leaned down and shook Dominic's hand. "You're fast becoming my favorite, Dom, since you're the only man left not sleeping with one of my sisters."

"Hey," Bethany exclaimed, her spine snapping straight. "I'm not sleeping with Wes."

"Give it time," Stephen muttered on his way out the door.

And then there were four.

Wes looked like a pig in shit. "Give you a ride"—he paused to sip his drink—"home, Bethany?"

With a shriek contained in her throat—mostly—Bethany stood and marched out. Wes followed a moment later. Rosie and Dominic turned to each other and burst into laughter. He caught Rosie as she toppled sideways, her head landing against his chest, the musical sound of her amusement warming every corner of his insides. He couldn't help it when the laughter died in his throat. Couldn't stop himself from pulling her into his lap in one desperate move and burying his face in her neck.

"I'm proud of you, Rosie."

He took a deep inhale of her and let it out, trusting the prodding in his gut. They were one entity. They shared a life. They either moved forward in the right direction or they would end up off course again. Dominic didn't think he could survive losing her a second time.

"I'm proud as hell. I believe in you." He swallowed. "I'm also selfish when it comes to my wife and I don't like the idea of everyone else taking a piece of you."

Rosie lifted her head, a line forming between her brows. "What do you mean, everyone taking a piece of me?"

"I mean . . ."

Dominic sounded as if he'd been running, his attention landing on different spots around the vacant restaurant. Hell, maybe therapy hadn't been such a stupid idea, because when he normally would have balked at sharing his feelings, they lifted to the surface now without effort. Apparently his stiff upper lip was loosening up.

"All these people around you. Asking for things. Stressing you out. Even the good they get—the things you want to give them, like comfort and happiness? I've had them all to myself for a long time. I'm greedy with you. And I know, honey girl, I know that has to change so you can have your dream and be happy. I want that. I want your dream for you so fucking bad. But it means letting you fly without me. I'm scared of that."

His wife took his face in her hands, her breath coming in short puffs. "Dominic—"

"Scared of you finding happiness in something that has nothing to do with me." *Unlike the house I bought for us.* "That makes me a bastard, and I don't know how to change it."

She stopped his flow of words with her mouth, staying there until the rise and fall of his chest wasn't so severe, then pulling back an inch. Searching his eyes.

"There are parts of me that I will never share with anyone else in this world. Not a single soul. Only you. And that is never, ever going to change," she said.

She turned in his lap, straddling him, laying soft kisses on his mouth, his cheeks, ruining him. Winding him all over again.

"No one is ever going to see me cry or be at my weakest inside these four walls. That's something I'll always save for you, because you're the only one who can make me stronger. No one is ever going to turn me on and piss me off at the same time or make me feel protected. Or alive. You're the only one who'll ever do that."

Every word out of her mouth stitched shut the gaping wound inside him, tied knots, made sure it was securely closed. Maybe his wife wasn't the only one who craved words. And Jesus, he hadn't cried since he was a kid, but he was suspiciously close to it right now. Had to drop his head back and look up at the ceiling, so the suspicious moisture in his eyes wouldn't escape.

"Dominic, do you honestly think I could ever love anyone the way I love you?"

That snapped his head and eyes forward, sent the organ in his chest into a frenzy. Had he heard her right? "You're back to loving me?"

Rosie made a small sound, her expression a mixture of regret and love. "I'm sorry I said that. Maybe at the time I was angry enough to convince myself I meant it. But, Dominic, I couldn't stop loving you if they cut the heart out of my chest."

With a gruff exhale of her name, he shot forward and snared her mouth in a rough kiss. Oh Jesus Christ. His heart was going to beat hard enough to incite an earthquake.

Rosie loved him. His wife loved him and nothing else on this fucking earth mattered but thanking her for it. If he took his mouth off hers, he was pretty sure poems were going to come tumbling out and he'd never written a damn poem in his life, so he pried her lips apart with his own instead, licking into her mouth and intercepting her unrestrained moan.

Dominic knew his wife's signals better than the back of his hand, so when her thighs got restless around his hips, he wasted no time standing. It would be a cold day in hell before he fucked this incredible woman on a floor covered in sawdust and dirt.

When Dominic reached his full height, her thighs tightened around him like a wrench, her hands busy stroking his face, mewling coming from her throat. It was everything he could do to stumble toward the back of the empty room, toward the kitchen, when all he wanted to do was jerk down his zipper, impale Rosie, and bounce her to an orgasm. They'd ripped some of the paper coverings off the window throughout the evening, however, so anyone passing by would see them—and he wasn't having that.

"Please, baby, please," she whimpered in his ear, her teeth tugging on the lobe—hard—making his cock swell like a motherfucker in his pants. "Now, now, now."

Dominic strode toward the kitchen with the word "baby" tumbling through his head. "You haven't called me that in a long time. God, Rosie. I've missed it. I had no idea how much."

"Baby," she whispered, working the juncture of her thighs against his erection. "Baby."

His groan echoed in the dark kitchen when they stumbled inside, ramming into a metal storage rack and sending it flying into a nearby wall. Not that either of them stopped kissing long enough to care. Dominic took two steps and threw his wife up against the first flat surface he encountered. A stainless steel fridge. Having her sexy body cling to his made Dominic feel like a god, so he flattened his palms on the steel above her head and forced her to cling harder. And when he looked her square in the eye and started to roll his hips, she climbed higher, her head falling back on a moan of his name.

"Dominic."

He reached down and lowered his zipper, releasing a rough expulsion of breath when his dick finally had the room it needed. "Going to give this to you, honey girl." He stroked himself a few times and felt moisture bead at his crown. "Take your pants off and tell me how you need it," he rasped, nipping at her chin with his teeth. "You always want it hard enough to last the week, but we're not doing that shit anymore. No more games. No more building up until we're ready to explode. I'm going to satisfy my wife's tight pussy every night of the week."

Her eyes were dazed and glowing as they locked on him, wicked intentions like he'd never seen before in Rosie's expression. She leaned in and spoke just above a whisper at his mouth, her tongue sliding out to taste him, slowly, teasingly. "I want to satisfy my husband's huge cock just as much."

Dominic growled and thrust himself against the seam of her jeans involuntarily, his blood heating to a fevered state over the wetness of the material. Their mouths fused together, heads tilting, and fucking hell, she tasted so sweet, he had to bang his fist against the fridge. Dominic was two seconds from ripping the crotch out of her jeans so he could get inside his wife without losing the perfect death grip of her thighs around his hips. Before he could proceed, Rosie's legs dropped, her palms pushing against his heaving shoulders to ease him back. Away. Confused, needing more, Dominic didn't want to go—but then she dropped to her knees and swirled her tongue around the head of his dick.

"Rosie." Watching from above as half of his inches sunk into Rosie's mouth, Dominic beat off the remaining length of his stretched cock, angling himself toward her giving lips. "Ohhh. Jesus. Jesus. You're asking for it."

Looking up at him, she nodded, her plump, wet mouth riding up and down his erection. They were tempting fate with him so clearly ready to burst, but when was fucking Rosie not a combination of pain and perfection? That's how it would be until the end of time. The attraction was too fierce, too consuming. They challenged, they taunted, they didn't hold back a single thing. No choice but to savor this, Dominic planted one hand on the fridge and wrapped the opposite fist in Rosie's hair, slowly fucking her mouth, his hips pitching forward and stopping short when he felt resistance, well aware she needed a little longer before welcoming him into her throat. He anticipated that moment the way a prisoner anticipates getting sprung from prison. His queen might be on her knees, but he was the one begging for that reward, harsh pleas falling from his mouth without permission.

"So good, Rosie. Honey, can I, please. Please. Rosie."

Her eyes teased him from below, that pink tongue dancing up the side of his length in a featherlight lick before she wrapped him in a fist and went lower to draw one of his balls into her mouth. Sucking hard while he shouted epithets in the dark kitchen. She moved on to the other one, and Dominic reached down, pinching himself in the right spot to stave off release. His wife took mercy on him, but by no means was she finished. Letting go of his sack with a pop, she took his cock back between her lips and consumed the entire length.

Dominic bit down on his lower lip so hard he tasted blood. "Shit," he gritted out, his fingers tightening in her hair, his thighs quaking, his hips remaining still despite the overwhelming urge to rock deeper. "Can't. Ah, Christ. Can't take any more. Stand up," he ordered raggedly, dragging his dick out of her mouth with a curse.

No sooner had she swayed to her feet with a feline smile did Dominic strip off his shirt. Her smile disappeared, her eyes glazing over more than they already had. Smirking as much as he could when his balls were full and welded against his lower body, he yanked the jeans down Rosie's legs. The button ripped off and pinged on the floor, but Dominic could only shove at her panties with frantic movements, wanting them out of the way. They landed on the floor with a soft whoosh that could barely be heard over his and Rosie's uneven breathing. Dominic stooped down, picked her up, and urged Rosie's thighs back around his hips, sinking his teeth into her neck and making her cry out, her fingernails breaking the skin on his shoulders.

Finally, finally, he guided his cock to her drenched entrance and thrust inside, pushing her a good foot higher against the fridge. He caught her scream in his palm at the very last second, but could do nothing to muffle his own deafening groan. The walls of her pussy wrapped around him, clenching, her scream rising another octave, making it almost impossible for Dominic not to ejaculate on the spot. How he resisted when his wife was shaking and coming for him, her knees digging into his waist, he had no goddamn clue.

Commanding his body to hold off, Dominic dropped his head to her shoulder and breathed through his nose. In, out, in, out, all while Rosie clawed at his back, her pussy squeezing on and off around his aching sex. A month ago, he would have already been driving into her almost angrily— and now, in this moment, he realized he'd been searching frantically for their old connection. The one he'd known was there, but had been buried deep. It wasn't anymore. It was a burning flame between them, more real than anything he'd ever known. His wife. God, he loved her so much, his heart threatened to crack under the pressure.

"Tell me you'll come home tonight. To our home." He caught her chin in his hands, tilting her face up and waiting for her dazed eyes to focus on him. To see him. "Give me that, Rosie. Say you'll come home and I'll fuck you harder than I ever have in our lives. Your screams will still be echoing in this kitchen when you open for business."

Her breathing accelerated. "I never knew you could play so dirty," she murmured.

"Yes, you did." He flicked open two of her blouse buttons and yanked the material aside, licking the swell of her breast, his tongue sneaking under the lace cup of her bra to graze her nipple. Maintaining eye contact, he trailed his tongue across to her other breast and loved it with a growl. "You want a preview? Will that help you decide?"

"I'm afraid to say yes."

Dominic clamped his teeth around the lace hiding her tits, pulling it away from her body, farther and farther until the material started to tear. Only when it was a limp tatter did he let it go. Rosie made a soft exclamation, her back arching, inviting him to suck her tits—Dominic had already planned on complying. She turned into a shameless little attention seeker, her pussy growing more and more slippery around his cockstand the longer he licked at her nipples, drawing them deep into his mouth and rolling them around on his tongue.

Only when she was sobbing his name did Dominic take her ass in both hands and position her against the fridge. "Time for that preview." He tucked his hips back, pulling several inches of his cock from her wet, warm body, before ramming himself deep. Again, he caught Rosie's scream with his mouth. "Keep quiet," he growled, molding the supple flesh of her butt in his palms. "Don't say another word, unless you're telling me you'll come home."

"I . . ." She sucked in a shaky breath. "I'm—"

Dominic let loose on her. Maybe he didn't want to hear

a no. Or hell, maybe he simply couldn't deprive his body of her perfection any longer. Whatever the cause, he fucked her like an animal against the refrigerator, rocking the foundation of the appliance, muffling her cries with his mouth. Her thighs held on as long as they could to his bucking hips, then lost purchase, jostling around him with every savage drive. He could feel blood trickling down his back, thanks to her nails, but the evidence of her pleasure only curved his lips against her mouth.

Rosie's head tossed left, right, fingernails clawing at his chest. "I'm coming," she whimpered, the slap of his flesh entering her pussy almost drowning out her voice. "I—I'm coming again. Yes. Oh God. Dominic."

The refrigerator groaned and rocked with the force of one more thrust before Dominic ceased all motion. Ignoring her frantic protests, he released the right cheek of her backside and cupped the back of her head. He dragged their foreheads together. "Mine. Tell me I'm bringing home what's mine." He pushed his cock deep and ground down, making her cry out. "That's yours. That's what you get for belonging to me. And my—" He cut himself off to gather his emotions, but it was impossible. "My heart. You get that, too. All of it. I'm begging you to take it back before it stops working. You're my home. I need you with me, Rosie. Please."

"I was trying to tell you . . ." she panted, her hands dragging across his shoulders, over the curve of his neck to clasp his face. "I was already planning on coming home."

Dominic couldn't breathe. "You were?"

"Yes." She kissed him so sweetly, with such trust, his

head grew light. "What part of 'you make me feel alive and protected' didn't you understand? What part of 'I love you' didn't you understand? I'm coming home."

"God, I love you, too," he breathed into her neck. Relief set him free. Driven by a primal need to please now that the weight was off his shoulders, Dominic angled his dick and pumped deep, grinding himself on her clit with every rough, deliberate thrust. They both looked down, watching the sexual friction take place between their bodies, their breath coming in accelerated puffs. Rosie started to tighten up again almost immediately, her snug, wet pussy pulsing, pulsing, constricting. With a guttural groan, he picked up the pace, his satisfaction speeding closer from watching her perky tits bounce in the opening of her blouse, witnessing her beautiful eyes go blind.

"Yes, baby," she whined, pressing her middle finger to her clit and rubbing in quick circles, the walls of her cunt swelling and leaving him almost no room to thrust. "Yes."

The second she broke, Dominic lost it, too. He fell on her with a snarl, sandwiching her between himself and the refrigerator, rocking the appliance as he fucked his release into his wife's body. Into the woman he loved beyond all recognition. Her screams of his name were trapped by his palm, Dominic setting his own growls of pleasure into her neck, wave after wave of bliss pulling him under, deeper, so deeply in love with this woman, he wasn't sure his head would ever comprehend the magnitude.

That love only increased when she kissed him with soft, smiling lips and said, "Let's go home."

It wasn't until minutes later, when they walked hand in hand out of Rosie's future restaurant, did Dominic remember how he'd made it possible . . . and a tiny ribbon of dread slithered into his stomach. Ignoring it, he scooped Rosie up into his arms and carried her all the way to his truck. Nothing but blue skies ahead.

CHAPTER TWENTY-THREE

Rosie hadn't stopped smiling in a week.

A whole host of old behaviors had begun making appearances. She started singing in the shower again, for one, which Dominic took great pleasure in teasing her about.

On her way down the supermarket aisle, Rosie fanned herself thinking about Dominic's brand of teasing. After a particularly loud shower-singing session, he'd caught her on the way into the bedroom in her towel, tossing her into the middle of the bed and tickling the terrycloth right off her. Pinning her to the mattress with his long-lost grin—one she'd missed so much without realizing it—he'd kissed down the middle of her shower-softened belly and back up to her mouth.

And they'd made out. They'd spent the whole morning making out like teenagers, laughing and groaning and petting until Stephen called to find out why Dominic wasn't at the work site. Rosie couldn't contain her laughter at the sight of Dominic, flushed and aroused, trying to form coherent sentences on the phone . . . all with his erection standing at a ninety-degree angle.

Best not to think of the frantic quickie against the front

door that came after. Or how he'd still been hard enough to spin her around and give her a second orgasm from behind, all while chanting "I love you" in her ear.

Yes, best not to think about *that* in public.

Rosie blew out a choppy breath and continued down the aisle.

It wasn't all physical, this shiny new hold her husband had on her. Where before she might get a grunt as a hello, he'd started commenting on everything. His contributions ranged from unnecessary—*those tomatoes look ripe . . . thinking I'll wear my green hoodie today . . . nicked myself shaving*—to perfect and sweet. Little gifts of insight to let Rosie know he was always thinking of her and paying attention.

Wear a scarf, honey girl, it's cold.

It makes me so happy when I hear your car pull up in the driveway.

You're not going to believe what happened at work today . . .

His voice had been missing for so long and having it back felt like having a major part of herself back. She couldn't wait to hear it again. Every morning, every night. As if thinking of Dominic had made him appear, something brought her up short while reaching for a can of diced tomatoes. A familiar scent.

Her husband's scent, to be specific.

Before she could turn around fully to search for the source, two strong arms slipped around her waist, a pair of beloved lips climbing the back of her neck.

"Dominic," she sighed, turning and wrapping him in her arms. "What are you doing here?"

They swayed for a few beats in the brightly lit aisle. "I decided to take a long lunch. The kind that lasts until Monday morning," he said gruffly, rubbing circles on her back. "I missed you."

"I missed you, too."

Their mouths met in a kiss. A quiet one where she could hear their hearts pounding in unison.

"I got to thinking how . . ." He trailed off to rub his lips against her temple. "We never went out on that date. Ditch these groceries and let me take you somewhere."

If he'd asked her to rappel down Everest, she'd say yes. "Where?"

Was it her imagination or did some redness appear high on his cheekbones?

Tongue tucked into his cheek, he stared just over her shoulder for a moment, before his gaze ticked back to hers. "Was thinking we could go ice-skating. You in?"

Rosie was positive her feet weren't touching the ground. Dominic had taken her ice-skating on their first official date and the symbolism was far from lost on her. Here they were, essentially learning to be together all over again. And she could see from the sudden gravity in Dominic's expression as he kissed her brow that he'd thought of the significance, too. God, she loved this man.

"I'm so in."

Rinx wasn't usually in service until closer to winter, but the temperatures had been unseasonably cold for the last week, so the small penned-in oval of ice situated on the harbor was open for business. Since it was a weekday, the local kids were in school, and thus, Dominic and Rosie were virtually the only ones there. Cold, crisp wind bit her cheeks and picked up the curls of her hair as she glided out onto the ice. She looked back over to find Dominic pushing out after her, the same way he did everything else. Casually, expertly. Brutally masculine in all endeavors. Given his height and mass, if someone had slapped a hockey stick in his hands, he would have resembled an NHL star.

"We haven't skated in years." She wobbled and righted herself. "How dare you look so good doing this."

With a snort, he caught Rosie around the waist and tucked her into his side. "I look good? Honey girl, I was just thanking God I'm the only man here." He shook his head. "Christ, you're the most beautiful woman on earth."

"Thank you," she whispered, swallowing through a veritable heat flash. "Last time, my father was here watching us, remember?"

"Remember?" he returned drily. "I was innocently trying to keep you upright and he thought I was copping a feel."

"Innocently." She raised an eyebrow. "Sure."

He winked. "Come on, now. I was the perfect gentleman."

Rosie hummed, letting Dominic turn her in a circle on the ice. "My father called you Octopus Hands for a year."

Dominic's head tipped back on a laugh. "He did, didn't he?"

"Yes. And it was well earned." They skated in the direction of the water, and the sounds were so soothing. The breeze, blades on ice, her husband's voice. "He was wary of you right up until the day of the snowstorm."

He shivered and squeezed her closer. "Don't remind me."

She ignored his gruff request. "Sophomore year, wasn't it? They dismissed school early because of the blizzard and I never made it home. The snow was too thick to see my hand in front of my face. I had to wait it out in the pharmacy, but the power lines were down so I couldn't call anyone." Rosie tugged him to a stop at the wall of the rink and cuddled into his warmth. "You searched for me for hours. Almost gave yourself hypothermia."

"Found you, though, didn't I?" Dominic said quietly, cradling her cheeks and sinking toward her for a kiss. "I'd still be looking if I hadn't. I'd look forever. You know that, don't you?"

"Yes." She slid her hands into his coat and settled them on his stomach, fingertips tucking into his waistband. "You'll always love and protect me. Through everything, I never lost faith in that. Not for a second."

He made a sound and pulled back, seeming to gather himself. "Good."

Dominic went down on one knee and pulled a ring box from the pocket of his coat—and Rosie almost collapsed.

"Rosie Vega, marry me again." His voice had a deep resonance that rivaled the power of the water stretching out behind them. "Please give me a chance to do better this time. I don't want to start over—there's no way to do that when I've already loved you for a millennium. I just want to start stronger." He opened the box to reveal her mother's wedding ring, except the missing stones had been replaced. Rosie's hands flew to her mouth and she started to shake, overwhelmed by love for this man. Her husband. "Hell, we know I can be selfish when it comes to you, honey girl. I want you to commit to loving me again in front of God. I want to lock it down."

"You have," she wheezed, her words muffled by her palms. She dropped her hands away from her face. "You have my love already, but I'll give it to you a second time. Yes. Yes, Dominic. Let's get married again."

He started to stand just as Rosie stooped down. They collided and toppled toward the ice, Dominic catching her in his arms before she could hit. Her husband's panicked expression sent Rosie into a giggling fit, and after taking a few recovering breaths, Dominic joined in. For what seemed like hours, their laughter bounced around the skating rink in rich echoes that reminded her of the past, the future. Reminded her of them.

Rosie had everything. Her soul mate back.

Her dream coming true.

It seemed like nothing could go wrong.

Rosie turned in a mid-living-room pirouette, a stack of laundry on her hip. There were definite perks to being temporarily unemployed. This morning, she'd slept late and taken a bubble bath. After that, she'd met Bethany at an indoor antiques mall in Farmingdale and found some perfect pieces for Buena Onda. A shabby chic chandelier for the center of the dining room, a vintage chalkboard for the specials, Spanish-style doorknobs for the bathrooms. Deciding on the smallest details put big, whopping butterflies in her stomach, especially knowing that Dominic, Stephen, and Travis were spending their spare time making repairs and remodeling the restaurant space to her specifications.

Earlier that week, Dominic had surprised Rosie by taking her to the Brick & Morty office, where she'd sat on his lap while Stephen drew up a blueprint. God. She'd never felt more special in her life—and every day, she believed more in her ability to command a restaurant. She *could* do this. The way she walked felt different. Her voice was stronger, full of conviction. No one was doing her any favors. They really believed in her dream.

Rosie continued to the bedroom and dropped the stack of laundry on the bed, plopping down beside it and sighing at the clock. An hour until Dominic got home from work. He would be dusty and grimy. Which of course meant she'd be forced to strip him naked in the bathroom and bathe the poor man. Such was her lot in life.

She squealed inwardly and glanced down at her new engagement ring for the thousandth time that hour. There would be no recovering from that proposal. Days later and she still risked floating to the moon every time she thought about it. How lucky was she? Most people didn't find their soul mates during their lifetime. She'd found Dominic twice.

The kitchen timer went off, and Rosie went to check her Chipa. She'd been experimenting with several recipes in the last few days, determined to nail down a short, tasteful menu, and Dominic was not complaining. He'd been going to the gym every morning to work off the food she fed him at night. When she'd scratched Dominic's inked abs and mentioned she would love him even if his stomach wasn't made of corrugated steel, he'd scoffed.

"Told you, honey girl," he'd drawled, pushing her down onto the couch and unzipping his pants, dragging his tongue across his lower lip. "Not going soft when I've got a ten at home."

An hour later, she'd had to apply Neosporin to the scratches on his back. He'd done the same to the rug burns on her knees.

They had a unique marriage.

"Wouldn't trade it," she murmured, taking her Chipa out of the oven, coaxing them from the pan, and setting the cheese-flavored rolls on the cooling rack. She took a knife from the drawer and carved off a small piece of one roll, popping it into her mouth—and threw her hands up in victory. They were perfect.

Having mastered one of her menu items, Rosie got the sudden urge to look at the restaurant blueprint. Just to remind herself this was happening. It was real.

Dominic had left the big rolled-up plan on top of the kitchen cabinet, and she retrieved it now with the help of a step stool. After moving the napkin rack and some bills out of the way, she unrolled the blueprint—and stopped.

"What's this?" Rosie murmured, running a finger over the slope of a roof. It looked more like the blueprint for a house. That theory was bolstered by the typed address at the bottom of the page. It was located in Port Jefferson. Instead of taking the restaurant blueprint from Stephen's office, they must have grabbed the plan for one of his flips.

Rosie was getting ready to roll the paper back up when she caught Dominic's name at the very bottom, alongside her own. Homeowners.

She double-checked the address, positive she'd never been there.

What was this?

A weird shift happened under her feet. As if she'd been speeding along on a moving walkway at the airport and then stepped right in molasses. For over a week, everything had moved forward at such a rapid pace. Maybe she'd been in desperate need of some easy happiness. Some positivity. Because she hadn't really stopped to think of the how.

How could she own a restaurant?

How could Dominic replace the stones in her mother's ring?

The building materials seemed expensive, but she'd assumed they were left over from a flip. Or . . . donated.

Rosie swallowed the growing lump in her throat. She memorized the address on the blueprint and walked like a zombie to her car. Maybe the dread tickling her gut was unfounded, but something told her to go see the house. So she tugged the car keys out of her purse, got in her Honda, and drove . . .

CHAPTER TWENTY-FOUR

When Dominic arrived home and Rosie's car wasn't in the driveway, he battled his disappointment. She'd probably gone down to the restaurant to check the progress, and he needed to get used to coming home from work and not finding her there. It wasn't the first time since she'd moved back in that he'd returned to an empty house. And while he always counted the minutes until she darkened the doorway, Dominic found it wasn't as hard as he thought to wait for his wife. Whenever he got the urge to get back in his truck, drive into town, and fireman-carry her home, he remembered her face when she'd become the owner of her own restaurant. He thought of the light that danced in her eyes every time she said Buena Onda.

Rosie had attained something she'd wanted her whole life. He'd worried he would be resentful of the restaurant consuming her time, but he only found himself feeling . . . lucky. Lucky as hell. He'd won back the love of his life and handed her the keys to her dream. The trust was rebuilding between them—and she couldn't keep her hands off him.

There honestly wasn't a damn thing to be resentful about.

Except maybe the length of time it took to get them both undressed. His wife was smiling at him again. Laughing. They'd started talking about their days at work, vacation plans, musing about mundane things and having deep conversations late into the night. Last night, Rosie had remained sprawled on his chest for hours while he trailed his fingertips up and down her spine, listening to her reminisce about the past, fill him in on the present, paint a picture of the future.

He'd never been more content in his life.

So why couldn't he sleep?

The happier Rosie became, the more his nerves seemed to pop and race. Their growing bond was like concrete being poured onto a cracked foundation. No matter how many times Dominic told himself she would never find out about the house. No matter how many times he convinced himself he'd done the right thing, sleep never came. He woke up in the dead of night with sweat on his forehead, fresh from a nightmare of Rosie walking out the door again. Only in the nightmare, he couldn't find her.

I should have told her about the house.

Now it was too late, though. What was the point when it had been sold?

He had no regrets over selling the house to give Rosie her restaurant, but he couldn't help but wish she'd had a chance to see it.

Regret ate at Dominic's gut as he let himself into the house. Rosie's coconut scent lingered in the air and he sucked in a lungful, issuing a silent plea to his maker that he'd never have to walk into his home again without Rosie's presence coasting over him and settling his blood. She equaled home for Dominic and that would never, ever change.

He walked straight past the blueprint where it sat open on the table and stopped, denial ripping through his veins. His surroundings fuzzed at the edges and pared down until he had tunnel vision, his quickening breaths scraping his eardrums. He didn't want to turn around. Didn't want to look. But based on the quick glance he'd thrown at the plan as he passed . . . it wasn't for Buena Onda. No, that plan was rolled up and sitting on the dashboard of his truck. He'd looked at it less than half an hour ago, relaying the square footage of the bar area to Travis over the phone.

Ice encased Dominic's spine as he turned and confirmed his worst fear.

Rosie had seen this. She'd been here, looking at this. One of the discarded blueprints for their house. Had she . . . gone there? This was bad. This was worse than bad. He'd bought and sold a house without his wife's knowledge. That alone was unforgivable. But they'd gone to therapy to learn how to be honest with each other. It had worked. Except for this one thing. This secret he'd held on to instead of coming clean. And now it could screw him.

He could lose his wife again.

"No. No, Jesus," Dominic breathed, snatching up his keys and sprinting out the door. His hands shook violently as he unlocked the driver's-side door and lunged inside, turning over the engine and peeling out of the driveway. He knew the route by heart, but nothing seemed familiar when he was facing the loss of Rosie. "Why didn't I tell her? Why didn't I tell her?"

As soon as he pulled into the driveway, his heart dropped into his stomach and his fingers turned to ice on the steering wheel.

Rosie was sitting on the front step of the house. Wasn't it the ultimate kicker that she looked perfect surrounded by the old ivy-covered brick and wraparound porch? He'd pictured her in front of the house so many times, but his imagination hadn't done it justice.

They watched each other through the windshield.

Get out and apologize. That's what he should do. It was the only option. But he was so righteously pissed at himself for fucking up the best part of his life—again—he could feel the anger curl in his belly like a rattlesnake.

Dominic threw the truck door open and climbed out, his self-disgust forcing the wrong words to come out of his mouth, in place of an apology. "I sold it to pay for the restaurant, Rosie. That's what you wanted."

"No." She stood, fists balled at her sides. "No, don't act like I had anything to do with this decision-making process. I didn't even know we owned a house in the first place."

Despite the cold October air, sweat slid down the center of Dominic's back. "It had to be done. If I'd told you about the house, you wouldn't have let me sell it."

"We'll never know, will we?" She broke off on a sob, looking around. "It's beautiful. Damn you, Dominic." He took a step forward, eager to comfort her, but she held up a trembling hand. "How long have we owned it?"

He hardened his jaw and didn't answer.

"Tell me."

"A year," he croaked, unable to look at her. "Maybe a little longer."

A sound of disbelief from Rosie had him glancing back to find full-fledged betrayal on her beautiful face. She might as well have rammed a screwdriver into his chest.

"Rosie, since we were kids, I've only wanted to give you everything, but it wasn't until I grew up that I realized how . . . *impossible* that is. I had my hands and my work ethic. And that's all." He couldn't fill his lungs enough. He needed to hold her, but couldn't. "When I was deployed and I met these men . . . God, Rosie, the *plans* they made. The places they'd been, places they'd go. Until then, I didn't realize how simple this life would be. How inadequate for someone as incredible as you.

"I'd only learned one way to cope with those fears and I followed that example. Head down, bust your ass. Earn. It took me four years of setting aside money until I could afford this house, and by then, I'd had my head down so long, I forgot to look *up* and see you needed something else. The restaurant, yeah. But me, too. You needed me.

"Your love would have been powerful enough to overcome everything if I hadn't shut you—shut *everything* out. I'm here now, though. Just forgive me for this. Please."

For what seemed like an eternity, Dominic stood there while Rosie digested his words. They were coming far too late, that much was obvious. Her eyes were glazed with pain, the heel of her hand pressed to her chest.

"Even if you'd told me about the house this morning . . . I think I would have understood. We could have talked it out. But knowing you were going to keep this from me forever . . ."

"I'm sorry," he said raggedly, the apology like a last-ditch life preserver. "I just got you back, Rosie. I didn't want to remind you why you left."

She took several breaths with her eyes closed. "I need some time—"

Panic clobbered him. "No."

"You have to let me process this," Rosie burst out. "Goddammit, I'm so mad at you."

"I know. Let's just sit down and talk about this."

"It feels like the last few weeks are tainted now. All this time, we were supposedly making progress, but we weren't. Not really."

Dominic dropped his head into his hands, his thumbs biting into his eye sockets. "I don't fucking get this. I don't get how we can love each other this much and not stick." He banged a fist against his chest. "Look at me. I love you. I'm sorry."

She turned in a circle and looked up at the house before stumbling away, stopping in front of him, her body language warning him not to touch her. "I love you, too," she whispered. "I'm sorry you were living with enough insecurities that you kept something so huge from me. That must have been hard." She opened her mouth and then closed it, her eyes touching on everything but him. "I—I just don't know if I can get right with this."

He could only stand paralyzed as his wife walked away. Again.

Rosie sat in the parking lot outside Armie's office, trying to psych herself up to go inside. Or move. Or think straight. Her mind couldn't seem to hang on to any single thought for longer than a few seconds before it flew off like a flock of startled birds.

There was a divider straight down the middle of her mind, like a mental pro/con list. On one side, all the bad stuff bumped around. Suffering in silence before she'd left Dominic. Feeling unsupported. Schlepping into the department store every day, her dream moving a little further and further out of reach. The other side of her brain housed all the progress they'd made. Not to mention all the revelations she'd had since she and Dominic had reconnected.

Her husband hadn't been ignoring her all those years. She'd been his center of gravity, just like always. To a fault.

Yes, she'd found that out today the hard way.

A house.

He'd bought her a secret freaking house.

Who did that?

Rosie reached up to massage the pounding ache in the center of her forehead. There had been a moment back at the secret house when she'd wanted to throw herself into Dominic's arms and tell him the house was beautiful. That he was a ridiculous, romantic, complicated man and she loved him in spite of it. But as she'd sat there on the porch watching him approach, she'd heard the therapist's voice.

I'm afraid your marriage isn't going to make it.

Could they have a successful union if he kept these kinds of things from her? After everything they'd been through over the past few weeks, if he still couldn't be honest, what hope did they have of him opening up in the future? She'd been so positive they'd laid it all on the line, but it turned out she didn't even know where the line was.

She just needed to talk to someone. Her friends were an amazing choice, but honestly? Rosie was almost embarrassed to tell them about the secret house. How could she have been kept in the dark so long? So here she was. Not only did she need to vent, but she wanted to know why Armie didn't think her marriage to Dominic could work. What had he seen?

Anxiety turned over in her stomach as she climbed out of the Honda. She closed the driver's-side door and idled there for a few seconds, measuring her breathing and fingering the shoulder strap of her purse. Armie was definitely open for business—she could smell the pot wafting from beneath the building door. When she walked inside, she found him in a meditation pose in the center of his waiting-room floor.

She shifted. "Um . . ."

His eyes cracked open. "Mrs. Vega." A smile lit his face. "Hello."

"Hello!" Rosie did her best to subdue her too-bright tone. "I know we don't have any more appointments scheduled, but I was hoping we could speak for a few minutes."

Armie rose to his feet, not without some effort, and tucked the end of a joint into his shirt pocket, patting it closed. "Dominic isn't with you?"

"No."

He studied her expression. "I see," he said, nodding once and turning. "Come on into my office. Something to drink?"

"Tequila, please."

His crack of laughter almost made her smile. "You're not the type to show up for a spontaneous therapy session." He leaned back against the front edge of his desk. "Why don't you tell me what's happened?"

Rosie fell onto the couch and stared at the therapist, although she wasn't really seeing him. Visions of flower beds and patios and a dock extending into the sound played in front of her eyes like a slideshow. "Last time we were here, you said our marriage wasn't going to work. That you could tell these things." She blew out a breath. "Well, I guess we didn't believe you, because . . . hearing your opinion only seemed to bring us . . . closer. Dominic talked to me about his insecurities and he really came through, supporting my dream of opening the restaurant. He even proposed a second time."

Armie only rested his hands on his belly and nodded. "Go on."

Rosie swallowed hard. "The whole time, he was keeping something from me. I found out by accident that he bought us a new house with money he'd been setting aside since he returned from Afghanistan. He bought it a *year* ago—and never told me."

Armie whistled through his teeth. "Oh dear."

"Yes." She threw her purse to the side. "He sold it to pay for the restaurant."

A beat of silence passed. "To give you your dream."

Rosie nodded and trained him with a look, nerves building in her stomach. "You said our marriage can't work. Why? Is it because he can't be honest with me?"

Armie sighed and rounded the desk, settling into his chair. "Rosie, I know you're not in the mood to hear you've been duped twice in one day, but I have to come clean." He tapped his fingers on the desk. "I knew you and Dominic were going to make it the day we met."

"What?"

He definitely looked like he wanted to light up his joint again. "Not only had I never seen two people who love each other more, I've never seen two people whose hopes, fears, and sexualities are so intertwined. You share a heart." He laughed a little under his breath. "Not to mention, there wasn't a chance in hell that man was letting you go."

A vision of Dominic walking into Bethany's kitchen to ask for a second chance caught her off guard and she had to take several deep breaths to kick-start her lungs.

Rosie spoke through numb lips. "So why tell us we wouldn't make it?"

"A little wake-up call, to present you both with the reality of living without each other. Permanently. Kind of a scared-straight program for husbands and wives." He arched an eyebrow in her direction. "Tell me it didn't work."

"It worked," she mumbled, thinking of how Dominic had arrived in the club that night, his heart in his eyes. How he'd let her shine. Encouraged her.

"I didn't see the secret house coming."

She leaned her head back. "That makes two of us."

Armie stood up again and came around his desk, sitting beside Rosie on the couch with a kind smile. "It wasn't right for him to keep the house from you, Rosie. Both spouses should be involved in decisions regarding household finances." He started to hedge.

She turned her head. "But what?"

"Change within a person doesn't happen overnight. They have to work on it every single day. Their significant other has to help," Armie said. "Dominic bought this house a year ago, when communication had broken down between you. It's reasonable for him to think revealing it now might cause the worst damage."

Rosie chewed her lip and waited for him to say more.

"Let's untangle this. The fear of losing you trumped honesty, in this case. Not an excuse, just a reality. And we've both learned that Dominic expresses his love and appreciation through deeds." He shifted on the couch, moving his raised hands around as if feeling her aura. "Close your eyes. Let's put you in Dominic's shoes." Rosie complied. "Go to the moment your husband realized he could present you with your dream of the restaurant and avoid losing you again in one fell swoop. What do you think he's feeling?"

"Duty. Love. Some self-doubt," she whispered. "Mostly, the need to make me happy."

"You need words, Rosie. We've discovered that. Do you think there are words Dominic could have said that would have given you the same feeling as realizing your dream? Having him help you realize that dream?"

"No," she said quietly, aching to feel her husband's arms around her. "No, I can understand why he might have made that decision, even if I don't agree with it."

Those words settled in the room, but she kept her eyes closed.

"You have the restaurant. What is Dominic's dream, Rosie?"

Her heart pounded loudly in her ears. When was the last time she asked him that question? "Being a provider. He lives to provide."

"For you."

"Yes," she whispered in an uneven tone.

An idea came to her, real and vivid. It was beautiful. So right that her blood started to flow at high speed, nearly propelling her off the couch.

"I have to go make this right," she said, standing and reaching for her purse. "Thank you, Armie."

Before she could reach the door, his voice stopped her. "Rosie."

She glanced back over her shoulder. "Yes?"

"If I may," he said, smiling. "Remember, Dominic needs deeds. Actions."

"I understand." She rushed back into the room to hug the therapist, plans formulating in her head faster than she could catalogue them. "What are you doing tomorrow afternoon?"

Rosie jogged from the therapist's office with purpose.

And love. So much love for her stubborn, old-fashioned, complicated, sexy husband, she worried she wasn't capable of waiting until tomorrow to pull off her plan.

Yes, she was definitely floating on cloud nine.

Until she realized she wasn't finished being duped.

CHAPTER TWENTY-FIVE

*D*ominic threw a right hook at the punching bag and listened to the satisfying rattle of the chains. A left jab came next, followed by a series of rapid punches. Sweat poured down his forehead and into his eyes, but he continued to punish the bag. Finally, when his arms were spent, he stepped back and doubled over, his sides heaving with exertion.

When he could manage to stand up straight again, he squinted at the clock. Twenty-four hours had officially passed since Rosie had walked away from him in front of their sold house. The more time slipped by, the less likely it was she could get right with his lie of omission. And the rage he'd been directing at the punching bag for the past hour was aimed at himself. There were no excuses to fuck up so spectacularly this time around—he'd learned the tools to communicate with Rosie and he hadn't used them.

God, there was no worse fate than this. Losing her twice. The Groundhog Day from hell.

The first time Rosie had left him, he'd been devastated. His wife had left him. His pride as a man had been hurt on top of the loss. The loss of the only woman he'd ever love.

It was different this time. It wasn't just the loss of his wife, this woman he'd sworn to love and cherish all the days of her life. It wasn't just losing the woman with whom he shared a past. Those things were true as hell. But he'd also lost Rosie, the girl he'd just fallen in love with all over again. They were old love, committed love, and fresh, insatiable love all rolled into one.

And he was fucking aching for her.

He'd gone so long without sharing with Rosie. Talking to her. Listening to her. How had he survived? The sound of her voice fed his soul. He hungered for her nonstop. When she'd suggested therapy, he'd thought there was nothing in the world that could make him love Rosie any more than he already did. Turned out, he'd been wrong. The line that tied them together had been kinked in the middle, and now that their connection was flowing so free and easy, he was gasping for fucking air, trying to suck every nuance of her down.

When she told stories about her parents, her chin went up with pride. Early memories of Dominic and Rosie made her blush and duck her head. An adorable look of concentration came onto her face when they talked about anything restaurant related.

She'd unknotted his headphones this week. Twice. He'd watched her do it from the open door of their bedroom, holding his breath, loving her more with every pinch and pull of her nimble fingers. She'd given him a neck massage after a rough day on the job site—even started the shower for him. All these little things she'd started to do proved the progress had gone both ways. How had he managed to fuck this up?

Dominic reared back with his right fist and buried it in the punching bag. Again and again. This was the only way he could prevent himself from going to see her. Literally draining himself of enough energy to walk.

He would have continued whaling on the bag indefinitely, but he heard an *oof*—and found Stephen wincing on the other side.

"I'm fine," Stephen wheezed. "I should have known better than to walk behind the bag while you were trying to kill it."

"Time to hit the showers," said another voice. Travis. "We need you at the job site."

Dominic's right eye started to throb. "Said I wasn't coming in today."

"Yeah," Stephen said, tugging up his jeans and sniffing. "I'm pulling rank. Go clean yourself off and let's head out."

Dominic did his best to stare a hole into his boss. Why were these assholes getting in the way of his suffering? The sympathy in their expressions only reminded him of Rosie. Everything did. Breathing reminded him of his wife.

"Come on," Travis said, stepping into Dominic's line of vision. "If we don't get this stonework around the fireplace finished today, we can't put in the fixtures. And if we can't install the fixtures, we're looking at . . ."

Travis elbowed Stephen, prompting him to speak. "A two-week delay. Minimum."

All of this sounded ridiculous to Dominic, but his head

was having a hard time making sense of basic math right now, so what did he know? His sense of responsibility poked him in the gut until he had no choice but to gift both of his friends with a curse and stomp toward the locker room. He couldn't wait until the next time one of them was having trouble with his woman and felt like shit—he was going to find a parade and make him march in it.

The difference was, their woman trouble would be temporary.

It was very likely that his was permanent.

He couldn't help resenting them for that. Couldn't help resenting the shower spray, the towel that dried him off, the change of clothes he kept in his locker. They rode in silence, Dominic in the passenger side of Stephen's minivan, Travis in the backseat—quiet for once. Come to think of it, they weren't bickering, which was highly unusual.

Dominic frowned when Stephen took a right out of town, instead of going left toward the house they were flipping. "Where are we going?"

Stephen scrubbed at the back of his neck, and, suspiciously, he seemed to be subduing a smile. "Shortcut?"

Dominic turned in the passenger seat and leveled Travis with a look, but he only pointed at his phone and laughed. "Georgie is sending me dog memes again. She thinks I don't already know she wants a puppy for Christmas."

Something was up. Dominic faced front again, his muscles tightening up when Stephen took another right toward the water. Dominic knew this route so well, it was programmed into him. Driving there used to give him mixed feelings. Hope that Rosie would drive the same direction home from work someday. Fear that she wouldn't want to.

"I don't want to go to the house."

Stephen reached over and slapped a hand onto his shoulder. "Trust us."

Beyond throwing himself out of a moving vehicle, he didn't have much choice. He tried to keep his breathing even as they rounded the final curve and the house overlooking the water came into view. He barely registered the abundance of cars parked on the block because he was too busy remembering what happened the last time he was in that front yard.

He remained stationary as Travis and Stephen climbed out of the van. Might have stayed there all day, if Travis hadn't physically forced him out onto the driveway. They flanked him, giving him no choice but to walk toward the front door. They'd almost reached the porch when a jacket dropped onto his shoulders. A hat was fitted onto his head next. Dominic looked down, immediately recognizing his marines dress uniform. What the hell?

Stephen pulled open the front door of the house—

And Dominic was greeted by . . . applause?

Honest to God, if he hadn't seen Bethany and Georgie—not to mention a half-dozen Just Us League members he recognized, and their therapist, who had a shit-eating grin on his face—he might have left. This kind of attention was not his thing. But if those women were inside the house, there was a good chance Rosie was among them. So a sinkhole could have opened up and swallowed the front yard and he still would have followed Stephen and Travis inside without a backward glance.

There had been nothing but bare walls for so long, he wondered if he was in the wrong house. White cloth draped across the ceilings, wrapped in tiny lights. There were flowers everywhere. Music played softly. There was so much to take in, he almost lost his balance, but he continued to search the sea of faces for the only one he needed to see. The only one he needed to see every single day of his life. He couldn't find her, though.

Before disappointment could take hold, a figure appeared at the end of the hallway that led to the backyard. Backlit by the afternoon sunshine, her figure was shadowed at first, but a few steps forward—and there she was.

Dominic stumbled back and covered his face with a hand.

That was his only defense against Rosie in a wedding dress. The same one she'd worn a decade earlier when they'd married at the courthouse. As soon as she was out of view, he turned greedy for the sight of her. His hand dropped away and he could only stare, could only exist in a dreamlike state, taking in every beautiful detail. Her hair was up and clipped with something shiny; the skin of her face and bare shoulders glowed beneath the strings of lights. In her hand, she held a blue bouquet that, he realized after a quick glance down, matched a boutonniere that had been pinned to his jacket.

And she was smiling at him.

Christ, that was the best part of all.

It even topped the moment his father stepped out of the crowd and guided Rosie toward him, the music beginning to swell. He could barely tear his eyes off her long enough to notice there was a man holding a Bible beside him.

Wedding. This was a wedding.

Dominic wasn't a man given to tears, but hell if he didn't have to blink back moisture. What had changed since yesterday? What had he done to deserve this?

He wanted to ask his wife those questions, but when she stopped in front of him, he was only capable of asking her with his eyes.

She handed her bouquet to a nearby Bethany and swiped at the tears in her own eyes. Then she took his hands, squeezing them tight—his chest constricting along with the action.

"Rosie," he rasped.

"Dominic," she said, taking a deep breath. "First of all, I'm sorry for doing this to you. I know you don't do surprises and here I am in a wedding dress." Laughter rippled through the room. "But you . . ." She stepped closer and lowered her voice for his ears alone. "You love me fiercely and quietly—you always have—and you've started loving me out loud these last few weeks. Instead of letting one mistake detract from that, we're going to trample right over it, okay? I'm going to love you out loud, too. And since you need actions, deeds . . . here I am. I'm marrying you again in front of everyone in this house where we'll grow old."

"The house," he managed, reeling from the affection shining from his wife's eyes. "We don't have it anymore."

"Actually, we do." She smiled so beautifully, his whole body ached with the need to hold her and never let go.

"There's one person who has his finger on the pulse of Port Jeff real estate. Stephen. I knew he'd have the details. What neither of us knew is Brick and Morty bought the house, marking the second time it's been purchased in secret. Stephen claims he was going to flip it, but I think he was just waiting for you to realize you wanted it back. Or . . ." She blushed adorably. "Maybe he was waiting for me to storm into his office and demand the sale be canceled. It could have been that, too."

He shook his head, panic beginning to take hold. "But the restaurant. You need the capital. You're not losing it now."

"I'm not. We're not losing the restaurant." She laid his hand against her cheek. "I agreed to sell our other house. To Stephen. He's going to flip that one instead."

"Might even come out ahead on that one," Stephen told the crowd, only to be slapped on the shoulders by both of his sisters and his wife. "I'm just saying, it was good business."

Rosie laughed while Dominic tried his damndest to absorb the information.

"We don't love each other the easy way, Dominic, but our hearts are in the right place every single time." The lights caught the sheen in her eyes. "The words will come from you, the deeds will come from me. I trust that. But what we have between us is impossible to express sometimes. It's real and it's big and sometimes the magnitude of it creates flaws. I'm accepting those flaws because they mean I get to love the most wonderful man I know."

"I love you so much, Rosie," Dominic said gruffly. "Thank you for loving a flawed man."

She kissed his palm. "Thank you for loving a flawed woman."

"Flawed?" He swallowed hard and stepped closer to Rosie. "Agree to disagree." Forcing himself to stop staring at his bride, Dominic threw a look at the pastor. "Please make this official before she changes her mind."

Everyone laughed. Then they celebrated.

And that night, Rosie and Dominic camped on the living room floor in sleeping bags, making plans for their future home until the sun came up.

This was really happening.

Rosie stared at the row of order tickets attached to the silver kitchen rack, and both knees turned to goo. It was here. Opening night of Buena Onda was upon her, and according to the number of dinner tickets flapping in the kitchen breeze, the entire population of Port Jefferson had turned out. And they were hungry.

She took a deep breath and ran a finger down the list of entrees scrawled on the far left ticket. Her first-ever order. A Camarones al Ajillo appetizer, one serving of beef empanadas, and two orders of her homemade spinach-and-ricotta cannelloni. Good choices. She was prepared for this. Over the course of the past two weeks, she'd done two soft openings with friends only. And at least quadruple that number with just Dominic. The poor man had consumed enough Argentinian food to feed a small village, but he'd done it with a smile on his face.

Rosie brushed a curl back from her face and nodded at her newly hired sous chef, Marco—a local father of three with a positive disposition—prompting him to begin prepping the dishes. Her hands shook a little now that the moment was there, but she silently reminded herself of the rhythm she'd mastered with Dominic by her side. If she closed her eyes, she could feel him standing behind her, humming into her neck, his hands helping her mold pastry.

God, she loved the man she'd married. Twice.

Every day she swore she'd reached the final fathom of the depth of that love, but it continued to go deeper. And deeper. If it turned out there was no bottom, Rosie was just fine with that. She could go on swimming forever, because he'd be beside her every stroke and kick of the way.

In the weeks since they'd renewed their vows, life had been hectic, to say the least. Opening a restaurant and moving houses was something they'd just about managed, thanks to the love and support from their friends.

The house.

Sometimes she stood in the kitchen and felt as if they'd been living there all along. The walls hugged her close, sighed as they fell asleep, and greeted them like open arms in the mornings. It was heaven. At night, Dominic and Rosie sat wrapped in blankets on the dock and made plans. How they would extend the back patio and build a custom pergola. The parties they would host.

The children that would sleep in the rooms.

Rosie opened her eyes on an exhale and tried to focus on the moment. She already had so much happiness to revel in, but this. This opening night was just for her, the culmination of her dreams, and she needed to give it one hundred percent. Marco slid the prepared dish in front of her, cueing

Rosie to take over, but nerves started to build in her throat, leaving her hands feeling like lead—

"Honey girl," Dominic said in her ear, one large hand coming to rest on her hip, squeezing in a reassuring way. "You have got this."

"I know," she whispered, leaning back against his chest. "I think I just have a little stage fright. It was easy when it was just you or Bethany, but . . ."

"Everyone you meet becomes your friend." He kissed her neck. "It's only a matter of time before you're friends with everyone who walks through the door. That's what is going to make you and this place so special."

"And you're okay with that," she said. Not a question, a statement.

"More than okay." His lips grazed her temple. "I'm the one that gets your heart."

Rosie turned her head and they shared a lingering kiss. When she opened her eyes again, he was gone. With a surge of confidence bolstering her, Rosie plucked another order off the rack, smiling over her customers' choices. This must be Kristin's table, because she'd made about nine substitutions and asked for dressing on the side of her salad. Good thing Rosie was in an accommodating mood. She might stay there forever, truth be told.

Life was so good.

Dominic had always been the man of her dreams, but he'd learned how to express himself. Rosie had done the same, having learned what made him feel loved. Appreciated. It was as if they'd been living in the same house for five years speaking different dialects—and now? Now they used their love languages to translate affection into something each could understand.

How high could they soar? Not even the sky was a limit.

The night went by so fast, Rosie had an empty ticket rack in the blink of an eye. She peeked out from behind the silver station and her mouth dropped open. Ten o'clock? The bar remained open until midnight, but dinner service was over already. With a sense of disbelief . . . and bone-deep satisfaction, Rosie untied her apron and walked toward the kitchen exit, high-fiving the waiter who came through the double doors counting his tips.

She wasn't sure what to expect when she walked out of the kitchen, as she'd been completely absorbed in her own world for hours. But she definitely didn't expect a full dining room of familiar faces—Bethany, Georgie, Travis, Wes, Stephen, Kristin, Dominic's parents, and Armie—all seemingly waiting for her to join them. Whistles and cheers went up, sending her reeling back a step.

Buena Onda spread out before her like a glittering jewel. Lights were strung from the ceiling; black-and-white scenes from Buenos Aires graced the walls; the floorboards gleamed, reflecting the red candlelight. Her mother's portrait had been hung in two places. In the main dining room and above the cash register, where Rosie knew her mother would be standing were she alive, probably keeping an eye on the cash. A hiccup of emotion came unbidden to her lips, and she sought out Dominic for support. As she knew he would be, her husband stood at the forefront of the crowd, a look of fierce pride on his face. Rosie pressed a hand to her chest, hoping to keep her heart from bursting free.

"Thank you for coming tonight," she said, when the cheers quieted down. "You're all standing inside my dream and it wouldn't have been possible without all of you." She wet her lips. "But especially my husband, Dominic. His faith in me . . . well, it's unending, and I'd like to show him, in a way he'll understand, that he's always been the most important part of my dream."

Rosie walked over to the small section she'd had blocked off for opening night, sliding the temporary partition out of the way. Behind it was a small table with a single chair. On the wall, written in gold script, were three words.

Reserved for Dominic

She turned to find him standing beside her, his expression packed so full of heart, it was impossible to look away. Her husband needed actions to feel her love, and she would never stop finding new ways to show him, the same way he did for her with words. They would continue to grow a little more each day until they reached forever. They were best friends, soul mates . . . and perfectly, eternally flawed.

"You shine," Dominic said gruffly. "So bright."

Rosie twined their fingers together. "We shine together."

Port Jefferson isn't big enough for the both of them, so when Bethany and Wes are forced into close quarters, it can only spell disaster. Or make it a whole lot harder to deny what's happening between them . . .

Coming Fall 2020!

If you loved Georgie and Travis, don't miss their story! *Fix Her Up* is available now.